THE GIANT AND THE WITCH

WITCHES OF NEW YORK
BOOK 4

KIM RICHARDSON

KR PUBLISHING

www.kimrichardsonbooks.com

THE GIANT AND THE WITCH

WITCHES OF NEW YORK
BOOK 4

KIM RICHARDSON

KR PUBLISHING

CHAPTER 1

It had been one month since Shay and I moved into Valen's apartment above his restaurant, After Dark. It had also been a month since my little sister, aka Jewel of the Sun, had blown the Dark witch Darius into dust with a beam of her Starlight magic, which was basically the sun's energy only she could control.

As a Starlight witch, I was rare. As a Sun witch, as Shay liked to call herself, she was even rarer—probably the only witch who could conjure up the sun's power in my lifetime, possibly centuries.

And as Starlight magic went, my power was limited to a specific group of stars, a triple-star system called Alpha Centauri. Sounds eccentric, but the downside of having this type of magic was that it was restricted during the day. Add the sun—a bully star—blocking my reach to the stars, it doesn't sound so glamorous anymore.

The truth was, most Starlight witches couldn't call on their power in the daylight.

All except for Shay.

My little sister drew her magic from that bully star.

The gift had incredible power, passed on to her from our father, Matiel, the angel. And that power could be ultimately destructive and dangerous if the bearer didn't learn to control it.

Which explained why we were on the roof of the Twilight Hotel with the sun warming our faces, embarking on our daily morning practice sessions and getting our vitamin D doses.

"It's not working. I don't feel anything." Shay hung her head, looking like she'd rather be back in her room playing with her tablet than on the roof with me.

"Haven't you heard the expression 'practice makes perfect' before?" I angled my head to try and make eye contact with her. "You have to keep trying."

"Why?" Shay looked up at me, her green eyes sparkling with anger. "It doesn't work. I don't have magic anymore."

My heart gave a tug at the defeat in her voice. "That's not true. It'll come. Your magic can't just disappear. That's not how this works. It's still inside you. Now, you need to focus."

It was true that Shay's power hadn't materialized since that day Darius tried to kill me. We'd been at it practically every day since, trying to conjure it and help her wield it. But so far, nothing.

Shay had saved my life with that incredible starlight power, her sun power. She'd been so proud that day, having first believed she had no magic of her own. She'd surprised us all when a massive beam of sunlight had roasted Darius and some of his minions.

But Shay's joy had diminished when she'd tried to conjure up that same magic and failed. Every day since then, her resolve had been getting worse until she was almost right back to how useless she'd felt when she was too weak to save her mother from Darius.

Shay was only eleven and a half. This was too much for her to handle so quickly. Not to mention discovering that she had an older half sister she would live with until she became an adult. It was a lot to take in, and so far, I thought she was handling it exceptionally well, under the circumstances.

"Your power is linked to your emotions," I said. I'd seen it firsthand when Darius was trying to kill me, and Shay had blossomed into her power. "You need to tap into that. Tap into that well of emotions and grab on to them. It'll wake up your magic. Like a switch." I was sure of that. I'd watched it happen. The loss of her mother and then seeing the same bastard who'd killed her trying to kill me had awoken that power. But we hadn't seen it since.

I also wanted to test a few theories—the first being whether she could also draw on her power at night. Or was it limited to the day, like mine was limited mostly to night? But without her having good control over her abilities, I'd have to wait and see. First, she needed to be able to call upon her powers on a whim, and then we'd test the other theories.

"I don't want to do this anymore." Shay kicked a piece of roof shingle and then turned her back on me.

I sighed. That's not good. We were only just starting to get used to each other, and the last thing I wanted was for her to hate me. If I kept pushing her, though, I had the feeling that was exactly what was going to happen.

"Give the girl a break, Leana," said Elsa as she sat in her folding chair, massaging the vintage brass locket around her neck. I knew the Victorian mourning jewelry contained a lock of hair from her deceased husband. "You don't want to wear her out. She's allowed to have rest days between sessions, you know. You don't need to drill her so hard."

She frowned, her blue eyes crinkled with crow's-feet as she attempted to tame her unruly red hair that had been caught in a breeze.

"She's right." Jade stuffed her hand in her bag of microwave popcorn and tossed a few kernels into her mouth, the white plastic bracelets around her wrists clacking. She slid her round, purple sunglasses up the bridge of her nose. "Maybe we should break for an early lunch. I hear After Dark makes a mean eggs Benedict," she said and flashed me a smile.

Black curly hair replaced her usual blonde mane and was shaped in a mohawk style. Hopefully, it was some magical spell and not permanent. A white, ruffled shirt lay under her long, velvet purple jacket. It appeared she was going for a Prince look this morning. I was digging it.

"She needs to learn to control her power."

The faster she did, the better. I didn't know for sure if others had learned about my little sister's unique power, but word always got out somehow. If one douchebag Darius knew about it, I was positive others would soon. And when they did, I wanted to make sure Shay knew how to defend herself. We lived in a dangerous world, especially for young girls with incredible power.

Yet it seemed the more substantial the power, the harder it was to harness and conjure.

"Not today," said Elsa, giving me her motherly glare that I was sure she'd reserved for her son when he was disobedient.

I didn't like taking orders from the older witch, but she was right. The more I pushed Shay, the more she withdrew. We were at the limit for today. But I still needed to figure out a way to help her draw out that power of hers.

Maybe I was doing it all wrong? I was going with my gut, the way my mother taught me my Starlight magic. But Shay's was different. What if I was going about it the wrong way? It wasn't like I could ask another Starlight witch, who could control the sun's energy. I was at a loss here. The only other person who might be able to help was her father, *our* father, and we hadn't seen him since that night at the hotel.

How does one go about reaching out to an angel? I'd have to ask around.

I looked over at Shay. With her back to me, I couldn't see her face, but I was sure I'd find the same frustration as before. Poor kid needed a break. "Lunch sounds good. What do you say, Shay?"

At the mention of lunch, Shay whirled around. "Can I have pancakes? With real maple syrup?"

I laughed at the hopeful smile on her face. "Of course."

Shay's teeth sparkled in the sun, and for a second, I saw our father's face. "Cool." Without another word, Shay spun around and dashed to the emergency exit roof door.

"Wait for us!" I followed after her.

"Doubt she heard you." Jade folded her chair and stuffed it under her arm.

"Yeah." I sighed. "Or she did, and she *chose* not to hear. By the time we get to the lobby, she'll be sitting and waiting for us in Valen's restaurant."

"You're worried about her. Aren't you?" Jade's shoulder brushed up against mine. "About the no-magic thing?"

"A little." No point in lying. "She should be able to conjure her power by now. She needs to be able to protect herself. I mean, she used it to save my life. It's in there somewhere. We just have to figure out how to draw it out."

"She's young," said Jade, as though that explained everything.

"I was her age when I started to control my

power," I said, remembering how patient my mother had been with me and how frustrated and very much I'd been like Shay until my powers showed. "But her powers are different from mine. I'm thinking I might be doing this all wrong. Maybe I'm making it worse."

"I don't think so." Elsa was shaking her head, her face set in a deep frown as it did when she was thinking up a storm. "I think you're doing everything right. Your power is the closest thing to hers, and you're teaching her the way your power responds to you."

"So, why isn't it working?"

Elsa pursed her lips. "I don't know. I'm sure it will come. You just have to keep working at it with her."

I nodded, but it didn't help the feeling of trepidation slowly forming in the pit of my gut. Shay wasn't showing *any* signs of her power. And that was a problem.

I yanked out my phone. "I should let Valen know we're headed his way."

Me: *Heads up. Shay is on her way to the restaurant. She wants pancakes. Be there soon.*

"How's *that* going?" asked Elsa as she dragged her folding chair closer. "Still going well?"

I stuffed my phone in my pocket and made for the door. "Yes. Really well." I knew she was asking about Shay and not me. The move to Valen's much bigger, superior apartment had gone better than I'd hoped. Shay's room was double the size I had in my old thirteenth-floor apartment, not to mention she had her own en-suite bathroom too. She seemed much happier there than back at my old place. And I thought I knew why. "Valen spoils her."

Elsa chuckled. "I'm not surprised. He loves that girl."

My belly warmed at her comment. "You got that right. After what she's been through, she deserves to be pampered." As a giant, Valen was programmed to be a protector, a guardian. It was in his DNA. But I'd also noticed a fatherly side to him that had emerged when he first met Shay and it continued to grow. The two of them were close, and I loved seeing him dote on her. That side of him, for some reason, had my hormones out of whack. And it was sexy as hell.

"You know what's next. Don't you?" Jade opened the door, and we followed her inside.

Music, TVs, and the sounds of people conversing reached me as we stepped into the hallway of the thirteenth floor. I stared into my old apartment, the one I'd given to Catelyn, and saw the door open. But it wasn't Catelyn's home anymore. The giantess had moved back to be with her family a week ago since she could now control her inner giant, and gave me the apartment back. I'd accepted, of course, and now I used the space as my office and headquarters for my friends and me.

"What?" I asked as she and Elsa set their folding chairs at the entrance of our now office.

Jade's eyes widened. "Wedding bells."

Heat rushed to my face like I held a flamethrower to it. "It's a bit too soon to be talking about weddings. I've only been divorced a month and a half," I added as we crossed the hallway toward the elevator.

Elsa shrugged. "So? What does that have to do with anything? When it's right, it's right."

I pressed the down button from the elevator control panel. "I'm not ready for a wedding right now." But I *was* ready for a grilled double-cheese sandwich.

Not that I hadn't thought about it. I'd thought *a lot* about what it would be like to be married to a giant—a hot, uber-sexy giant, no less. But also strong, dependable, and charming.

Elsa scrunched up her nose in thought. "It's always best to marry a man your own age. As your looks fade, so will his eyesight."

I huffed out a laugh. "Valen hasn't popped the question either."

No. That was way too fast. And I had the feeling Valen wasn't ready. He'd lost his first wife to cancer, and no way would I pressure him into another wedding.

"Who's popped the question?"

The voice snapped my head around, and I found a tall, handsome male walking toward us, a snug white T-shirt making a show of his tight muscles and athletic body.

"Valen asked you to marry him?" Julian's voice echoed in the hallway like he was shouting through a megaphone.

"Shhh!" Mortified, I reached out and grabbed his

arm, pulling him close. "Quiet. No one popped any questions," I hissed, my face flaming anew.

I looked over his shoulder to an older female shifter named Linette, who was staring at me with a knowing smile on her face. I knew that smile said she was about to spread a rumor on the thirteenth floor. If she did, the entire floor would know of this "faux wedding proposal" by the time the elevator hit the lobby's floor. Fantastic.

"Okay, okay," chuckled Julian, running his fingers through his short brown hair. "Sorry. I heard wrong."

He didn't look sorry at all, more like he enjoyed seeing me red-faced and horrified. I pointed a finger at him. "I'll get you for this."

Julian laughed harder. "I said I was sorry."

With a *ting*, the elevator doors swished open. I stepped through and whirled around. "What about you? Have you proposed to Cassandra yet?"

Julian's face clamped tight, and I swear I saw something like fear in his eyes. He just stood there like a teetering zombie, not answering. Guess I hit a nerve with that.

"You coming to After Dark with us?" asked Jade, sensing a bit of tension as she stared at her witch friend with concern like he was sick or something.

Julian just nodded and stepped into the elevator after Elsa. I glanced at the tall witch, but he refused to make eye contact with me. If I were to guess, I'd say Julian *was* thinking of asking Cassandra to marry him. They had been dating for about a month now, and I knew he'd been in love with her for, like, forever. Plus, he loved her twin daughters. But as of right now, he looked like he was in hell.

I bit the inside of my cheek to keep from laughing as the elevator jerked and began its descent. A few seconds later, the doors opened, and we stepped into a spacious lobby with high ceilings, lots of glass, gray paint, and rich red accents.

A pale man fitted in an expensive, dark gray, three-piece suit stood behind a counter at the end of the lobby, typing on a tablet. Errol, the lizard shifter, and the hotel's concierge.

He looked up, his light eyes fixated on me for a few beats. A nasty cruelty lurked behind the calm of his features, a contemptuous grimace hiding within the ordinary posture of his body. Yup. He still hated my guts, but I didn't blame him. I had nearly killed him—the key word *nearly*—a month ago when I lost my temper and threw him across the lobby with my Starlight magic. Oopsie. The shifter was a creep, no loss of love there.

I followed the ladies out the hotel's front doors, and together we entered Valen's restaurant, which happened to be conveniently situated right next door. The storefront sat under a gray awning with a sign below that said AFTER DARK.

The restaurant door banged behind us as we wandered into the lobby. The modern interior had many dark gray furnishings in an open-concept room with twelve-foot ceilings and exposed beams and pipes, just like the apartment upstairs.

"Your juvenile delinquent is over there."

I spun to find my favorite hostess, whose name I never cared to remember, in a white shirt and short black skirt. She was staring at a young girl sitting by herself like everyone thought she carried the Ebola virus.

Said hostess, with her long, flowing brown hair and perfectly tight body, had the feel of a mermaid about her. If I looked closely enough, I swore I could see a pair of gills and scales.

She hated me from the start because I suspected she was in love with Valen. Looked like he preferred warm-blooded females as opposed to cold sushi.

"Thanks, Fish," I told her, smiling at her intake of breath, and moved between occupied tables. Paranormals glanced up briefly as I passed them, and reached Shay.

"You could have waited for us," I told her as I took the empty seat beside hers.

Shay's face was buried in the menu. "I was hungry."

I snorted. "You're always hungry." Thank God Valen didn't charge us for food in his restaurant. Otherwise, I'd be broke just feeding Shay. Who knew kids ate so much?

"You've been working the girl since eight this morning. Of course, she's hungry," said Elsa as she pulled out a chair and squeezed herself in. "Why is this chair smaller?" She shifted, trying to get comfortable.

Jade giggled. "It's not. Your butt just got bigger."

"It did not," snapped Elsa. Her cheeks grew a touch of pink.

"Well, the chair didn't shrink," laughed Jade as she stabbed her sunglasses into her hair.

Julian let himself fall into his seat. He rubbed his hands together and said, "After all the workouts with Cassandra last night, I could go for a big steak."

"Ew." Jade grabbed the empty chair next to him and sat. "No talk of whoopee, please. We're about to eat."

"Please." Julian leaned over the table. "I know you've been having plenty of sex with Jimmy. Boning every day, twice on Sundays. Am I right?"

"What?" Jade hid her face with her hands but not before we saw how red it got.

I glared at Julian, flicking my eyes over to the little person who was now fully attentive to our adult conversation. He mouthed a "sorry" between the goofy grin on his face.

"Your banana pancakes are on their way," said a deep, husky voice.

I turned my head to feast on the man who'd appeared at our table. His handsome face pulled into a smile that sent hot tingles over my skin. The black shirt he wore had to be made of some stretchy material. Otherwise, all those large muscles would have ripped it by now. The tattoos that peeked out from under his sleeves only added another layer of sexiness and danger. I liked it. I liked it a lot.

"And *real* maple syrup," said Shay as I pulled my eyes away from the giant to see her smiling face.

Valen gave a soft laugh. "And real maple syrup." His dark eyes flicked to mine, burning with a kind of intensity that had my insides churning.

I had assaulted his broad chest with my face two months ago. He'd been unforgivably rude. But now... now we shared a bed, among many other things.

The giant pulled out a small notepad. "I'll be taking your orders." He brushed back a strand of his dark, wavy hair, streaked with gray at the temples, which only made him more attractive.

"Well," said Elsa, her reading glasses tipping the edge of her nose as she read the menu. "I'll have the chicken parmesan. Please ask your cook not to burn the cheese. I hate it when the cheese is burnt. Takes away from the flavor."

Valen's lips twisted in a smile. "Noted." He looked at me. "And what will you—"

A scream split the air.

I jerked around in my seat in time to see a female customer dashing out of the ladies' room.

"She's dead! She's dead!" screamed the same female, her eyes wide as she pointed in the direction of the bathrooms. Her gray-white hair was a matted mess like she hadn't brushed it in years, and her blue eyes brimmed with tears and fear. Our eyes met, and her lips trembled, but no other words came out. I had the fleeting feeling I knew her, but the thought vanished just as quickly.

"What the hell?" I stood up, my heart thundering,

and ran toward the bathrooms, which were to the left of the entrance.

I dashed into the short hallway and rounded the corner. I pushed open the door, with the picture of a werewolf in a dress, holding a parasol, and froze.

A wave of nausea hit as I stared at an emaciated, mummy-like face and withered body. She was lying on her side. Female from her sheer size and the width of her shoulders and delicate, tiny hands.

The skin over her face, hands, and neck was dried as though all the blood and fluids had been drained from her body. Her teeth were too large, and barely a hint of a nose was left.

My lips parted as I ran my eyes over the body. Because, yes, it *was* a body. No one could be alive and look like that.

Whoever she was, she was dead.

CHAPTER 2

I stared, both repulsed and strangely curious at the same time. What did that say about me? In my defense, I'd never seen anything like it—the way the body had been sucked dry of all its liquids. I couldn't see any puncture marks from where I was standing, which would have helped to explain what had been done to her, but that didn't mean there were none.

Without magic, it would have taken some kind of lab or medical equipment to do it. No person in a bathroom alone without any gear would have been able to pump all the liquids out of a body. The simple explanation was that magic had done this.

There was only one way to find out.

Focused, I called out to my starlight. Even though it was broad daylight, when my magic was most limited, I didn't need much for this.

The slight tug on my senses meant my starlight was answering. With a mental push, my starlights thrust forward like white dandelion floaties and settled over the dead woman, covering her in brilliant bright lights. Since my starlights were like miniature sensors, I sensed what they sensed. And right now, they felt a whole lot of nothing.

I tried to feel for any paranormal energies around her that would help differentiate between races, but I got nothing. There was no substance to her. No blood. No essence. No magic. Not anymore.

I felt a presence behind me and saw Valen step into the bathroom, a horrified look on his face.

"She's dead," I told him, not that he couldn't tell just by looking at her. Daring a step closer, I knelt next to the woman and brushed her hair away from her face. "Ah. Hell. Her neck is broken. Pretty nasty." It was bent at an odd angle. Still, one thing struck me as familiar. The way her neck was broken looked like when Catelyn had killed the White witch Adele by snapping her neck with her giantess hands. But that was not the case here. Weird.

"Cauldron save us," said Elsa as she stepped into the bathroom. She gripped her locket close to her chest, the way I'd seen many Catholics grab on to their rosaries, searching for comfort in prayer. Unfortunately, no amount of praying could save this woman.

"Holy shit." Julian skidded to a stop at the sight of the dead woman, making Jade crash into him from behind.

Jade poked her head around Julian. "Oh my God. Her face." She covered her mouth with her hands as a whimper escaped her.

I looked over at Valen. His jaw was set as he stared at the dead woman like he was about to punch a few walls and maybe rip out a few toilets while he was at it.

"Do we know who she is?" Elsa had braved a step forward, her facial muscles twitching with whatever she was feeling. "Is she one of us?"

"I'm not getting any paranormal vibes from her," I said as I let go of my starlights. "But that could just be because very little of her is left to sense any connection." Plus, the fact that it was daylight out, my starlights were subdued. But it could also be that whoever killed her made sure we wouldn't find out. Yeah, this was no accident. This was done on purpose. But why?

"Whoa." Shay squeezed herself between Julian and Elsa. "Is that a mummy?"

"Shay!" I jumped up, grabbed my little sister by the shoulders, whirled her around, and pushed her out of the bathroom. Once we were in the short hallway, I leaned over her and said, "Go back to our table and wait for me. There's nothing to see here. Okay?"

Shay crossed her arms over her chest defiantly. "Why? I saw it. I'm not scared. I'm not a baby."

I sighed, seeing that she was going to make this difficult. "I know you're not. But this is not something I want you to see. No eleven-year-old should see this."

"Eleven and a half."

"This is really bad, Shay." Nope. She was way too young to have seen something so disturbing. If that had been me at her age, I'd have had nightmares. Even more concerning was that she didn't seem that affected by it. I'd think about that later. "And this could be a crime scene. No one should be there before I've had a chance to work it."

"You think she was murdered?" asked Shay, her green eyes round and her brows high with interest. She angled her head to try and sneak a peek behind me.

I hauled her in front of me, using my body to shield her view of the bathroom. "I don't know yet. I need to do a bit of investigating. It might take a while."

"I can help," said Shay. "I know things. Stuff. I can be your assistant," she added with a hopeful smile.

Ah, crap. She was doing that face again, the one with the big puppy eyes that I found I could never say no to. But I had to stand my ground. I didn't want her near the bathroom. "No. Just... go sit and wait for me. Okay?"

Shay made a face, but she turned around and stomped all the way back to our table. Damn that kid. She was as stubborn as me.

I waited until I saw her throw herself down in her chair and start hitting her glass of water with her fork before I returned to the bathroom.

Valen looked at me as I entered. "Is Shay back at your table?" The evenness in his voice failed to hide his tension at the situation. He was just as upset as me that Shay had witnessed this.

"Yes."

"Good. That's good," said the giant, his voice full of worry that only added another layer to my own tension. "She shouldn't have seen this." His attention turned back to the dead woman.

"I know." And it was too late for that.

"You think whoever did this is still here?" asked Jade as she looked over her shoulder like she thought she was about to be attacked, like she was next.

I thought about it. "I don't think so. They're long gone." Because whoever did this, to this extreme, wouldn't want to be caught. "This couldn't have happened that long ago. Maybe a few minutes."

"But she looks like a corpse." Julian grimaced.

I looked at the tall witch. "I know. But this is a busy restaurant. She couldn't have been dead that long. Someone would have seen her." Which gave me an approximate time of death, more like a window.

"Are there cameras in here?" I asked the giant, hoping to catch a glimpse of our killer.

Valen was silent for a moment. "No. Not inside. Outside in the back."

"Hmmm." That wasn't helpful. We'd just have to make do with what we had. My eyes fell back on the victim. "I've heard of old, ancient vampires who can drain a person of all their blood. You think a vampire did that?" I threw the question at Valen but also at my friends.

I was an experienced Merlin, but this was a first

for me. I'd need all the help I could get, assuming I was working this as a case. Was it even a case?

"Maybe," answered Elsa, her tone bitter. "Though I've never seen a vampire do *this*, even an ancient one. This isn't exsanguination."

"More like mummification," mumbled Julian.

Elsa pointed in the general direction of the victim. "If it was a vampire, you should look for puncture holes near her jugular or wrists."

Valen moved first, kneeling next to the dead woman, and I watched as he carefully moved the collar of her shirt to see if he could find any such markings.

I kneeled next to him, trying not to get too close to her neck or the bone that was sticking out. "Anything?"

The giant shook his head, darkness brewing behind his eyes. "Not on her neck."

I traced my eyes over the woman's neck. It wasn't even a neck anymore. It looked more like a knee, a broken one. It was even worse up close. A tip of white bone perforated her skin like a chicken leg snapped in half. But no blood was oozing from the wound, as though her neck had been snapped post-mortem. But even then, you'd see some evidence of bodily fluid. Here, it was as dry as a pretzel.

"Check her wrists," instructed Elsa, her tone expectant as she flung a finger at me.

I didn't mind that she was barking out orders. We were all pretty shaken up at finding this dead woman. I inched closer and grabbed her hand, trying not to wince at how light it felt and how small her wrist was. I folded over the sleeve of her blouse and turned her wrist. "Nothing on this one." I crab-crawled over to the woman's other side and did the same to her left arm. "Nothing."

"Old vampires have magic to subdue their victims," said Julian as he walked into the bathroom and pressed his back against the far wall. "It's possible she didn't even resist. Or move. Would be harder to detect the teeth marks."

"Still, we'd have some sort of hole that would suggest the evacuation of bodily fluids." I pinched her skin just above her wrist. It stayed there like I was fondling clay. "You can't just take blood without leaving a hole. Teeth or needle."

Unless I was wrong, but the fact that no one contradicted me said I was right. I shook my head.

"Unless they're microscopic, there're no puncture wounds." I met Valen's eyes. "I'm not a hundred percent sure, but it's not looking like a vampire did this. Not a sick vamp or even an ancient one. This could be something else."

When he didn't comment, I added, "Do you recognize her? Does she work here?"

This was his restaurant, so the odds were that she was either a customer or maybe one of the staff. But with the way she looked, I doubted even her own parents would be able to recognize her.

Valen shook his head. "No. I don't recognize her or her clothes. She doesn't work here. She must be a customer."

"A dead customer," muttered Julian, his face wrinkling in an ugly scowl.

"Check her pockets for her ID," commanded Elsa.

"Yeah." Wincing, I slid my fingers into her pant pockets, doing my best not to look at her face. After searching both pockets, I leaned back. "Nothing on her. She probably came in with a purse or something. We should check the customers. See who's missing among them." Cauldron forbid she was a mother and came here with her family for brunch.

We had no idea who she was or why she was killed. But what I really wanted to know was why here? Why Valen's restaurant?

"Who could have done something like this if not a vampire?" Jade wrapped her arms around her middle, looking like she wished she'd never laid eyes on the dead woman. I didn't blame her. It was pretty horrific. But I was a Merlin. Gruesome came with the job description.

"I don't know. But look at her neck," I said, pointing to the obvious. "Vampires don't break the necks of their victims. Not that I remember. And judging by the way the bone sticks out, I'm guessing she was hit with brute force. Something or someone really strong snapped it."

"Demons?" Jade took a careful step back, her face wrinkling in shock, though the fear in her eyes was real.

"No," I answered. "Not in daylight." Demons couldn't have done this, but it was something equally strong.

"A giant."

We all turned and looked at Valen.

"Only a giant could break the neck of a person like that," he said, his voice low in the sudden, poignant silence. He gestured at the woman's neck. "See how there's barely any bruising? It was one hit. One strong hit."

Dread clasped at my throat, making it hard to breathe, like I had a broken neck. "What are you saying?" I knew precisely what he was saying. I just wanted to hear it from his lips.

Valen's dark gaze settled on me. "I'm saying a giant did this. That's what it looks like to me."

"I thought no other giants were here," I said, feeling my friends' attentive gaze on us. "Your friends from Germany are gone. So that leaves…"

"Catelyn and me." Valen let out a breath.

Fear stabbed my insides. "You don't think… You can't possibly think Catelyn did this?" I didn't want to admit it, but Catelyn was a freshly turned, or rather *made*, giantess. It was possible she was still struggling with her new abilities and had accidentally struck out and killed this woman.

"I thought you said Catelyn was doing great," said Julian, his voice high with accusation. "That's why she moved out and gave you back your apartment so she could be with her family?"

"I know I did. Guess this warrants a visit to her." I didn't want to have to admit that Catelyn might have killed this woman. Still, I had to check with her to remove her from my list of suspects. Guess I had a list now.

"And there's me," said Valen.

I snapped my eyes back on the giant. "No. You didn't do this." I rose to my feet, hating how my knees burned in protest from crouching for so long. Valen, in his giant form, would have trashed the bathroom. He wouldn't even fit.

"I didn't," began the giant, "but the Gray Council will still want to interrogate me."

"Why? Because we need to call it in?" asked Elsa, her features twisting like she was trying to think of an excuse not to inform the Gray Council.

"We do." I ran a hand through my hair. I met Valen's dark gaze. "You got any enemies I don't know about?"

The giant's forehead creased. "You think someone's trying to frame me?"

"Catelyn aside, this looks like it. I mean, why do this and leave the body in your restaurant?"

"Holy shit, she's right." Julian dragged his fingers through his hair. "Dude. Someone's playing you."

Valen's jaw tightened, but he remained quiet.

"But something doesn't add up," I said to no one in particular.

"What is it? What's wrong?" Elsa angled her head to get a better look at me.

I glanced at my friends and Valen. "Yes, someone with extreme force broke her neck, but as far as I know, giants can't suck someone's bodily fluids." Or maybe they could? Giants were still a newer subject for me. I still had a lot to learn about that race of paranormal.

"Right." Julian was nodding his head. "A giant vampire?" he offered.

If I wasn't so distraught, I might have laughed. But maybe... "Does that even exist?" I asked Valen.

The giant looked at me. "I don't know. But if they do... we're in serious trouble."

The hairs at the back of my neck stood at the tension in his voice. A giant with vampire traits? Yeah, I didn't want to think about that.

"What's going on? Ah! What is that!" howled my favorite fish-hostess as she stepped into the bathroom.

Valen grabbed her by the shoulders and ushered her out. "Simone. Listen to me. Close the restaurant. Tell the guests their food is on the house," I heard Valen say as I sneaked closer to get a view of both their faces.

Right. Her name. Did I care to remember it? Nope. It was already gone.

"B-but what do I tell them?" said the hostess, standing in the tight corridor, her eyes filling with tears. Even Shay hadn't cried.

"Nothing. Just get them out. All of them. I have to contact the Gray Council. Simone? Did you hear me?"

The hostess bobbed her head up and down. "Okay," she said in a dazed state. "Okay. Okay. I'm on it."

For a second, I thought she wouldn't move, but

then she whirled around, stepped around the corner, and disappeared.

Valen glanced at me. "I'll call the Gray Council," he said, heading to his office.

I stood there watching as he opened the door and moved to his desk to pick up his landline. His back was stiff, his movements heavy with tension.

I was left wondering if some connection existed between Valen's restaurant and the dead woman. Who could have done this? Someone who wanted to blame Valen? It was very possible.

But the real question was, *Was this a one-time thing, or would it happen again?*

CHAPTER 3

I woke up early the following morning, feeling tired and groggy but excited at the same time. I'd stayed up until 2:00 a.m., back in my old apartment on the thirteenth floor of the Twilight Hotel, going over the case of the dead woman we'd found in Valen's restaurant.

The cleanup crew had taken the body to the paranormal morgue in New York City. They'd camouflaged the dead woman with an invisible spell to hide her from nosy customers or human bystanders who might be outside the restaurant waiting to catch a glimpse of why the restaurant had to close abruptly. She'd been cataloged and taken away but not before I took loads of pictures to document the scene myself.

Valen had been especially quiet while the cleanup crew did their thing. He just stood there with a predatory glower on his rugged face, his fists clenching and unclenching like he was waiting for the right opportunity to pound someone's face in.

I got his frustration. Not only was the body found in his establishment, but the way she'd been killed suggested that perhaps a giant was the culprit. I was leaning toward the theory that someone was trying to sabotage Valen's reputation. They wanted to pin this on him. Who? Did Valen have enemies? That was the billion-dollar question.

Once the medical examiner could identify the victim—with dental records, no less—we would know who she was. There was no point in taking her picture. She wouldn't look at all like the same woman to her family since she'd been all but mummified.

I'd spent most of the night on the Merlins' mainframe database, reviewing the list of creatures and beings known to exsanguinate their victims. Vampires mostly, and the incubus and succubus demons were among the few. But none of them ever broke their victims' necks.

That was still a mystery, and I didn't like what it implied. Something big and robust had done it, like a giant.

Yet the main reason I went to my old apartment to work was, first, it was my new office, and second, I didn't want to wake Shay because she needed all the sleep she could get.

Because today was the day I was enrolling my eleven-year-old half sister, Shay, in a new elite school for the paranormals, Fantasia Academy. It was meant for witches, weres, shifters, faeries, and all other manner of supernatural beings like us. We had other schools, but Fantasia Academy was the crème de la crème when it came to scholastic achievement in our world, reserved for only the best, those who showed the most potential and were the most prominent. Shay would be lucky to learn from a school like that. Not to mention meet paranormal kids her own age and hopefully, make a few friends.

And it was all due to Valen.

The giant must have pulled some heavy strings to have Shay accepted into such a prestigious school. He had mentioned to me a few weeks ago that he thought he could get Shay in. My eyes had bugged out of my skull when he'd revealed the tuition fee, but he had paid for that too. He'd insisted when I told him I didn't even make that much in a year.

Things like that made me fall for the giant even more. How could I not, when he was so generous, so loving, and so, so incredibly hot.

Luckily for us, Fantasia Academy was in Manhattan, only a few blocks from our place.

Rubbing the sleep from my eyes, I glanced around my bed and found Valen missing. He hadn't been in bed when I'd climbed in during the early morning hours either, but I figured he'd been patrolling the streets in his giant form. He should have been back by now, though.

I let out a sigh, rolled out of bed, and headed for the connecting bathroom. After a quick shower and dressed in whatever was clean—a pair of dark jeans and a black V-neck T-shirt—I went to Shay's room.

I knocked twice and pushed in. "Shay? It's time to wake up." I stared at the bundle under the light-gray-and-white-striped comforter. It shifted.

I smirked and tapped the bundle where I believed her head was. "I know you're awake. It's time to get up, Shay. You need to get ready for school." I gave the lump another tap for good measure.

The bundle groaned, and the covers flapped, revealing an eleven-year-old's head. "I don't want to go. I want to stay here. Why don't you want to home-school me like other normal paranormal kids?" she grumbled.

Here we go again. "Like I told you, I'm not adept enough to homeschool anyone. I can barely take care of myself—*and* I text with one finger at a time."

Shay laughed. "Lame."

"So, you see, I don't want to be responsible for ruining your education. I'm a horrible teacher."

"Why can't Valen teach me, then?" she asked hopefully. "I know he'd be good. And he has giant magic."

Damn. "Because he's busy. He has a restaurant to run, he has employees, and he has his giant responsibilities. He doesn't have time." If she kept staring at me with those desperate puppy eyes, I might give in.

Shay crossed her arms over her chest and wrinkled her face into a pout. "I'm not going. You can't make me. You're my sister not my mother. I don't have to listen to you."

Ah. She was going to pull *that* card. I'd been wondering when it'd show up. Since I knew it would, I'd prepared for it. The bed squeaked and bounced as I sat down next to her. "I know I'm just your sister. But your father left you in my care."

Shay's cheeks flushed. "I'm not a baby."

"I know."

"I'm old enough to make my own decisions."

"I know that too."

"Fine. I'm not going."

I sighed. "Listen. This is a *good* school. The very best in our community. Hell, I would have loved to go there if I'd had the chance. But I couldn't. *You* can. You've been given an opportunity to go. You're very fortunate, Shay." Not like we had the money to send me there either, at her age. "Think of all the wonderful things you'll learn." I pulled out *my* card now. "Valen wants you to go too. He had to pull lots of strings to get you in." If I couldn't convince her, I knew using the Valen card might work.

Shay blinked and then threw the covers over her head. "I still don't get why I have to go at all," she said through the sheets. "I can teach myself."

Oh boy. "Shay, you know you're not like everyone else. You're an exceptional girl with incredible power."

"No, I'm not. I don't have them anymore."

I felt pricks in my middle at the sound of misery in her voice. "They will show up. And when they do, you need to learn how to use them. To control and develop. This school is the best place for you to learn how to do that."

Shay peeked out from under the covers. "But you were teaching me." Sadness flashed in her eyes. "You don't want to teach me anymore?"

I felt like I'd been kicked in the gut by a mule. "That's not it. You saw me. I'm not able to help you. I don't even know what I'm doing half the time. I've tried, but I just don't know how to help you reach out to your powers. This school is filled with trained witches and wizards and other magical practitioners who can help. Trust me. They know what they're doing." I also had the feeling that if we kept going along that route, I would surely lose my temper, and Shay would eventually resent me. I didn't want that. Our relationship was still fresh, fragile, and I didn't want to ruin the work we'd already put in. No, Shay needed to be trained by others who weren't me. I did not want to screw this up. It was too important.

Shay watched me. "But I don't want to be with paranormal kids all day. They're weird."

I couldn't help but laugh. "You realize you're a witch too. Right? And that you're just as weird as they are? Maybe more?"

Shay scowled. "I'm not weird. I'm eccentric. And I don't want to go to that school."

I stared at my sister's face, seeing the first signs of fear in those big green eyes and how she bit the corner of her bottom lip, something I'd learned she did when she was frightened or nervous.

"Look, I know it's scary to go to a new school,

especially one where you'll be learning about things that are still new to you. But trust me, once you get there, you'll realize that everyone is just like you, like us. They're all figuring things out too." I took a breath. "And… if you hate it, I mean, like, *hate* it hate it, I won't force you to go."

Shay finally pulled herself up and rubbed her eyes. "Really?"

"Really."

"Okay. I'll go to your stupid school."

I grinned. "Deal. Now, get ready. We don't want to be late for your first day."

As Shay shuffled out of bed and headed for her bathroom, I left her room and made a beeline for the coffee machine.

Once the coffee had brewed and I made myself a cup, I yanked out my phone, swiped the screen, and texted Valen.

Me: *Where are you? You didn't come home last night.*

If I were in my twenties, I might have struggled with some insecurities about my man not returning home. But in my forties, I had the attitude of "if he's gonna cheat, he's gonna cheat," and I could do nothing to stop him. If that was his way, he'd lose me forever.

It didn't help that Martin, the ex-husband, had been a big ol' cheater. It had hurt in the beginning, but after that, I'd been numb and just focused on work so I didn't have to think about being married to a cheater. But that was over. And I'd changed. I was strong, and life had made me hard. I wasn't about to go out of my mind looking for Valen either. I was done with that.

Besides, I trusted Valen. I knew the giant was looking for the killer or an explanation of what had happened to that customer we'd found dead in his restaurant. He was taking it hard. And that worried me.

Once Shay was out of the shower, and after a quick breakfast of box cereal—whatever I'd found in the pantry—we climbed down the stairs from the apartment above the restaurant and headed out.

"Are we taking a cab?" asked Shay, looking cute in a new pair of jeans, black Converse sneakers, and a cute top with her favorite Marvel character, whose name I couldn't remember.

"No. It's not far, only a few blocks from here, actually," I said as we started walking south on Fifth Avenue. I eyed her backpack. "Did you really have to bring that with you?"

Shay narrowed her eyes at me. "Yes. Why? What's wrong with it?"

"Nothing." I looked away. I knew that dingy backpack of hers was a sort of security blanket. She never left home without it. I just hoped the school would let her keep it.

We walked for another fifteen minutes, me checking my phone's digital clock. Shay was silent, and I had no idea what she was thinking.

We meandered along the bustling streets of Manhattan, my eyes scanning the crowded sidewalks for any signs of the hidden school. I had no idea what it looked like, just that it was hidden from humans by a glamour, like the Twilight Hotel.

My heart raced with excitement as I approached the spot where I knew the school was supposed to be on 777 West Nineteenth Street, between Sixth and Seventh Avenue.

"This is it," I told Shay, and she lingered beside me.

As we drew closer, I felt a strange energy emanating from the area, as if the very air around me was infused with magic. I cast my gaze around, trying to find any sign of the school.

Then I saw it.

Nestled between two other buildings, the structure was old and weathered, but it had a strange beauty to it. The enormous castle-like building had towers and turrets, tall and proud against the sky. It stood out from the other buildings on the block as if it was a beacon of power and mystery.

The glamour was almost imperceptible, but I could see it, as though a veil had been lifted from my eyes, revealing the true nature of the building. It was definitely a paranormal school hidden from the eyes of ordinary humans.

"Doesn't look like a school," said Shay, and I could tell she was hoping this was a mistake and we'd turn back.

"Come on. We're late." And we were. Two minutes late. Damn it.

I noticed a set of metal gates surrounding the property. They were tall and imposing, with intricate designs etched into the metal. Without hesitation, I pushed them open and stepped inside.

The moment I crossed the threshold, the air around me crackled with magic. I felt a rush of energy coursing through my veins, making me feel more alive than ever before.

Wow. If this place made me feel this good, I wanted to go too.

As I explored, I couldn't help but feel a sense of wonder and excitement. This was a place of magic and mystery, where my little sister could learn and grow as a witch—a place she could truly belong.

As we walked through the gates, I could see the apprehension on Shay's face. I quickly looked away so I wouldn't change my mind and do something foolish like grab her and run.

I stepped up a stone platform and knocked twice on the massive oak double doors.

"If we run now, they'll never know we were here," whispered Shay.

I looked over at her. "Why are you whispering?" I said, my voice equally low.

Shay shrugged. "Everyone knows magical school walls have ears."

"They do?" I had no idea. But before I could ask her some more questions, the door swung open to reveal a tall and lanky man with thin shoulders below a shiny, balding head, a pointy nose, and a crooked leer.

"Yes?" said the man. His voice had a sort of oily tone with traces of false airs. The scent of incense and something sour assaulted my nose, and I did my best not to grimace. A gust of air wafted through the opened doors, thick with the aroma of herbs and spices, and I could feel the hum of magic all around me.

He reminded me of Errol, but I plastered on a smile. "Hi. I'm Leana Fairchild, and this is Shay." I slapped her on the shoulder a little too hard. "She's starting school today." I waited for the man to speak. When he didn't, I prompted, "Um. Well, I believe you were expecting her." Did I get the dates wrong?

"Yes," he said, his voice oozing with false charm. He looked down at Shay. "We've been expecting you. Though I am astonished how you managed to get enrolled when the first term has already started. Usually, late-registering students must wait for the second term."

Valen. "Luck, I guess."

The man scowled, his eyes narrowed until they nearly disappeared in the folds of his brows. "There is no such thing."

"You're just all rainbows and sunshine," I snapped, not appreciating his tone. "Wouldn't kill you to put on a smile either."

"Leana," hissed Shay, and I reeled in my temper when I spotted the redness on her cheeks.

When I looked back at the stranger, he was watching me with a smile reminiscent of Errol. Maybe they were brothers. "She'll have to work twice as hard to catch up."

"She's a hard worker."

The stranger's smile widened. "Only three out of ten students ever graduate. I'm afraid the odds are not in her favor."

Instant magma anger filled me. "You listen here, you son of a—"

Shay yanked my arm. "I can do it."

"You sure?" *I* wasn't so sure anymore. "I've changed my mind," I told her. Valen was going to kill me. "You don't have to go to this stuck-up school." This school was supposed to be for witches and other supernatural beings like Shay, but what did that really mean? Would she fit in? Would she be safe? If the asshat who greeted us at the door was an indication of what waited for her inside, I wasn't so sure any longer.

Shay smiled at me in a way that told me that her mind was made up. "I'm going." And with that, she stepped up and joined the lanky Errol-wannabe on the threshold.

He stared down at Shay like her presence had soiled the halls of this great school. "Your first class is in room 101. Your teacher will give you your schedules and maps in your welcome packet."

Shay put on a brave face, yet I could see the fear lingering behind her eyes despite how she did her best to hide it.

I made to follow, but a firm hand pushed me back.

"Only students allowed inside the school," said the doorman or whatever he was.

I cocked a brow. "You don't look like a student. Unless you've been held back a few centuries."

"Students and *faculty* only," he corrected with that sneer I wanted to kick. "You can claim her at three p.m."

Claim her? What was she, a puppy? "Okay. I'll be here." I raised my hand to wave goodbye, but the man had already pushed her forward, his body hiding her from view. And the next thing I knew, the door slammed shut in my face.

"Nice school. Hope they teach good manners," I yelled at the door.

Realizing I had attracted the attention of a few humans walking along, I spun around and headed back through the gates and into the crowded streets.

My face flamed with anger and trepidation. I felt like the biggest fool in the universe. What if this had been a terrible mistake? What if this school wasn't what I thought it was?

It didn't help my mood that I had a dead woman on my hands. I was still unclear as to how she'd been killed, who had killed her, and most importantly, why.

It looked like this would be one of those weeks.

CHAPTER 4

With a heavy heart, I walked into the Twilight Hotel lobby, my legs feeling like they were filled with lead as I tried to avoid making eye contact with anyone. I kept wondering if I'd done the right thing leaving Shay at that new school. Part of me wanted to rush back and haul her away with me. But that was just stupid. She needed schooling, and I was the last person who could offer that to her.

But the other part worried I had messed this up. After my grandmother's and mother's passing all those years ago, I was left feeling alone and without a family. I couldn't count Martin as family. He was more of the bloodsucking-tick variety.

So when Shay appeared in my life about a month ago, I felt like I'd been given a second chance at a family. Cue in Valen, and I was set for life.

But now... now, I just didn't want to make a mess of things. I didn't want to lose Shay.

I shook my head, clearing it of those morbid thoughts. Nothing had happened yet. Besides, I had a death on my watch that I needed to solve. I needed to focus on that.

As I walked through the lobby, I noticed something was off. The marble floors were covered in a bright pink shag carpet, and a glittering disco ball hung from the ceiling, reflecting light on every inch of the lobby. Strobe lights flashed to a thumping bass beat.

I halted as I glanced around and couldn't believe my eyes. "What is this? It's like the Bee Gees came to party."

The lobby was transformed into a 1970s disco club.

"That, my dear, is the sound of funk," said a man, strolling my way. "Welcome to the seventies." A dark suit wrapped his lean frame. His light hair was shorter than it had been, telling me he'd gotten a haircut. He smiled at the guests, his back straight, as he walked with a nice confident gait.

"Hey, Jimmy." As the hotel's assistant manager, he looked cool and collected, as if nothing was out of the ordinary, and a giant disco ball wasn't hanging over our heads with a shag carpet under our feet.

I thought of the first time I'd met him, as a wooden toy dog, a curse from the haggard sorceress Auria and how much he'd changed since that the curse was lifted.

"So," he said, flashing me a smile. "What do you think?"

I laughed, gesturing to the disco ball and the pulsing lights. "Was this you?"

He grinned from ear to ear. "I thought we needed to change things up a little bit. The guests seem to like it."

I glanced at some guests with bell-bottom pants, frayed jeans, midi skirts, maxi dresses, tie-dye, peasant blouses, and ponchos. A vampire group, by their exaggerated good looks, sported some chokers, headbands, scarves, and jewelry made of wood, stones, feathers, and beads.

He was right. The guests loved it.

I couldn't help but laugh at the absurdity of it all. But I remembered Jimmy telling me that after the success of Basil's Casino Week, the hotel "themes thing" was going to be a monthly endeavor. "Well, I have to say, you've outdone yourself this time. I never thought I'd see a disco ball in this hotel."

Jimmy chuckled. "It's all about surprising people. Making them feel like they're going on an adventure. You never know what's going to happen next. The hotel's never been this busy."

"I'm happy for you, Jimmy." I truly was. "Have you seen Valen?"

"No. Why?"

"Just need to go over some stuff with him."

"About that dead woman you found in his restaurant?"

"You've been talking to Jade." I wasn't surprised. The two of them were a hot item.

Jimmy shook his head. "I haven't seen him since last night."

"Leana!"

I whirled at the sound of my name and spotted Elsa and Jade. Well, what I believed were Elsa and Jade.

"Oh. My. God. Is that... is that Sonny and Cher?"

Sure enough, Elsa had stuffed her curly red hair into a short brown wig with a thick mustache taped below her nose. She wore a pair of bell-bottom jeans under a red, psychedelic shirt.

And Jade, well, she had on a long, straight black wig with a headband wrapped around her head. Red-and-gold-striped bell-bottoms finished the look with a fringed vest. Of course, we all knew Jade was into the eighties and loved to dress the part. Apparently, that also included the seventies.

"We're celebrating the seventies, baby," cheered Jade, beaming as she and Elsa joined us. "Where's your outfit?" she asked Jimmy.

The assistant manager chuckled. "Upstairs. I haven't had time to change."

Jade smiled, seemingly accepting his excuse not to be walking around in bell-bottoms. Her eyes widened as they settled on me again. "Oh! I have a Lynda Carter Wonder Woman outfit in my closet if you want," offered Jade. "You'd look amazing."

I don't know why, but I stared down at my chest. "Thanks. But I have work to do." God help me, I didn't want to wear that. I remember it being skimpy, and I didn't have Lynda Carter's long, lean body either. No one wanted to see me in that. Trust me.

"Any idea who she is?" asked Elsa, scratching the top of her wig. "That poor woman. Dreadful what happened."

"Not yet. We didn't find a purse or a wallet. I should hear back from the morgue later today. Hopefully, they'll shed some light on who she is." I hoped. Fact was, I couldn't build a solid case without at least the woman's identity.

"There you are."

I turned around to face the hotel manager, Basil. His white hair was slicked back, and he wore a bright orange polyester suit.

"Holy hell," I muttered, making Jimmy laugh.

"Leana, I need you to help me with the festivities." The aroma of wildflowers and pine leaves filled my nose as he approached, the scent of White witches. "It's the nineteen seventies," he said, his voice tense.

I smirked. "You sure? I wouldn't have guessed."

Basil narrowed his eyes. "The seventies were an exceptionally colorful era. And I want the hotel to feel like you've stepped into a time machine."

"Mission accomplished."

"We've got a boogie showcase tonight," informed Basil, a smile spreading over his face like this was the best news to ever hit the hotel. "Disco dancers."

I snorted. "Are you one of them?"

Basil gave me a pointed look. "Of course not. I

have two left feet. The point is, I need you to help set it up. Greet the guests; don't forget to tell them you're the hotel Merlin, that sort of thing. And we need more glitter," he said, holding up a small bottle of some sparkling gold substance. "And you're just the person to get it for me."

Jade giggled, and I tried to keep a straight face as I replied, "Sorry, Basil, I'm busy investigating the death of the woman I found in the restaurant next door. You know, the one who looked like she was embalmed? I gave you a full account yesterday. Remember?"

Basil gave me an incredulous stare. "What does that have to do with anything? The death happened at the restaurant, not the hotel. You're not supposed to be involved."

I rolled my eyes. "I am. Sorry, Basil, but my Merlin work comes first. Maybe next time."

Basil huffed and puffed like he was hyperventilating, clearly unhappy with my response. "Fine, but don't expect to get paid for today."

"What? You can't be serious?"

Basil lifted his chin. "As I recall, you work for the hotel. Not your boyfriend."

"This has nothing to do with him. There's a victim."

"That doesn't change the fact that the hotel pays you to keep an eye on the *hotel* guests, tenants, and staff to make sure everyone is safe. *That's* your job."

"Which is precisely what I'm doing. Guests and tenants eat at that restaurant."

Basil's grin faded, and he leaned in closer to me. "Listen here, Leana. That murder happened in the *restaurant*, not the hotel. It's got nothing to do with us."

I cocked a brow. "It does. That woman might have been a guest at the hotel. Have you considered that?"

Basil waved a dismissive hand. "Doesn't matter. You're not a detective. You're a Merlin. Let Valen take care of it, which I'm sure he has already. It's his bloody restaurant. We've got guests to attend to. And I need you here right now."

"I can't."

Basil propped his hands on his hips. "I'm your boss, and I say you stay."

I gritted my teeth. That little shit. "Oh, you do, do you?"

Jimmy cleared his throat. "I think that lady over there needs help."

I frowned at my friend as he walked away, pulling Jade and Elsa with him. Looking back over her shoulder at me and smiling, Jade started to sing the chorus to Cher's "Do You Believe in Life after Love."

Well, at least she was having a good time. Not like me at the moment.

I groaned, knowing that arguing with Basil was pointless. "Fine. I'll help you. What do you want me to do?"

"Great!" Basil exclaimed, clapping his hands. "I need you to help with the decorations. As I said, we need more glitter, more neon lights, more... well, more everything!"

I wanted to throw up.

"My Disco dancers don't start until tonight," continued the hotel manager. "See to the glitter. I'll check with Polly to make sure she's got everything ready for tonight."

I watched as Basil hurried over to the dining hall, his legs stiff from his outfit and his knees not bending as though they were made of wood.

As he walked away, I couldn't help but feel a sense of relief. I wasn't in the mood to dance to "Stayin' Alive" with a bunch of strangers.

So, when Basil wasn't looking, I snuck away and sauntered up to the desk, my shoes clicking on the marble floor. Errol refused to make eye contact with me as I approached and instead fiddled with papers.

Errol, the lizard shifter and resident concierge, hated my guts. I had no idea why. Oh, fine. Of course, I did. I'd purposely blasted him with my starlights. Oops. He'd deserved it, though, and worse. It was a bad move. Unprofessional. I'd lost my cool and assaulted a coworker. Not good. I knew we'd never be friends, but now I'd lost all thought of civility from him. He always sported a nasty attitude toward me, even from the first moment we'd met.

Plastering on my best fake smile, I leaned forward, resting my elbows on the counter and knowing he hated when I did that. "Hey, there, Errol. Anything for me?" My voice was smooth and pleasant, without a trace of disdain. See? I could do civility.

He refused to make eye contact, instead staring intently at the computer screen in front of him.

"Go away. I'm busy," he snapped.

"Can you tell me if I have any messages?" I replied, trying to keep my tone light, though he was already ticking me off.

Errol let out a disgusted sigh and turned to rummage through the papers on his desk. After what felt like an eternity, he finally turned back to me, a smug look on his face.

"No messages for you," he said, handing me an empty tray. "Nobody cares about a worthless witch like you."

"Ouch. You hurt my feelings." I laughed and touched my heart. "How can I keep on living?"

"I don't have time to speak to stupid people," hissed the concierge. I could practically hear his tail twitching in annoyance.

I suppressed a growl. "Always a pleasure, Errol."

"Always a bitch, Leana."

Clenching my jaw, I spun around and walked away before I did something stupid again.

"Oh. I forgot. There *was* a message for you."

I turned back to face him. "There is?" I walked back.

Errol tossed a message card to me like it had soiled his fingers just by touching it.

I snatched it off the counter.

Dear Leana Fairchild,
Your presence is requested at the Gray Council headquar-
ters building in New York City at 9 a.m. We have learned
of the recent death of a female found at the After Dark
restaurant. You will provide us with your account of
events.
Yours sincerely,
Clive Vespertine
Gray Council Investigator

Dread hit hard. Clive Vespertine had arrested me for the murder of Adele, his late girlfriend. We weren't exactly on good terms.

He was a Gray Council investigator, and the last time I'd seen his chain-smoking ass was when he smiled at me and shut my cell door in the bowels of the Gray Council building here in New York City. I hadn't planned on seeing him again—ever. And why was he interested in this one death? That didn't make sense.

I glanced at the clock on my phone. "It's almost ten." Crap. I was already unforgivably late. But that didn't make sense. The message card couldn't have arrived just now. "When did this come in?"

Errol shrugged. "I can't remember."

"You *can't* remember?" Anger flushed my cheeks.

"I'm swamped today. Maybe it came in last night. I must have forgotten. And maybe I just don't care enough to remember."

"How about I remind you for the next time with my foot up your ass."

Errol stiffened. "Are you threatening me?" He looked over my head. "I will go to Basil this time." He pointed a trembling finger at me. "Don't think I won't."

"Why didn't you give me this message?" Damn. Missing an important meeting with a member of the Gray Council would not look good for references. If I had Clive's number, I would call him. I didn't.

The lizard shifter just gave me a blank stare. He didn't have to say anything. I knew why. It was because I'd blasted his ass and humiliated him.

I might not be able to blast him again without reaping repercussions. But I had something else in mind that might help.

I leaned farther on the desk until my upper body was propped over it. "Errol, honey, I just wanted to let you know that I forgive you for whatever is causing this tension between us," I said, my voice dripping with faux sweetness. "Maybe one day we can be friends."

Errol's eyes widened in surprise before narrowing in suspicion. "I'd rather drink a bucket of cyanide."

"Well, you let me know. I'll be there."

Errol glowered and turned his back on me.

I tucked the card into my jeans pocket and whirled around, leaning my back on the counter and feeling a little lighter that I had Errol all hot and bothered again. Yes, that was a tad immature, but he started it.

Yet my glorious victory smile was short-lived as a man walked through the hotel's front doors.

He wore a black suit of some expensive material and a familiar frown. His light eyes found me as he took a drag of his cigarette.

Clive Vespertine.

CHAPTER 5

Ah, hell. Clive Vespertine was the last witch I thought I'd see today. His ugly face making an appearance at my place of work didn't settle well. Maybe he hadn't *seen* me seen me.

With that in mind, I whirled back around, leaned over the counter, and pulled myself over it until my entire body was horizontally splattered over the top. Then I slipped off the edge on the other side in a very unattractive fall of jumbled limbs, my face hitting the floor first.

"What are you doing?" cried Errol.

I glanced up at him from the floor. "Thought I'd give you a hand. Isn't it Assisting Errol Day today? Thought we could start with a little foreplay? What do you say?"

Errol grabbed his chest, looking like I'd just assaulted him with my lady bits. Jesus. I didn't think I was *that* repulsive.

I made a face. "It was a *joke*. Keep your gecko pants on."

"Get out!" Errol yelled. "Only the concierge and hotel manager are allowed back here. The *help* is not!"

"Shhh," I hissed as I rolled around and eventually got to my feet in a crouch. I wanted to tell him that he was also considered "the help," but I was too busy trying to stay low. "Just pretend you're working. Ignore me. I'm not really here." I wiggled my fingers like I'd seen magicians on TV do.

"If you don't leave now, I'll call... I'll call security!" threatened the lizard shifter.

"News flash. *I'm* security." This guy was just not lightening up. I glanced to the side, looking for my way to escape. The only route was Basil's office. So be it.

Ignoring Errol's continuous outburst, I crab-crawled my way to the left, seeing my freedom only a few feet away—

"Leana Fairchild," said a voice above me that I knew wasn't God.

I flinched, turned my head, and looked up. The bastard Clive Vespertine was staring down at me from the opposite side of the counter.

"Are you trying to avoid me?" accused the male witch, a sneer in his voice.

"'Course not." I stood, wiping the dirt from my jeans.

The witch's face twitched, and then he took another long drag of his cigarette. "Thought you could hide from me? Me?" he repeated, as though I didn't get it the first time.

"This is a nonsmoking hotel. Tell him, Errol." I turned around, but the concierge was at the opposite end of the counter, his back to us.

Clive blew out a shoot of smoke through his nose. "You're not as smart as they say you are."

I perked up, smiling. "People think I'm smart?" Go me!

He regarded me for a moment, thoughts formulating behind his eyes. "A smart witch wouldn't ignore a meeting with the Gray Council."

"That was a mix-up," I said, staying behind the counter like somehow that would protect me from him. Not that I was afraid of this witch... Well, maybe I should have been, but the last time I'd seen him, he cuffed me with some anti-magic cuffs and dragged my ass to a cell. I did not want that to happen again, especially now that I had Shay in my life. She needed me.

The male witch observed me, his eyes flat and empty, before he said, "You were always a liar."

Anger bubbled up. "I'm not lying. I wasn't given the message in time. I had no idea about the meeting. Errol. Tell him." I turned my head in the direction of the lizard shifter, but again, he chose to ignore me. Of course, he would. He was probably relishing this, his success of getting me into trouble. Possibly fired.

The male witch moved closer and rested a hand on the counter. The light from the hotel lobby gleamed on his dark, slick hair.

I'd never paid much attention to his face before, but now it was right front and center. It reminded me of an old scab—dark and ugly.

A small laugh emitted from Clive, and he took another drag of his cigarette. "I don't particularly like you," he said. "In fact, I despise you."

"Ah. And here I thought we'd have nothing in common." For some strange reason, that made me happy.

Clive's eyes went hard. "You took someone from me, and that deserves a lifetime in Grimway Citadel. You shouldn't be walking the streets, enjoying your life. You should be behind bars, enduring a lifespan of misery and torture."

"I was acquitted of those charges, just FYI." Damn. He was still not letting go of the fact that Adele was dead. More like she was killed. Not by me, but by Catelyn, and rightfully so. The giantess had come forward to the Gray Council, explaining that she had killed the White witch after she'd been kidnapped and transmutated against her will from a normal boring human to a massive giantess.

Adele suffered from taking too many crazy pills. Yet she'd been taking her orders from Darius. Another nutter. And I was glad they were both gone.

Clive's teeth showed as his lips curled into an ugly smile. "Yes. How convenient."

I shrugged. "It was only a matter of time before she was stopped. You do realize she was involved with a lot of *illegal* stuff. Right?" Unless he knew all along and had agreed to it. The fact that he didn't answer *was* my answer. He knew. He knew, and he was on board with it.

"You are a despicable, interfering witch," accused Clive, his tone as cold as his white skin.

"I'll take that as a compliment."

I felt eyes on me, and I turned to see Basil, his eyes locked on us with an expression like he thought Clive's presence would ruin his seventies' theme. More like *I* would ruin it. He caught me staring and threw up his hands, his eyes accusing like this was my fault. I guess it was.

Clive leaned on the counter with his cigarette dangerously close to my face. The first hints of stubble were showing on his chin. "But it's not just you. Is it? Your... *friends* are just as meddling as you."

I clenched my jaw, doing my best not to let my temper get the better of me. "You leave my friends out of this, Clivy."

Clive smiled without humor. "Or what?" he asked, shoots of smoke coiling out of his mouth. "Are you threatening a member of the Gray Council?" When I didn't answer, he continued, "Do you know what happens to worthless witches who threaten the council?"

I blinked. "If I say yes, will you go away?" Bastard. I didn't do well with authority figures. It explained why I liked the Merlin gig, which enabled me to work independently and be my own boss most of the time. I rarely had any of the Gray Council members involved in my work. Well, that was *before* I took the job at the Twilight Hotel. Now it seemed they were always involved in some way. It didn't help that they owned the hotel.

"They're never heard from again." He laughed harshly and made an excited sound in his throat. When he flashed me his teeth, they were yellow and speckled with brown stains.

"Is there an end to this delightful interrogation?" I'd had enough of this. "What do you want? So I missed a meeting. Big deal. It happens. It's not the end of the world. Reprimand me for missing a meeting or whatever, and leave. It is why you're here. Right?"

Clive's gaze moved to my hands for a moment, and I thought I saw something flick behind his eyes like he was refraining from pulling on his magic to kick my ass with it. Then he focused back on me. "I'm here about the dead witch found in the restaurant next door."

That piqued my interest. She had magic, yet that wasn't enough to save her. But we all knew not all witches were created equal. Besides, she might not have had the knowledge or the experience to defend herself. Take me. I was practically a dud during the day.

I swallowed. "She was a witch? How do you know that?"

A sly, satisfied grin appeared on the male witch's face. "You would have known if you'd cared to attend a meeting when you were ordered."

Ordered? I wasn't a dog. "Like I said, I never got

the message." I inched back. The cigarette smoke was making me light-headed.

"Strike one, Leana. Strike one," said Clive, his tone light as he spoke to me as though we were old friends having one of our usual conversations.

I really hated this guy. "What's the Gray Council's interest in her?" From what I knew, they didn't send their dogs unless they valued something as important. A single dead witch shouldn't involve them. Something else was up. Or they knew something I didn't.

Clive pulled back and flicked the butt of his cigarette on the floor. "Funny thing, though. Isn't it?"

Okay, I'll bite. "What is?"

"The way her neck was broken. It looks almost like... almost like a *giant* snapped her neck like a twig. Wouldn't you say?"

My pulse pounded on my forehead. "No."

"Well, that's not what the coroner had to say. Something you'd also know if you cared to show up when summoned to a meeting."

"I know what you're doing. He didn't do it." I didn't like the fact that the coroner's results were in, and I didn't get a copy. I made a mental note to call them after I dealt with this asshat.

Clive smiled. "Maybe he did, and maybe he didn't. Still. Anything suspicious that revolves around you... is now *my* business. That means anything that happens in the hotel or your boyfriend's restaurant is now my concern," said the male witch. His voice remained casual like he was commenting on the fabric of his suit, but somehow it reverberated over the sounds of the guests in the hotel and the seventies' music.

"Why? I'm a Merlin. I'm perfectly capable of handling this case on my own. I don't need a babysitter."

At that, Clive laughed. "Oh. But you do. See, you're under suspicion. The Gray Council feels you're a dark mark on them, even the Merlin organization. You're like a weed that needs to be taken care of—a bad apple."

Ah. Now I get it. "So, you're *watching* me? That's really pervy. Can't you just Facebook stalk me like the rest of the world?"

"Everything you do now goes through the Gray Council." Clive's lips spread into a slow smile as he said, "Me."

I let that information settle for a moment. The Gray Council had lost faith in me. Can't say I'm surprised. I did expose one of their own as a fraud. I had a feeling it would someday come back and bite me in my witch ass. And I was fairly certain Darius wasn't the only bad apple sitting on the Gray Council. Likely others wanted to discredit me as well.

Well, it wasn't like I was going to let them.

If there were weeds, they were in the Gray Council, and I was about to meddle in that garden.

When I looked over to Clive again, his face held traces of deep satisfaction and something I couldn't quite understand, like he was holding something back that was worse than stalking me. What was worse than him stalking me? Him stalking me while he was naked. Yeah, definitely worse.

"There's something else. Isn't there?" I didn't know why, but my muscles tightened.

The smile Clive gave me turned my blood to ice. "There's a rumor going around about a young girl. A young girl with *incredible* power."

Oh, shit.

"The Gray Council is *very* interested in this little girl," he continued, and a twinge of fear hit me. "They say she has an extraordinary gift. One in a billion. And I hear she's staying with you."

My heart was pounding so hard against my chest that I was sure everyone in the lobby could hear it. "I don't know what you're talking about. Have you been drinking the shower water while showering again?"

"I know you've got her."

Heaps of anger replaced my fear and sanity, cementing in my gut. I knew this might happen after what Shay had done to Darius and some of his minions. Some of them had escaped, and apparently they'd blabbed. I should have killed them, but I wasn't a cold-blooded murderer. I had a conscience. I just wasn't ready to face this yet. I didn't have a plan of action. I felt trapped. And I hated that Clive knew this.

"Yeah, you do. I can see it on your face," said Clive, looking mildly entertained with what looked like a laugh quirking his mouth.

"That's called a bitch face. It's what I usually wear

in the presence of assholes."

"You're a terrible liar," said Clive, a sly smile on his lips. "And a terrible witch. It's funny, though, because I heard another rumor. They say she's your sister." He reached inside his jacket and yanked out a flat metal box. Flipping it open, he plucked a cigarette to his lips and lit it with a metal lighter.

Something feral and violent raged inside me, and I strained every nerve in my body to keep it on its leash.

"You stay the hell away from her," I snarled. There was no point in lying anymore. It was obvious someone blabbed, and he'd done his research.

Call it maternal instincts or just the overwhelming need to shield any child, but that triggered a primordial sense of protection in me, a feeling born ages ago, before reason or logic—a maternal instinct ruled by the overwhelming drive to protect our young. That instinct shackled me.

The male witch puffed briefly and then dropped the lighter and metal box inside his jacket pocket.

Clive blew out rows of smoke from his nostrils. "I don't think so. See, the Gray Council would very much like to meet... *Shay.*"

"Over my dead body." I knew what a meeting with the Gray Council would mean. They would take her away, and I'd never see her again. They'd probe her and test her until nothing was left of that cute, independent, fiery little girl. Rage shook me violently, and I leaned forward until I was even with Clive.

"You come near her, and I'll kill you." Yeah, really, not the way to go here, but I'd lost it.

Clive laughed, actually laughed. "Is that a threat? You know I can have you arrested for that."

"Arrested?" came a voice, and I lifted my gaze to see Elsa and Jade stepping up to the counter. "Leana? What's going on?" asked the older witch.

I didn't look away from Clive's smug face. "Nothing." It wasn't nothing, but I had the gut feeling he wouldn't arrest me. At least, not yet. I could tell he wanted nothing more than to haul my ass back into that cell, but he had nothing on me. But if he was watching me like he'd said, he would wait in the shadows until I screwed up, which happened a lot.

Elsa, still in her Sonny costume, pressed her hands on her hips. "Are you charging her with anything?"

Clive flicked his gaze on Elsa and blew smoke in her face. "Not yet."

"Then leave her alone," said Elsa, just as her mustache slipped and came off, hanging from just one corner. "Or I'll file a complaint of harassment with the Gray Council. Don't think I won't."

"It's okay, Elsa. He was just leaving." I wanted to tell her that his being here was a result of the Gray Council's wishes. I'd tell her later. The fact that he hadn't arrested me proved he had nothing on me, except for Shay. That was a colossal problem.

"I'll be back soon," Clive assured me. His face creased into a wicked smile as he said, "And I'm not going to rest until you're behind bars, stuck in a cell for the rest of your miserable life." A dark glee simmered in the backs of his eyes, evil and absolute. "I'll be in touch."

"Screw you." I glared at him as he turned around, sucking on his cigarette like it was oxygen, and walked away.

"Ugh. That witch is vile," said Elsa, her fingers twitching at her sides as though she was silently cursing him.

"What's his problem?" asked Jade as she leaned against the counter, throwing evil eyes in Clive's direction.

I sighed and said, "Me. I'm his problem."

And I knew this wasn't the last I'd see of him.

CHAPTER 6

"Hi. Welcome to the Twilight Hotel." I forced the millionth smile as an elderly werewolf female stepped through the doors of the Twilight Hotel, the scent of wet dog loud on her like she'd taken a shower with *eau de dog*. She didn't smile back. But she did give me her stink eye. Granny Wolf did not like me.

My facial muscles protested as I tried to pull them into another smile, though it could have looked like I was constipated. Most likely. I'd been at it for more than four hours and didn't think my face had any smiles left. I was all smiled out.

I despised this part of the job, hostessing or whatever you want to call it. I was a Merlin, damn it, not some glorified entertainer. But Basil had made it clear that if I wanted to remain an employee of the hotel and get paid, greeting guests from time to time was part of my job. He wanted me to tell everyone who walked through those doors that I was the Merlin staffed here, like that was supposed to put the guests at ease. The hotel had acquired a new reputation as of late after a string of demons and other unfortunate encounters.

I never did. It felt stupid.

Besides, my head and heart weren't in it. I was still reeling from my encounter with Clive at the front desk. Now that I knew he'd be watching me, it was a problem. It meant he was waiting for me to make a mistake he could use to throw me back into that cell.

I knew he hated me, but I'd figured once the Gray Council knew of Adele's duplicitous—and let's not forget illegal—behavior with using humans in her guinea pig experiments to turn them into paranormals, he'd leave me alone.

I was wrong.

It appeared he was even more adamant about framing me or just seeing me live out the rest of my life in the Grimway Citadel, the witch prison in Upstate New York. Clearly, he blamed me for his girl-friend's death. I was vaguely connected to it, but Catelyn had killed her. Adele deserved what she got.

Shaking Clive off my back was going to be complicated. After our little encounter today, I could tell he would never let it go until *he* felt I got what I deserved.

The chain-smoking investigator was building a case against me. Three strikes, and I was out. From now on, I was going to have to do everything by the book, the Merlin book, if I was to avoid prison time.

I was pissed, furious that I'd have to deal with

this idiot, but I could handle whatever he threw at me and then some. I wasn't scared by his tactics. Quite the opposite. If he was Adele's man, it was plausible that he knew of her plans and agreed with them. Yeah, he was oily and dubious, and I had the feeling he was working with the shady members of the Gray Council who still sat on that board of directors.

To get rid of him, I'd have to get rid of them.

Still, I was less worried about me than I was about his sudden interest in Shay.

Shay, my only living family member and half sister, was on the Gray Council's radar. I didn't like that. What if they came and took her away? Could I even stop that from happening?

My mind was going wild. I had thoughts of running away. Maybe I should. Maybe I should hide Shay. But would living in hiding be the best thing for her? She'd just started school. I didn't want to take that away. But if it meant I could save her life, I would. I would do anything.

I yanked out my phone and tried Valen again. I needed to talk to him. Maybe he'd have a few ideas about Shay. After four rings, it went to voicemail, so I hung up. I'd already left him two messages. That was enough. I knew he was busy at the restaurant, but I was tired of waiting and force-smiling at strangers.

By the time a group of four paranormal guests walked through the doors, their clothes and expressions oozing money and disdain, I was done.

I needed to find Valen.

Just when I turned to leave, Sonny and Cher made their appearance with their bell-bottom pants and colorful blouses that practically glowed under the dim lights of the lobby.

"You've been stuck here this whole time?" questioned Elsa, her mustache back on correctly.

"Lucky me, huh," I said, eyeing their outfits again with amusement. I wanted to match her authentic smile, but my face lacked the necessary motor skills like it was numb from excess Botox. I couldn't help but chuckle at their antics and how they fully embraced the 1970s' vibe.

Jade brushed a strand of her long, black wig behind her back. "You look exhausted."

"Exhausted from smiling and pretending to love my job," I told them.

Elsa swirled her glass of red wine around in her hand. "I should have words with that Basil, making you work like this."

"It's fine. It's part of my job description." The part I hated. "If I want to keep working here, I need to greet the guests every now and then."

"So?" Jade leaned forward and whispered, "What about that Clive guy? He's a real jerk. What are we going to do about him?"

My heart tugged at the use of *we*, like my problems were her problems. Having such good friends willing to take on a Gray Council investigator was still very new to me. "For now, nothing. But I will try to dig up some dirt on him."

Jade's eyes rounded. "Oooh. Sounds like fun. Count me in."

"Me too," said Elsa. She rubbed her locket with her hand for a moment. "But be careful, Leana. I sense a sort of desperation about him, felt it in his aura. A man who has nothing to lose can do almost anything."

I nodded, having sensed the same thing. "I know. He blames me for Adele's death. I have a feeling he's just waiting for me to screw up."

"So don't screw up," said Elsa, sipping her wine.

I gave her a pointed look. "I'll try." I wasn't planning on messing up. But I didn't think it would matter with Clive breathing down my neck. I had the feeling he was going to make trouble for me or blame me for something I didn't do. Yeah, that was more like him. "But I'm more worried about Shay."

Color left Elsa's cheeks, and she clasped her locket. "What are you talking about?"

I looked between my friends. "The Gray Council knows about her."

"That Darius," growled Jade. "He told them."

"Maybe, maybe not," I said. "Some of his goons escaped before Shay could blast them away. I'm pretty sure they blabbed to other members of the Gray Council."

"Maybe having the Gray Council know about Shay is a good thing," offered Elsa.

I shook my head. "Not the way he was talking. More like he would take her, and I'd never see her again."

Jade sucked in her breath through her teeth. "They can't do something like that. Can they?"

"Sure they can," I told her. "The Gray Council can do anything they want. If they take Shay away from me, they can hide her or put her in a school in another country. I'll never see her again."

"So we hide her first." Elsa's mustache fell into her glass of wine with a soft plop. "We put her somewhere they'll never look to find her."

I scratched the back of my neck. "I thought of that. But I don't know if she'll be willing to live her life on the run. I mean... do I really want to do that to an eleven-year-old kid?"

"You might not have a choice in the matter," said Elsa. "You need to put her first. If you think her life is in danger, you need to act fast."

"You think they'll hurt her?" Jade's eyes glistened with unshed tears.

I swallowed hard. "I don't know." I let out a breath. "Maybe. If we're talking about those shady characters on the council that were Darius's buddies, yeah. He wanted her for her power. I'm pretty sure it's the same with them."

"Where will you go?" Elsa's face had turned red, and I could tell by the roughness of her voice that she was trying hard to keep it together. The idea of me leaving them was just as hard for them as it was for me.

"I don't know. Haven't thought that far ahead yet." Which was true. "I'll need to speak to Valen and Shay before I make any decisions."

"What about your father?" asked Jade. "Surely he can help."

"Yes, good thinking, Jade," said Elsa, and she went to take a sip of her drink—

"Wait!" I pointed to her glass. "You dropped something."

"Oh, dear." Elsa laughed, and I could see tiny tears at the edge of her eyes as she fished out her wet mustache. "Wouldn't want to choke on that. But what about your father? Maybe he can help."

I had thought about it. "Maybe. I'll just need to figure out how to make contact with him. I've never had to get in touch with an angel before. But I'm sure I'll manage." I had come across some information in the Merlin database about summoning angels. I might have to give it a try.

"I bet Valen has other houses all over the world," said Jade. "Being a giant and all. Maybe even in New Zealand," she added with a smile. "You could do the Hobbiton tour. I'd love to live in the Shire."

I let out another breath. "I hate to do this to Shay. For now, I'm going to talk to her and see what she thinks."

"Yes," said Elsa. "But don't worry. Kids are more resilient than you think. They bounce right back."

I nodded, hoping she was right. Shay had been through enough hardship and loss. I didn't want to have to add to that. I'd wait to speak to her before making up my mind. She had a say in this.

"Doesn't Jimmy look dreamy?"

I followed Jade's gaze and spotted Jimmy in a

white polyester suit, a black shirt, and a wide collar. I could spot his chest muscles, a little hair, and a pair of sunglasses. He looked like John Travolta in the movie *Saturday Night Fever*.

"He's really rocking that look," I told her, which was the truth. That only made her look more adoringly at him, staring at her boyfriend like he was a celebrity and she was his groupie.

"Leana. Why aren't you dressed?" Elsa's eyes narrowed like she was trying to scry into my mind. "There's still time to put something outrageous on."

I shook my head. "I'm not really in the mood for disco tonight. Besides, I have work to do."

Elsa rolled her eyes. "I think you've done enough. It's time for you to relax a little. You need to let loose every once in a while."

"I'll relax when I'm dead."

Elsa pointed a finger in my face. "Don't joke about things like that."

"Why not?"

"Because they might come true," added Jade, though her eyes were still fixated on Jimmy. He caught her looking, and she gave him a finger wave.

Man, those two were cute. So cute, it made me want to hurl.

"You can take a ten-minute break and have a drink with your friends. Can't you?" Elsa waited for my reply like she anticipated me not having a choice in something like that.

Jade spun around. "You know... I have another

Cher costume you can borrow. We could be Cher twinzies!"

"Ah…" I shrugged again, unsure of what to say. They had a point, but my mind was still focused on the case. And even more on Shay. "Maybe later," I said finally, trying to sound noncommittal. "I need to talk to Valen."

Jade raised an eyebrow at me. "Okay, well, if you change your mind, we'll be right here."

As I started to leave, Elsa grabbed my arm. "Leana, seriously. Take some time for yourself. Don't let work consume you."

I sighed, knowing she was right. "Thanks, Elsa. I'll try."

"Good," she said, patting my hand. "Now, go have that giant of yours give you some of that fun you're missing."

My face flamed, but I laughed. "I just might."

"Here comes Basil. Duck!" hissed Jade as she made a curtain of her long, black wig to go over her face like that was supposed to hide her.

Me? It was too late. The hotel manager had spotted me and was heading my way.

"Why aren't you in costume?" Basil came strutting forward, giving false smiles to guests as he walked past them. "I left a very nice metallic-gray disco jumpsuit for you at the front desk with Errol."

"He burned it," I lied, though that was a possibility. "The lizard hates me. You can't trust him with anything that belongs to me." Like messages.

Basil was wearing that same orange one-piece suit and a scowl. "You need to change."

"I need a break. I've been at this for more than four hours."

Basil cocked his head to the side as though pondering a response. "I guess a ten-minute break couldn't hurt the hotel's image. You know, I've been telling the guests all about you—"

"Later." I slipped away before he could stop me, laughing all the way out the doors. I noticed a para-normal female about my age giving me the eyes reserved for those who laugh by themselves—the crazies, like me.

I laughed harder as I made it to the sidewalk, walked another twenty seconds, and popped into Valen's restaurant, my mood marginally lighter. Maybe they were right. Perhaps I did need to take a break and let loose a little.

Good thing I knew just who could remedy that.

CHAPTER 7

Valen sat at his desk in his office, his eyes on his laptop, looking too big for that simple swivel chair and devastatingly handsome in his crisp white shirt and dark jeans. Whatever he was looking at held his full attention.

He hadn't even seen me standing in the doorway, watching him like the stalker I was. I'd much prefer to stalk him when he had no clothes on, like while he slept.

I cleared my throat. "Maybe if I take off my clothes, I can get you to finally notice me."

"Leana?" Valen stood up from his chair. "I know. I should have called. I'm sorry. I've been going over the coroner's report."

I frowned. I really needed to get my own copy. He made to come over, but I stopped him with a wave of my hand.

"Sit. I'm more curious to know what the coroner has to say." I grabbed the only other chair in the office and pulled it around next to him so I could get a good look at the screen from his laptop and sat. His scent of musk and some aftershave wafted over me, and I drank him in. Yum. He did smell amazing. Who knew giants smelled so damn good.

Valen let out a breath and sat. "Nothing we didn't already guess. The victim died of heart failure. Her body shut down after it was drained of every liquid. That's the official cause of death."

I leaned forward. "So she felt it. Damn it." I pushed down the queasiness in my stomach. She'd been alive when someone drained her of her blood and bodily liquids, and it must have been excruciating.

The giant looked at the screen. "Her neck was broken postmortem."

Gross. "Do they know how she was drained? Did they find puncture marks?" We didn't find them on her, but that didn't mean there weren't any. They could have been too small for us to detect.

Valen's dark eyes settled on mine. "None." His gaze sharpened on me. "They believe her fluids were removed by *magic*."

My mouth fell open. "By magic."

"Yes."

"How's that even possible?"

"You're the witch. I thought you'd have an idea."

I cocked my head. "I'm not that kind of witch." I was a Starlight witch, and my magic resided in the stars. But that didn't mean I hadn't studied and read about what the White and Dark witches could do, mostly because I envied them.

I clicked my tongue as I thought about it. Remembering something I'd read, I said, "Could be a demon. Demons are known to suck the life force out of mortals, but it was daylight. Demons can't walk around in daylight." Unless we were dealing with a new type of demon?

"Then who?"

Now that I knew magic had done this, something occurred to me. "Dark witches can do this. Whites, too, but mostly Dark. They drain the other witch of her powers. In turn, it makes them more powerful."

"Really?" Surprise etched Valen's brow as he leaned back in his chair, crossing those large, manly arms over his chest. I really liked those arms. "But we don't know who she is. She could be human."

"She's not. She's a witch."

Valen blinked. "Who told you that?"

Here was the part of the conversation I wanted to avoid. "Clive came to pay me a visit."

A flicker of anger lit through his expression. Valen looked away, the muscles on his neck contracting as he lowered his hands on his desk, trying to compose himself but failing. His features twisted into a scowl. The realization of my words hitting him showed in the stiffness of his posture and the tension along his expression.

I knew the mention of *that* name would set him off, reminding him of the time when he felt powerless to help me. He couldn't save me when those

Gray Council bastards took me away, unable to do a damn thing about it.

None of that was his fault, but he'd blamed himself anyway.

Valen turned his head slowly. "What did he want?"

Damn, if the tone of a voice could kill, Clive would be dead. "I was summoned to a meeting this morning. Errol neglected to tell me I had a message. Anyway, Clive came to tell me. He told me about the dead witch and that the Gray Council was interested in her. He basically told me he's going to stalk me from now on and wait for me to screw up so he can lock me up again."

"Not going to happen," growled the giant. Was it wrong for that to turn me on?

"He's going to keep a close eye on me, on what happened here with the dead witch, and whatever other misfortunes might come my way. He's got a vendetta against me since he still blames me for Adele's death."

"You didn't kill her."

"I know that. He knows that, but he chooses to blame someone. Me." My eyebrows lowered, my mood souring at just mentioning that chain-smoking bastard. "He implied that a giant killed this witch, which we now know is impossible. Says so on the coroner's report, though if Clive had a brain, he would have read the part where it says her fluids were removed by magic. Giants don't do magic. No giant could have done this. Right?" I felt a release of tension that Valen and Catelyn were in the clear with this new information. I think I'd text Clive and tell him to suck it, if only I had his number. Oh well.

"Not necessarily."

I stared at the giant. "Meaning?"

"Giants *can* do magic," he replied, as though everyone knew that detail. "In fact, they are very good at it."

I made a face. "You're shitting me."

Valen shook his head. "I'm not." He tossed his hair from his eyes and pulled up the sleeves of his shirt, revealing a compact and tattooed, muscled forearm. Very pretty.

I knew giants possessed a sort of innate glamour magic and some healing abilities. I just never saw them as wizards. I tried to imagine Valen with a tall, pointed wizard hat, and robe. Didn't work.

"Are you telling me some giants are wizards and witches?" I didn't care to hide the shock in my voice.

The giant nodded. "Not in the way you are a witch, but yes. A few have been known to dabble in the arts."

"This is crazy." But it now explained why Clive still thought it possible for Valen or another giant to have killed the witch. But things still didn't add up. "Why would a giant kill some random witch? And then drain her of her bodily fluids. No, her magic?"

Valen exhaled. "My guess is the same as yours. To take more power onto themselves? I don't know."

"But you're the only giant here. Well, you and Catelyn. No way you did this. You're too smart.

You'd never kill in your own restaurant. That's just stupid, which you're not."

"Thanks," said Valen, a tiny smile reappearing on those damn fine lips. "Have you reached Catelyn?"

"No," I said, not believing for a second that she would do this. Besides, she'd only just started to get used to her new giantess self. No way did she have the time for that and to learn advanced magic. Because from what I saw and knew, doing that to another witch took some serious badass magical mojo.

"I'll keep trying until I do." I reached out and rubbed my hand over his thick forearm. "You're worried about this murder."

"I don't like having a killer in my city. Especially one who killed in my restaurant."

"You think it's a message."

The giant was silent for a moment. "I do."

Damn. "You have a list of enemies?"

Valen gave a dark chuckle. "Too long to write down. I've made many enemies since I moved here. Had to break a few bones to get the message across to a few werewolf packs that weren't following our laws. And a fair number of vampires. Some faes as well. Trolls. Ogres."

"Ugh." I sighed and let my head fall on his arm, struggling with what he'd said but more so for what I had to say next. "There's something I haven't told you about Clive."

My forehead slipped as the muscles on his forearm tensed.

"What?" asked Valen, his tone harsh, and I could tell he was doing his best to control his temper but failing miserably.

"It's about Shay—"

Valen's forearm shot up, making me jerk back my head. "What about her?"

"He knows about her. The council knows," I said quickly. "He said, and I quote, that 'the Gray Council was *very* interested in this little girl.' You know what that means. It means they aim to use her and her special sun magic." No doubt in my mind that's what the council planned on doing. Just like Darius had wanted to do. Use her as a tool to their advantage.

Valen grabbed the edge of his desk, his knuckles turning white. "They won't touch her. We'll hide her from them."

"That's what I thought. But where? And for how long?"

Valen looked at me. "For as long as it takes. They're not going to take Shay."

My heart just about exploded at his fierce love for that little girl. "I was hoping you had a house somewhere up in Canada that no one knows about."

The giant released the edge of his desk, and I saw grooves in the shape of fingers pressed into the wood. "Not in Canada. But I have a cabin in Wolf Brook, New York. It's a four-hour drive north. I use it to get away from the city. No one knows about it."

"Perfect. I can take Shay there. I don't know if she'll go willingly, but I think she's old enough and smart enough to understand the danger she's in."

Still, I didn't want to hide out forever. Sooner or later, I'd have to take care of Clive and the council members he was working for.

"I won't let you go without me." Valen watched me, his eyes alight with the confidence of violence toward anyone wanting to hurt Shay. It was an amazing quality for a man, a giant, and I felt myself fall for him even more. Plus, it did all kinds of things to my libido.

"But what about your restaurant? Your life here? I don't know how long we'll be there." In hiding.

It sounded so weird. Even to me. Was I ready to let go of my new job? My new friends? Just when I'd finally found where I truly belonged and was finally happy, I'd have to leave it all behind. It was excruciating just thinking about it. But for Shay... for Shay, it was nothing. She was more important to me.

"I can have Simone manage things while I'm gone," said Valen.

"Oh, right. Fish."

"What?"

I shook my head, trying to look innocent. "What?"

Valen watched me for a beat. "The restaurant manages itself. And I can do most of the office work remotely. I don't need to be here."

"Okay. If you're sure. Thank you." I was a bit selfish when it came to my giant, but I was glad he planned to come with us.

Valen slipped his hands around my waist, and the

next thing I knew, he pulled me onto his lap, my legs straddling him.

I smiled. "Is this my employee evaluation?" I purred, leaning in. *Oh, please let it be it!*

The giant grinned sheepishly. "Something like that."

"I see." I stared at his lips. His hands felt good around me, and his eyes held lust and desire. I felt my arms move up to slide around his neck. "Was I a good employee? Did I follow the rules?"

He drew me closer until my breasts smashed against his hard chest, and his arms around me tightened. "You came in late a few times. And no. You didn't follow the rules. That deserves a punishment."

"What kind of punishment? The naked, tie-me-up-on-the-bed kind?"

His gaze was heady. "Maybe. You have been really, really bad. Worst employee I've ever had."

I laughed, imagining pushing Fish's head down the toilet. "When does my punishment start?"

He leaned in closer until his lips grazed the side of my jaw, sending tiny electric tingles in my middle. "Patience, my little witch."

"I'm not patient, or haven't you noticed?"

His lips parted, and he breathed in my scent, his eyes widening as they traced my face and then my mouth.

I licked my lips, teasing. "If I don't get punished soon, I don't know what'll do."

Valen let out a growl that sounded like something

from a werewolf's throat. "Oh, you're going to get it."

I giggled, though my lady bits were beating out a tune. "Hurry up, boss. Or I'll go seek other employment."

Valen's breath came and went as his hands tightened around me. I felt his desire and his need in them. He dipped his head and kissed one corner of my mouth. Then the other side, pulling gently on my lips and teasing the hell out of me.

He slipped his hands under my T-shirt, and my skin tingled where his fingers touched my back. Heat pooled in my middle, the need for him pulsing within me.

And then he covered my mouth with his and slid his tongue between my lips. My breath came fast as he darted his tongue deep into me. I let out a little moan and wound my fingers at the nape of his neck, pulling him closer. His kisses made me ache for more.

Part of my brain shouted this was insane at a time like this, but we both needed it—a reminder that we were here for each other. A release.

I kissed him deeper. He made a surprised sound as his kiss turned more aggressive. A thrust of desire went straight to my core and sent a surge of heat to my nether regions.

A wicked part of me wanted to rip off his clothes and feel his hard body against my skin. I loved spontaneous sex. It was exciting, thrilling. Maybe we had time.

And maybe I should have closed the door.

"Valen! Blake is dead!"

I jerked and spun my head around, seeing a short, skinny male with the yellow eyes of a cat.

Valen picked me up and settled me on the floor. "What do you mean Blake's dead?"

The male shifter, probably a werecat, was visibly trembling, his forehead beaded with sweat. "He's in the kitchen. He's... he's... Something happened to him. His neck's broken, and he's all... fuck... he's all dried up or something."

I looked at Valen, seeing the same conclusion mirroring in his eyes.

Damn. We had another victim.

CHAPTER 8

I stood in a large, commercial-style kitchen with bulky, high-end stainless-steel appliances that probably cost more than my yearly salary. Cooking stations and prepping areas sparkled under the lights. I'd never been in the restaurant's kitchen before. It was just as neat and clean as Valen's apartment and the rest of his restaurant. All except for the dead guy spread out on the tile floor.

The male, called Blake, lay crumpled on the kitchen floor. The smell of death filled the air, and I had to fight the urge to gag. His back was against one of the prep stations, his skin emaciated, dry, and lacking any echoes of his blood or fluids. And yup, his neck was broken, bent at an impossible angle with some bone perforating the skin, suggesting brute force was involved.

It was undoubtedly the same way that other witch had died. We had another body on our hands —another body found in Valen's restaurant, no less.

If I had any doubts before that this was planned or that these killings were the result of someone sending Valen a message, they were gone. Whoever had done this wanted Valen to be blamed for it.

The giant was pacing back and forth, clearly agitated. I could tell this was taking a toll on him, and I wished I could do something to ease his mind. Valen halted, his face deep in a frown as he stood above the body of his employee. Blake was a cook, by the looks of his white uniform, or someone who worked in the kitchen. Valen remained silent, his expression stern, but his eyes danced with fury.

"Is Blake a witch?" I had to ask. If we were going with the theory that whoever was doing this was removing a witch's power by sucking out their fluids, their magical blood, and essence, I had to assume he was also a witch.

"Yes." Valen's jaw clenched and unclenched, his tension shifting from anger to sorrow. "A potions witch and an excellent cook."

I wanted to ask Valen more about giants manipulating magic, but I didn't know where to begin. If this was the work of another giant, who were they? And why were they doing this? To become all-powerful? It had to be more than that. But maybe it wasn't. Maybe the answer was the simplest one. It usually was. Either way, it was all connected. I just didn't know what that connection was yet.

"All the customers are gone," said the same werecat male from before as he appeared in the kitchen. "Simone's told all the staff to go home and use our sick days."

"Thanks, Vince," said Valen. He turned his head and glanced at his employee. "Go home. I'll call you."

The werecat gave a slight nod, his fingers twitching at his sides. His yellow eyes lingered on me for a second before resting on the dead witch again. A twinge of fear marked his face, mirrored in his eyes. He spun around, disappearing out the kitchen doors like he couldn't wait to leave. He was scared. Frightened that he might be next.

I didn't blame him. The body was ghastly to look at. But Vince wasn't a witch, and if our theory was sound, he was safe. But he didn't know this.

I didn't have to be a medical expert or a para-normal coroner to know this male witch had died in the exact same way as our first victim, whose name we still didn't know. It was the same MO. The same killer. I was sure of it.

Did this mean we had a serial killer on our hands? A witch killer? I surely hoped not.

Dread sat heavily in my gut as I did my best not to look at the victim's face. His eyes were the worst, soulless, and it creeped me out.

"I don't think I have to tell you how bad this looks, Valen," I said, glancing over my shoulder and making sure the kitchen was empty so no one could hear me. When he didn't answer, I added, "You know what this means. Right? That someone's trying to frame you for this."

The giant had said he had many enemies, and whoever would do something so extreme, something so vile and gruesome, really had it in for him. It was the only thing that made sense. But who? Who would do this to Valen?

"I need to shut down the restaurant," said the giant in the stillness. His tone held a faint ribbon of worry at the revelation of someone doing this on purpose.

"Really?" I didn't know why I said that. I knew he had to. Who would want to eat at a restaurant when you might be dead by the time they served you dessert?

"Until I find the sonofabitch who did this." The giant's hands were fisted, and it looked like he was about to smash in a few appliances, possibly some faces. "No one is safe here. They're using my restaurant as a pool to pick out their victims. I won't have it."

Ripples of energy flowed around us, more like beating down on us, and I knew it was Valen's giant magic. He was controlling his inner beast, his giant. Not that I would complain seeing him strip down naked, but the timing was all wrong. Darn.

"This isn't your fault, Valen. I hope you know that."

The giant looked at me. "Of course it's *my* fault. Two witches died in my restaurant. *My* restaurant, Leana. It doesn't matter how you look at it. It is my fault."

"You didn't ask for this."

A muscle feathered along Valen's jaw. "Doesn't matter. They did this. Made sure I'd go down for it." Stress laced through his body, tightening his posture.

I would never let that happen. "We'll find them." I stepped forward and rested a hand on his shoulder. "Even if it means we need to go through your list of enemies one by one—and I know it's a long list—we will find them and stop this." Preferably with my boot up their ass.

The quivers in my belly competed with the yearning that surged in my chest at the sight of his distress. I didn't like seeing Valen so distraught. I didn't like someone picking on my giant. That's right. I said it—*my* giant. If they messed with Valen, they messed with me. We were a unit now, a witch-giant package.

"Well, well, well. Isn't this interesting?"

I flinched, though I didn't need to look to know who that voice belonged to. Gritting my teeth, I turned around slowly, my heart pounding in my chest.

Clive stood in the kitchen, a cigarette in one hand as he gave us a flick of his rotten, winning smile. "You've practically made my case. I couldn't have asked for more valuable evidence to pin this on the giant." He laughed, spreading out his hands. "This is way too easy. I thank you."

Fury flared, and I stepped forward. "Valen didn't do this." I pointed to the dead witch, though I don't know why. It wasn't like you could miss him.

Clive blew a shoot of smoke from his mouth and

came forward. His pale eyes rolled over the witch called Blake, resting on his neck. "That's not what it looks like to me. It looks like your giant lost his temper and killed this poor bastard. Funny. Looks exactly like the other victim. Doesn't it?" He wiggled a finger at Blake's broken neck. "The way his neck is all fucked up. Like I said. Way too easy."

"He's being set up," I said. "No one with a brain would kill someone in their own restaurant. Anyone with a little intellect would know this. Like you said, too easy."

Clive snickered. "Nice try. We all know giants have tempers. They're more bestial than you and me. Sometimes they just lose control. They can't help it. And then they kill."

"Blake was Valen's employee." I seethed, feeling myself losing my cool. "You don't just kill your employees because they came in late."

Clive looked up and met Valen's murderous gaze. "Looks like this giant did."

A slow burn of rage took root, and I had to restrain from tapping into my Starlight magic, though it wouldn't do much at this time of the day. I just needed enough to send a blast at his man berries.

"Look at him," I said, flinging my finger in Blake's direction. "You need magic to do that to a witch. Says so in the autopsy report. The report you read. Valen doesn't have magic," I said. Though technically that was a lie, Clive didn't need to know that.

The male witch looked unimpressed. "Any idiot can obtain the necessary spells and hexes. Someone with means, like your giant here, can easily have bought a spell that can remove a person's life force. Their magical essence. Any troll can do magic. Your point is weak."

His words knocked through me like a mallet to the gut. I ground my teeth. "What the hell are you doing here?" Valen and I hadn't even had the chance to call it in. No way the Gray Council had known about this killing. Not yet. So how the hell did he know? Unless he'd been spying on the restaurant. My insides churned at the realization. Yeah, the bastard had been waiting for something like this to happen. He'd basically told me so himself.

"Saw the commotion outside, customers being ushered out," said the male witch as though he'd read my thoughts. "Thought I'd come over and check it out."

"Thought you'd come over and manipulate the scene, more like it." Damn. I hated this guy. Why did slime like him always manage to get themselves to the top?

Smoke billowed from the witch's nostrils. He stared at me and then at Valen. "Looks like I got here just in time. Did you inform the Gray Council?"

"Not yet," said Valen, his gaze lethal on the male witch, though Clive didn't even flinch.

A normal, decent person would probably have shat themselves if a giant regarded them in that way, in the I'm-going-to-pound-your-brain-into-mush kind of way.

Clive snorted. He moved closer to the body and

kicked it as though he was making sure Blake was *dead* dead, or maybe because he was just vile and liked to kick people when they were down—in this case, dead. The fact that he would do something like that, so uncaring and disrespectful, made me hate him even more.

"Hmmm," said the male witch, his face pinched like he'd gotten a bad smell.

I crossed my arms over my chest. "What do you mean, *hmmm*?"

Clive met my gaze and said, "Looks to me like you were about to cover it up."

My mouth flapped open. "What? You can't be serious. No, we weren't."

The witch showed a slip of teeth. "That's not what it's going to say in my report. It's going to say the two of you were about to hide the body before *I* intercepted you."

"You son of a bitch!" My legs were moving before my brain caught up, and I was rushing over to the witch, my fists ready. If Valen hadn't seized my arm, I would have punched the witch in the face.

"Careful," whispered Valen in my ear. "This is what he wants. He's playing you. He wants you to screw up. Remember? Don't give him that. You need to relax."

Though I wanted nothing more than to strangle the damn witch, I let go of my anger—well, some of it—and relaxed, knowing Valen was right. I'd lost my cool. If I had hit Clive, he would've dragged my ass back to that cell, and I'd be no use to anyone there.

Clive shook in mock fright. "Oooh. Temper, temper. Females are so emotional." He looked at Valen. "You need to control your little bitch."

Oh, no, he didn't. "What did you call me?" I'd been called worse, much worse, but something about being called a bitch was so offensive, especially coming from him, that it just hit me in all the wrong places.

"Leana," warned Valen, but he didn't need to. I wasn't going to risk getting myself dragged back to jail again, not when Shay depended on me. And not when it looked like Clive was trying to pin all this on Valen.

"I'm good," I told the giant. "I'm fine."

Clive's low, mocking laugh grew in depth but then faded with a bitter sound. "Not for long," said the male witch. "The Gray Council is not going to like what I have to say about the two of you. And boy, do I have lots to say."

Tension pulled me stiff, and in hearing the pleasure in his voice, I felt a snarl escape me. "We didn't do anything wrong. You've got nothing, you chain-smoking bastard." I wasn't sure if name-calling would land me a trip to jail again, but I didn't care at this point.

The male witch chuckled and took a drag of his cigarette. "That's not what it looks like to me." Clive looked at Valen with barely hidden disgust. "Looks like you're going to go away for a *very* long time," he said, a snicker in his voice.

"If you're going to charge me with something, do

it," challenged Valen. I watched him force the tension out of himself. He was wired just as tightly as I was. If I didn't lose my temper soon, Valen would beat me to it.

Clive sneered. "Not yet." He looked at me and said, "From what I understand, there are two giants in this city. This one and a female. She's a friend of yours. Isn't she?"

Catelyn. "So? She didn't do this either."

The male witch laughed. "Well. One of them did. And I'll find out soon enough. You can't keep covering for them. I will discover who did this. And then... then their ass is mine."

Damn it. I needed to warn Catelyn. She had to leave the city until we found out who killed those two witches.

Clive was still smiling at me like he knew something I didn't. I didn't like it.

"What?"

"With your giant out of the way and you joining shortly," he said, "Nothing will stand in my way of getting to your sister. Or should I say, the Jewel of the Sun?"

I balled my hands into fists. "You stay away from her. I don't care what council you work for. I'm warning you."

"*You're* warning *me*?" The witch laughed and flicked the butt of his cigarette on Blake like the body of that poor witch meant nothing, like it was garbage, an ashtray. "The Gray Council will have her whether you like it or not. It's not up to you."

"It is. She's my sister and a minor. You can't take her unless I let you. And I say a big fat *no*." From what I knew of the laws of our world, you couldn't take a child without the parents' or their guardian's consent, and I didn't give it.

"True," said Clive, though he looked more victorious than I would have liked. "But when you're stuck in that prison hole again, you'll lose all your rights to her. She'll belong to the Gray Council."

Fuck. I flicked my gaze at the giant, seeing worry cross his brow. That was when I knew what the witch said was true. "She doesn't belong to anyone. She's a person. Not an object."

"She belongs to the council," repeated the male witch, and a ribbon of panic pulled me. "That school is a good choice. Yeah. We know she's there. The Gray Council approves. But she won't be there for long."

"You can't do this," I said, hating the fear and desperation in my voice. A wave of despair hit me repeatedly until I felt as though I were drowning. I felt like I'd failed Shay.

They couldn't take her from me. They couldn't. I wouldn't let them. Looked like we were going to run away after all, much sooner than I thought.

Clive pulled out a cell phone from inside his jacket pocket. He pointed at us. "Don't go anywhere," he said, though I didn't know whether he meant right now, or he could sense what I was planning to do. "I'll be right back."

I watched the hateful witch turn his back to us and walk out of the kitchen, his cell phone to his ear.

"Shay," said Valen, and the fear in his voice doubled my own.

I looked at him. "I know… we need to…"

Oh, no!

"What time is it?" I went to grab my phone, but Valen answered.

"Four ten. Why?"

"Damn it. I forgot to go get her from school." And on her first day. *Nice one, Leana.*

Valen grabbed me and pulled me around, stepping over Blake to the other side of the kitchen. "There's the back door. Go. I'll stay here."

"You sure?" I hated leaving Valen with this mess, but I couldn't leave Shay.

"Yes. Go. Go get her. Hurry."

With a final glance his way, I slammed into the back door, pushing it open with my shoulder, and galloped into the alley behind the restaurant.

CHAPTER 9

Needless to say, Shay was in a foul mood by the time I'd reached Fantasia Academy's front gates, which were an approximate twelve-minute jog and then an unsightly limp away since I'd sprained my ankle on the uneven sidewalk.

Seeing her sitting alone on the steps shattered my heart. Her cheeks were red, and so were her eyes, like she'd been crying.

Damn it. I was a giant asshole.

She looked up as I hobbled forward. "You forgot me."

I wanted to die. "I'm sorry."

"Whatever." Shay stood, swung her backpack on her shoulder, and brushed past me.

Yup. She hated my guts right about now. I didn't blame her. I hated my guts too. It was a stupid thing to forget your little sister on her very first day at a new school, knowing how nervous she must have been. I must have looked like a horrible guardian to the school's faculty, but it didn't matter what they thought. It mattered what Shay thought.

I hopped after her. "Slow down," I groaned. "Ow. I sprained my ankle." Looked like my forty-one-year-old ankles didn't bounce back as fast as my twenty-year-old ankles had.

"I didn't even want to go to this stupid school," Shay shot back, her voice a little high. "And you didn't even show up."

I hobbled and shuffled forward, though she was still fifteen feet ahead of me. "I'm sorry. I can explain. Please. Just slow down. Let me explain."

"You made me look stupid," said Shay, as she continued just as fast—on purpose, I'm sure—down the street.

Human pedestrians laughed as they noticed me hopping along behind a girl.

"Nothing to see here. Move along. Move along." Yet that only made them laugh harder, and one of the young women flashed her phone at me, taking it all in on video. Fantastic.

"I know you're angry with me." I kept going, wincing as my ankle throbbed and seared with pain. "And you have every right to be."

"Whatever."

Were sprained ankles supposed to hurt this much? "Something happened at the restaurant," I said, panting and wincing. "And I just forgot." It was a lame excuse, but it was the truth.

Shay stopped and turned around. Her death stare made me stop mid-hop in an awkward tree-yoga pose. I thought she was going to yell at me or say something, but she didn't. Instead, the death stare turned into a wet-eyed one, and she quickly turned around before the tears fell. She didn't want me to see her cry.

God damn it. I made her cry on her very first day at this new school. I was the worst big sister ever.

Shay never said a word to me as I followed her all the way through the busy city streets and sidewalks until we finally reached our apartment above the restaurant.

She never slowed down or looked at me either, when she reached the door to the apartment and disappeared through it, not waiting for me.

My eyes went to the closed sign on the door, wondering if I should go and check on Valen. But if I did that, my relationship with my little sister would be over. She'd never forgive me for abandoning her. Twice.

I was terrible at this parenting, big-sister stuff—a colossal failure. I'd made her feel unwanted and forgettable. How would I ever make up for that?

The unshed tears were the worst, but I was fairly certain, with the sniffing I heard on the way over, she'd been crying.

I sighed and yanked the door open.

"Oh, crap." Then I cursed at all those stairs I had to climb. These were the times I wished I was a White witch where I could just magic my ass up the stairs with some spell or magic broom. My starlights could have aided the hike, but it was still daylight out, and for the amount of magic I needed, they wouldn't be enough.

With a sprained ankle and heavy heart, I climbed up the steps to our apartment—on my butt, no less—dragging myself up one step at a time until I finally reached the landing. At least she'd left the door open. On the other hand, maybe she'd just forgotten to close it.

I shuffled inside, not seeing Shay in the living room or kitchen. "Shay?" I called, moving slowly, like a hundred-year-old woman. With one glance at her bedroom and the closed door, I figured she was in there.

I felt at a loss. What should I do? What did parents do in these types of situations?

Food. "Are you hungry?" I waited. Nothing. "I'll make you a grilled cheese sandwich." I knew she liked those. Kind of her comfort food. Hell, it was my comfort food too. Anything with cheese usually was. It was also one of the only things I could make on a whim.

Using the wall as support, I lumbered to the kitchen, cursing the whole time. I grabbed the fridge's door and pulled it open.

"What happened to your foot?"

I flinched, nearly letting go of the door. Then, leaping on one foot, I managed to turn around. Valen stood behind me, concern on his brow.

"Sprained my ankle. No big deal."

"Looks bad. And you kept walking on it?"

"Didn't have a choice." I would have called a

cab, but I couldn't leave Shay. And she was ignoring me. She'd never have accepted a cab ride with me.

"Here. Come sit on the chair. I'll take care of your ankle."

I let Valen half lift, half drag me over to one of the dining table chairs. He grabbed a chair, set it in front of me, and sat. Next, he grabbed my foot and rested it on his lap.

"This should make it better," said the giant, and I felt a wash of magic tingle my senses, warm and light like a summer breeze. When he wrapped his hands over my ankle, a golden light emitted from his touch, and I felt a soothing sensation like he'd rubbed some lidocaine gel to numb the pain.

But he wasn't numbing the pain, I realized. He was *healing* my sprain.

"Tell me what happened," instructed the giant as the warm feeling continued to spread around my ankle and part of my leg. "How did you sprain your ankle?"

"By walking," I laughed. "Walking fast. I was trying to get to Shay." I let out a sigh. "I was late to pick her up from school. Remember?" My voice was low because I had a feeling she was listening. "She was waiting for me on the front steps of the school. She was pissed." I left out the part where I knew she'd been crying. I didn't want to embarrass her. I'd done that enough today.

Valen brushed his fingers over the skin of my ankle, sending warm tendrils of his healing magic into me that stirred every nerve in my body. Was that supposed to happen?

"Did you try to explain the situation?" Valen kept rubbing with his thumb now, and I had to resist the urge to moan. What kind of healing magic was this?

"I tried. She wouldn't have it. She wouldn't even look at me. I basically chased her all the way home. A hopping, one-legged freak." The memory of her tiny little self marching away, the stiffness of her movements, sent a pang in my chest. I hated that I'd hurt her. I just wished she would have let me explain.

"You know, I suck at this."

"At what?" Using both hands, Valen rubbed his fingers and thumbs over my ankle, like he was giving me a massage.

I didn't point out that I found the ankle rubbing relatively arousing. I was doing my best not to find it erotic, but the magic elevated the sensations to another level, and I struggled to keep my voice from growing croaky and horny. "Being a guardian, a big sister. It's not like our father gave me a manual to study. I've never been a mom. I've always been on my own. This is all very new to me, and I'm failing."

"It's new for her too," said the giant, his tone soft like this was really no big deal. "Fights are a natural process for families. You'll fight again. It's inevitable."

I shook my head. "This one could have been avoided. I wanted to know about her school. How she felt. If she hated it. If she made any friends." God, she needed friends her age.

Valen smiled at me, his gaze filled with emotion. "She'll be better tomorrow. Give her some time."

"I doubt it. You didn't see her face. See how furious she was." But I had a feeling she was more hurt than anything.

Valen moved closer, his hand reaching out to caress my cheek. "You're being too hard on yourself. Give it time."

I could feel his gaze on me, hot and heavy, and my body responded instinctively, flushing with heat. I suddenly felt too close to the edge of my control, and a brash part of me wanted to straddle him. Damn. What was *in* that magic of his? Instant horniness?

"Did you tell her about the Gray Council?" asked Valen as he dragged his expert fingers over my heel and up my leg again, sending delicious shivers over my entire body.

"How could I? She ignored me all the way here and then locked herself up in her room." She was so angry, I decided not to mention the fact that the Gray Council wanted her until she calmed down a little. Going away now, more like running away, might not go over so well. She was only just getting comfortable with our living arrangements, and she loved the thirteenth-floor gang as much as I did. So taking her away now might not be such a great idea.

"She just needs time," said the giant, rubbing that sweet magic into me. I had a feeling he was purposely arousing me simultaneously. "She'll come around. But she needs to know about the Gray Council."

"I know. I'll tell her. That reminds me," I said. "What happened with Clive after I left? He didn't arrest you, I gather." Obviously, since he was rubbing my ankle in a way that was probably illegal in some countries.

Valen stopped rubbing my ankle, leaving me disappointed. "No. The cleanup crew arrived moments after you left. He made some more idle threats about Catelyn and me." He let out a soft growl. "He has enough to arrest me if he wanted."

I jerked in my seat. "What? No. He can't."

"He can. And he will. As soon as he gets the okay from the Gray Council."

My heart was pounding in my ears. I glanced over at Shay's bedroom door. "Then we leave tonight. We go to your cabin."

A troubled crease etched Valen's brow. "I can't leave Catelyn. She needs to know that he'll come for her too."

"Then let's call her."

"I've been calling her since you left," said the giant. "She's not picking up."

Fear tightened my throat. "You think he has her?" Damn, maybe Clive had already arrested Catelyn and tossed her in some cell like he did me.

Valen leaned back and raked his fingers through his hair, leaving it all tangled and seriously sexy. "I'm not sure. I hope not."

"You think Catelyn could have done this?" I

hated to have to ask, but I needed to. I didn't think she did, but I didn't know what it was like to be a giantess and have to control those urges. Only another giant would understand.

Valen's gaze flicked to mine. "I don't know. Maybe."

"Maybe?" Holy hell. "But why? Catelyn adores you. You're like a mentor to her." I didn't want to believe Catelyn would do something so evil. But I wasn't an expert on giants.

Valen reached out and clasped my ankle again, though this time, I didn't feel any magic. "She might be acting out. She might have lost control over her giant. It can happen, especially in her case. She's not a born giant. She was made. She might not even know she's doing this."

"Wow. Somehow that's even worse." I shook my head. "I know Catelyn. She would never do this." At least not intentionally.

"I know. But like I said, she might not be in control of herself."

I let out a breath and leaned back into my chair, rubbing my temples. I tried to ease the tension that had built up in my head, sighing heavily. "Shay must be starving. She hasn't had anything to eat since lunch."

"I'll make her something." Before I could react, Valen slipped his hands under my legs and hauled me into his arms.

Grinning, I wrapped my arms around his neck. "What are you doing?"

"I'm completing the healing process," he said, his smile smug. The intensity in his gaze set my lady bits pounding.

"I thought you were going to make Shay something to eat?"

"I will. But right now, you need some more... healing... and she's still too mad to listen to any of us."

"Right. And how long will that be?"

"An hour should do it."

An hour to *do* it. "I think you're right," I said, trying to keep the excitement out of my voice but failing miserably. "I need lots more healing. What did you have in mind?"

Valen shrugged, a sly grin spreading across his lips. "Well, I'll start with some more rubbing."

"I like rubbing."

"And some nibbling and squeezing," he said, taking a few steps out of the dining area.

"Those are my favorite."

"You look like you could use a little release."

"I could. I really, really could," I said, my voice low and husky.

And then his lips were on mine, his mouth hot and insistent. I whimpered softly, my hands tangling in his hair as he pulled me against him, pressing his body against mine. We kissed like that for what felt like an eternity, lost in the heat of our passion.

When we finally pulled apart, panting and breathless, Valen whirled me around and headed in the direction of our bedroom.

"Come on," he said, his voice low and sexy. "It's time for your rubbing."

"Can't wait." No, I really couldn't. My lady regions were hammering away in time with my heart.

I'd been wire tight since I'd seen Clive today. If I didn't get my release soon, I might spontaneously explode like a piñata.

Valen hauled me into his bedroom, which was also mine now, and kicked the door closed.

"Won't she hear us?" The fact that my little sister was in the bedroom next to ours wasn't exactly helping the mood. The other times we'd bumped uglies, which weren't many, was either back in my old apartment, a few times in Valen's office, but mostly here when Shay had left to visit the gang on the thirteenth floor. It was all kept under wraps.

"She won't," said the giant as he lowered me onto the bed. "I made a few adjustments. Magical sound-proof walls."

I arched my brows. "Really? Wow." I sent out my senses now, and I could feel a slight vibration that hadn't been there this morning. But with my hormones raging, I would have missed it.

"You did this?" I asked. He had told me that giants were more than capable of magic.

"A buddy of mine did. He owed me a few favors."

"Nice." Really nice. And it came in handy because I had a feeling I would be really loud. Like scream-ing-banshee loud.

"Thought you might like it."

I laughed, feeling the tension and stress of the day melting away under his infectious grin. "You did not," I said, shaking my head in disbelief.

Valen shrugged, a mischievous twinkle in his eyes. "I did," he said, pulling me toward him, "and I have something else in mind too."

He lowered me onto the bed gently, and then he was kissing me again, his hands wandering over my body.

"I've missed this," Valen whispered, his voice low and husky while nipping at my bottom lip.

"I've missed this too," I replied breathlessly, running my fingers through his thick hair.

I smiled and kissed him, our tongues exploring each other's mouths eagerly. I moaned softly, my body tingling with desire.

"Damn, Leana," he groaned, his voice gruff. "You're so fucking sexy."

I giggled, feeling my cheeks flush. "I bet you say that to all the girls."

Valen chuckled, kissing me again before trailing his lips down my neck. His hands moved from my waist to the hem of my shirt, and I arched my back, silently urging him to remove it.

"Patience, baby," he murmured against my skin, his fingers fumbling with fabric. "Good things come to those who wait."

I groaned in frustration as Valen finally managed to slide his hand under my shirt, moving up to cup my breasts through my bra. He flicked his thumbs over my nipples, causing them to harden, and I gasped.

"Take your pants off before I kill you," I panted, my hips grinding against him.

Valen pulled back to look at me, a smug grin on his face. "Is that an order?"

I nodded eagerly, my eyes locked with his. "Yes. Now." Now, before I detonated.

He laughed, leaning in to kiss me again before breaking away to whisper in my ear. "As you wish, my love."

I was lost in the moment, lost in the heat of our passion. We kissed, touched, and explored each other's bodies until we were both writhing with pleasure.

Afterward, we lay there, sated and content, our bodies entwined in a tangle of limbs. Valen looked down at me, his eyes shining with love and adoration.

I could have drifted off to sleep, but I didn't.

I'd hoped to have more time to spend with Valen, enjoying his presence and relishing in living together, but these killings were putting a damper on the whole thing.

Besides, I needed to speak to Catelyn and warn her, if nothing else. I needed to find out if she was responsible for the two deaths.

No sleep would come until I did.

CHAPTER 10

I jumped off the N train and headed up Eighty-Third Street in Bay Ridge, Brooklyn. Yes, I said *jump*. Valen's healing magic had completely repaired the sprain in my ankle, making it as good as new, perhaps better. I still had no idea how his healing magic worked, but as long as it did work, I didn't care. I now had a fully functional ankle that I could walk and, if need be, run on.

After our magnificent round of one-hour love-making, Valen and I decided he would talk to Shay about the Gray Council, and I would try to find Catelyn.

"It'll be better if it comes from me," the giant had said, rubbing his thumb along my jaw as we lay on our backs, naked on the bed. "I'll make her favorite dish."

"Peperoni pizza," I said. At least I knew that.

"And we'll talk. She'll listen to me. Trust me. I'm good with kids."

"I've noticed." He was. He had a knack for it whereas I failed in every possible aspect.

"Shay's a smart kid," the giant was saying. "She'll understand why you were late. She'll forgive you."

I reached out and kissed his chest. "Will you tell her about our plans of running off to your cabin?"

"I will." His eyes locked on mine. "It'll be fine. I promise."

After I'd showered and got ready (and taking my sweet time to give Valen and Shay some privacy and enough time to talk while they ate together), I'd headed out just as I heard Shay and Valen talking in the kitchen. I hadn't looked back. I didn't want to ruin what Valen had already worked hard for. Besides, like he said, he was better at this than me.

Now, an hour later, I was in Bay Ridge, Brooklyn, on my way to Catelyn's parents' place, where I knew she was staying now. This was where she preferred to be, back with her family instead of living with the gang back at the hotel, which was totally understandable. She was, had been, a human, after all. She didn't grow up the way other paranormals did. But now she was part of two worlds. And I knew she struggled to fit in.

The buildings were a mismatch of brownstones, apartment complexes, a garage, and a few dingy-looking shops. It felt like I was in a more industrial part of the city, a man-made, concrete city of glass, steel, and stone. The streets were narrower than usual, and once the sun disappeared behind one of the tall buildings, everything was left in shadow.

My tension rose when I replayed my conversation with Valen about his belief that somehow Catelyn had lost control and had done those killings. A part of me didn't believe her capable of this. I had to believe that. It didn't make sense. Why would she do this? She didn't hate Valen. She respected him. He'd helped her, taught her to control her inner giantess. Why would she turn on him now? Unless she was sick or something? Having been made into a giantess was different than being born one. We all knew what had happened to those human-made paranormals Adele had created. They all spazzed out and went crazy.

Was that what was happening to Catelyn? Was she going mad? Lost to that same madness?

I'd thought she'd been safe from that. It had been months since she'd been changed, and she'd never shown any signs of aggression or mania. But maybe I was wrong. Maybe she was slowly turning into those mad, lab-made paranormals.

Speaking of labs, I wondered if I should try and contact Bellamy. If anyone could shed some more light on this, it was that witch scientist. Yeah, he was a little shit, but still, he knew a lot more about the magical transference than anyone else I knew.

I made a mental note to contact him if I didn't find Catelyn.

I felt a sudden rush of anger and violence at what Bellamy and his group had done to Catelyn. I moved my legs as fast as they would go without looking like a speed-walker on crack. A few humans, blissfully ignorant of the paranormal dangers and horrors that surrounded them, blurred past me as I ran up the street.

A sizeable four-story building spread before me at the end of the street. A few lights shone from the windows that lined most of the front. A name was stenciled above the front entrance, its washed out, weatherworn letters barely a legible shadow of what it once said. It could have been a department store once upon a time. The numbers above the glass doors read 858—the address Catelyn had given me.

Exhaust fumes, hot pavement, and the stench of garbage displaced the night air as I ran across the street. The gathering dark rushed in to fill the spaces where the streetlights couldn't reach.

I approached the apartment building, swung open the glass door, and moved inside. Her parents' place was on the fourth floor. Not seeing an elevator, I took the stairs, thanking Valen silently for his healing magic. I didn't feel any pain whatsoever from my ankle. He was a true miracle worker. The thought of thanking him later brought a smile to my face.

Burnt-out fluorescent light fixtures hung from the stairwell ceiling, their tubular bulbs covered in dust and cobwebs.

Pinching the cramp at my side, I gulped down buckets of air, feeling slightly dizzy as I finally reached the fourth floor.

"Damn. I really need to do some cardio." Especially for a Starlight witch like me, who couldn't fly or catch a ride on some magical broom.

I stepped into the darkened hallway, noticing that most of the ceiling lights were out except for one. Still, I was able find my way easily enough.

As I rounded the corner, I saw a door with a faded sticker denoting 4B. I reached out—and my hand froze in place.

The door was open, a barely visible crack in the opening.

Well, *that's* not good. An open door was a recipe for trouble. Good thing I dabbled in trouble.

"Hello?" I called as I knocked twice. I peeked through the gap, but I couldn't see much. "Hello?" I tried again. "Catelyn?"

My pulse pounded, and I opened the door as quietly as possible before stepping inside. The apartment was of moderate size by New York City standards, lit with nothing more than a few table lamps, which created long, creepy shadows. Great.

The ceilings were at least ten feet high, not unusual in the older buildings, and the walls were covered with wallpaper straight out of the eighties.

But that's not what had my arms and legs locked in place.

Two bodies lay on the floor in the living room, their skin gaunt and sickly in the dim light. The shadows caught their sharp cheekbones, pointy jaws, and hollowed eyes. Their mouths hung open as though in an attempt to scream or stop what was happening to them.

Just like the other victims in Valen's restaurant, their heads were bent at odd angles, glimpses of their cervical vertebrae poking through their withered skin. There was no smell of decomposition, blood, or signs of a struggle except for the broken necks.

It was nearly impossible to tell the man from the woman. The bodies were just too far gone, too emaciated to distinguish features. But from the clothes they were wearing, the one closest on the floor to me was female. The other lying next to the couch was probably male, judging by his clothes.

I was staring at Catelyn's parents. Had *she* done this? It was looking more and more like she was the guilty party here. Had she performed some spell to steal their life energy? To make herself... what? More powerful? As far as I knew, her parents were human without an ounce of paranormal blood in their bodies. So why did they look exactly like the witch victims?

Any enemy of Valen's wouldn't have known to come here and kill Catelyn's family. That didn't make sense. There was no motive here. No. This was a massacre.

And it looked like Catelyn had killed her family.

Dear God...

"Catelyn," I breathed. "What have you done?"

"Whoa," came a young voice behind me, making me jerk.

I spun around. "Shay? What the hell are you doing here?" Yup, my little sister, the one who was supposed to be hating me still right about now, stood but four feet from me. She had on her familiar backpack and a shocked expression.

"I followed you," said Shay with a shrug, like this was an utterly mundane thing to do.

Damn that girl. This wasn't the first time she'd followed me either. Nope. The first time was when I'd gone out to meet with Bellamy at the dingy hotel he was staying at and then the next was to the Gray Council building where Darius had tried to kill me.

"You followed me on the train?" That girl had more stealth in her eleven-year-old legs than I had in my entire body. She was born a spy.

Shay gave another shrug. "That was easy. You're not very good at hiding."

And here I thought my stealth had kept me in the Merlin business these last ten years. "You shouldn't have followed me. Weren't you with Valen? I thought he was supposed to cook you dinner and have a talk."

"He did. We did. You were in the shower. I snuck away after you left."

"How did you manage that?"

"Told him I was going to bed."

I raised a brow. "A bit early for you to go to bed."

Shay smiled. "He doesn't know that. I knew you were going to take the train. So I ran to the station, and then I saw you. Easy."

"My God, Shay." I walked over to her. "I thought you weren't talking to me."

Shay avoided my eyes. "Valen told me why you were late. He told me about the Gray Council too."

My throat clamped up. "He did. Okay. And... what do you think about that?" I didn't want to have this conversation now in front of these dead people, but she was talking to me. I didn't want it to stop. Until she was angry at me again, that is.

My little sister gave me a one-shoulder shrug. "Sucks."

She was right about that. "It does. Did he mention a cabin in the woods?"

"Yup." Shay glanced around the apartment.

"And? Is that something you feel *okay* about? I mean... going somewhere new again?" I hated doing this to her, but she wasn't safe. Not until I figured out who on the Gray Council wanted their hands on my little sister.

"Whatever. I don't care."

I stared at her, knowing that was code for she *did* care. "I'm sorry, Shay. I know this isn't what we talked about. We were supposed to be living with Valen, and you would go to that school. Oh. How did your first day go? Aside from the part where I came late."

Shay gave another signature shrug, still avoiding my eyes. "Okay, I guess. It wasn't as lame as I thought."

"Really?" That was interesting and heart-breaking at the same time. "You liked it. Didn't you?"

Shay glanced at me and then looked away. "Whatever. It doesn't matter." I watched as she walked away from me, clearly not wanting to discuss it. We would talk about it later.

"They look like mummies. Like the one in Valen's

restaurant." Shay stared down at the dead woman, which I presumed was Catelyn's mother.

"Yes," I said, stepping closer and joining her. "You know, you really shouldn't be here and looking at that. Why did you follow me, Shay?"

"I heard you talking in the kitchen," she answered, her eyes rolling over the victim's body. "I wanted to help you find Catelyn. Is this where she lives?"

"It is."

Shay's mouth fell open as I saw her connect the dots. "Are these people her parents?"

"That's what I think. And I think it's time for us to go."

A frown wrinkled Shay's face. "Who did this?"

I took a deep breath, not wanting to say what I thought. But Shay had a way of knowing if I was lying, and she always seemed to know things she shouldn't.

"I think... I think Catelyn did this."

"No..." Shay's face was set in a deep frown. "She wouldn't do this. You're wrong. Catelyn wouldn't do this. I know it."

"I don't think I am. The evidence all points to her." But the motive wasn't clear.

"You're wrong," repeated Shay, louder this time. "She's my friend. She's good. She wouldn't kill her mom and dad. She wouldn't."

I rested a hand on her shoulder, but she pulled away from me. "Catelyn is different from the rest of us. She wasn't born a giant. She was made."

"I know," said Shay, her jaw set in anger.

"And others like her who were made in that lab, well, they became angry. Violent. Really violent until they were lost to that madness. They killed a lot of innocent people. We thought—I thought—Catelyn was different since she didn't *turn* like the others. I thought she'd be okay."

Shay was shaking her head but not saying anything.

"She's my friend too," I told her. "And I want to help her. But I have to find her before she hurts anyone else."

When Shay finally faced me, she had tears in her eyes. "You're going to kill her. Aren't you?"

I stood there a moment, taken aback by her comment. "No. I don't want to kill her." That was the truth. I came here to warn her, and now seeing what she'd done to her parents, I was here as a friend to help her. She might never be able to live among us or humans again. There were places and institutions she could go, but I wasn't going to kill her. I just had to make her stop.

"You're lying," spat Shay.

"I'm not. Really. I just want to help her. I promise." I looked around the apartment. "She needs help. Our help. I have to find her before others do."

"Because they want to kill her," accused Shay, more of a statement than a question.

I nodded. "Yeah."

"I'll help you." Shay adjusted the straps of her

backpack. "I can help," she repeated, sensing my objection.

"Listen," I said, stepping closer to her. "Catelyn is not herself right now. She's dangerous. She's a freaking giant."

"Giantess," corrected my sister.

"Right. And really strong. Plus," I said, waving at the bodies, "she can handle magic. I wouldn't want anything to happen to you. Besides, you should be packing."

"I want to be here with you," said my sister. "Please. I can help."

The desperation in her eyes squeezed my heart. I knew this was her attempt to show me she wasn't useless. That she had magic. That she was strong.

"Fine," I said, and I couldn't believe I had just agreed. But the odds of finding the giantess tonight were slim. I'd take Shay on a search around town and then take her back home.

"Let's go," I told her, grabbing her arm and pulling her around with me.

"But what about them?"

"It's too late for them," I said. I would not call the Gray Council either. That would only alert them to Catelyn. I needed time to find her before they did.

"What are you doing here?" came a voice from the doorway.

Catelyn came walking into her apartment, a smile of surprise on her face at seeing Shay and me.

Looked like Catelyn found us first.

CHAPTER 11

Catelyn strolled into her parents' apartment, grocery totes in each hand. "Leana?" She looked from me to Shay. "Did we have something planned? Did I forget—"

Her eyes fell on the two bodies in the living room.

A smash sounded like the breaking of glass as her totes hit the floor.

And then, well, then came the screaming.

Catelyn released a heart-wrenching howl that I didn't think was humanly possible. The hairs on the back of my neck stood at attention as she rushed over and fell to her knees next to the body of her mother.

Shay looked at me, her green eyes round with fear and uncertainty.

I raised my hand, gesturing to Shay to stay where she was, as I moved over to stand next to Catelyn.

"No, no, no," wailed Catelyn, rocking back and forth with her mother's body clasped in her arms, sobbing frantically.

My chest contracted at her pain. I'd experienced loss before, the loss of a mother, but nothing like this. This was a mindless attack, and she'd lost both of her parents in one night. It was hard to imagine that kind of pain.

I watched Catelyn as she kept rocking, mumbling gibberish between sobs. With her mother's body still gripped tightly, she hit one of her fists on the wood floors. And then again. And again.

She was shocked. Devastated. Overcome with grief. It was not a reaction I believed possible from someone who had killed her parents. Quite the reverse. But it was still possible that she didn't *remember* doing it. That she'd lost control like Valen had suggested. It was what I had feared for her, that the madness that had taken over the other lab-made paranormals would, one day, take her as well. And now, I wasn't sure anymore.

"Leana?" whispered Shay, and I turned to the nervousness in her voice. She was shifting from foot to foot, looking like she was about to bolt out of the apartment.

I lifted my hand again. "It'll be okay. Just stay there."

I focused my attention back on the giantess, her screams having faded into a weeping, gurgling moan. Then she fell to the floor, her body curling into a shuddering fetal position next to her mother.

Damn it. I thought about whether I should call Valen, but I wasn't sure what he could do that I couldn't. Still, he should know that I found Catelyn and that Shay had slipped away.

I yanked out my phone, having decided to call my giant, and swiped the screen with my finger.

"Leana," came Shay's panicked voice.

"Don't worry. I'm calling Valen."

Shay let out a small, terrified sound. I looked over at her and noticed that she'd moved closer toward the door. But she was frozen in place, her eyes wide as she stared at something behind me.

Adrenaline soared as I spun around. Catelyn was standing and staring at me.

I cringed, not having expected that. I didn't even hear or feel her move.

"Wow. You got up pretty quick."

I stared at the woman standing before me. She was tall, perhaps almost as tall as me, but where I lacked in curves and bust, she had plenty. Her face was hidden by strands of light brown hair that stuck to her tear-stricken face and rested just below her shoulders. At first glance, you'd think this was just a normal, average woman. But she was the complete opposite of normal or even human. Not anymore. She was a giantess. But what reflected in those eyes now was only hatred… for me.

I slipped my phone into my pocket. "Catelyn?" My eyes swept over my friend, and I saw traces of suspicion cross her face, like she thought I had killed her parents.

Uh-oh.

"You killed them," she cried, her eyes wild, and I

knew I'd lost her at that moment. "You did this! You killed my parents!"

I raised my hands in surrender, aware that Shay was behind me and closer to the door. "I didn't. I didn't do this. I swear. I would never hurt your parents. You know me. You know I could never do this. Catelyn?"

Catelyn's eyes were lit with manic fury. "You murdered them. You killed my only family." She reached up and pulled at her hair. "I believed you but you're all the same. All of you! You don't care about us. You just *use* us. Kill us!"

A scream ripped out of her throat, and then she started to thrash and convulse as a thrum of magic pounded the air. With a flash of light, Catelyn fell to her knees again, howling as her face and body heaved and swelled to unnatural proportions.

Okay. *Now* it was time to panic.

Catelyn's face and body shifted and grew until they were triple her normal size. The floor creaked and trembled as she pushed herself up on her feet. My friend's face was still there, only bigger with a prominent brow and a protruding upper jaw, giving her more of a Neanderthal look. The clothes stretched and tore on her frame as she grew. They were now barely hanging on, like strips of rags showing off way more giantess skin than I would have liked.

Yeah, awkward.

She was hunched, her impressive head grazing the ceiling. Her fourteen-foot frame was too tall for these apartments. She might not be as enormous as Valen. But she was still frighteningly big and robust.

Too strong for me to fight while I had to protect my little sister.

My breath slipped from me. Catelyn, the human, was gone. It was over. We were screwed.

"*I will kill you*," growled the giantess, her voice so loud it shook the walls. She smiled at me, a twisted expression that was somehow wrong on her face, more hideous.

Keeping my eyes on the giantess, I took a few careful steps back, blocking Shay from Catelyn's sight. I turned my head slightly, and whispered, "When I tell you to run, you run. Got it?" I instructed my little sister.

"Okay," came Shay's reply close behind me, sounding scared, and it only fueled me with a sudden rage and crushing feeling of protection. I had to get her out of here.

I would never let anything happen to Shay. I didn't want to hurt or even kill Catelyn, but if she went for my sister... I'd have no choice. It would haunt me for the rest of my life, but I wouldn't think twice about doing it.

The sun had set, so Shay was defenseless. But I wasn't.

With my heart throbbing, I took a deep breath, tapped into my will, and reached out to the magical energy generated by the power of the stars. A cool shiver of magic washed over me, and I held it. I was ready for her.

But I was still hoping to be able to reach the giantess somehow. Part of the human woman who knew me, my friend, had to still be in there.

"Catelyn. You know me," I said and took another step back. "You know I would never do anything to harm you or your family. I helped you. I helped you settle in at the hotel. Gave you my apartment—okay, so you gave it back—but still, that means something. Right? It means we're *friends.*"

The giantess cocked her head like you'd see a dog do when it was trying to make sense of the gibberish you were telling it.

"*I will smash your brains,*" bellowed the giantess.

"Is that really necessary? I kinda like my brains where they are."

Her Neanderthal-like face creased into a wicked smile as she said, "*You're going to die now. I'm going to rip off your legs and your arms and watch as you bleed to death. And then I'll pound on you until nothing is left.*"

"And here I thought we were friends. I even let you borrow my hair scrunchy. It's yours, you know. You can keep it."

"*You murderous bitch!*" Spit flew from the giantess's mouth. "*You killed my parents. Why? Why? Doesn't matter. You're dead.*"

I let out a shaky breath. "Okay. Guess talking won't solve anything. Looks like it's going to be punches. Starlights and punches."

The giantess hammered her two fists on the floor. Wood splinters and fragments burst on impact. She reared back, and then with a powerful kick of her giant legs, she sprang at us, big and half-naked, bits flinging. Damn, I could never unsee that.

"Nice talk."

Okay, time for plan B. What was plan B? Oh yeah. Run like hell.

"Run!"

I spun around, pushing Shay ahead of me. A blast thundered in my ears like a grenade had just exploded. The floorboards lifted as a massive fist hit the spot where we'd been just a few seconds ago.

Shit. Shit. Shit.

"Hit the stairs!" I cried as Shay disappeared out the apartment's front door.

Me? I wasn't so lucky.

Something took hold of my leg, and the next thing I knew, I left solid ground as my body levitated horizontally. Okay, yes, I'd always wanted to fly, just not like this.

It was perfectly acceptable to panic at this moment.

So I did.

Terror welled, and I pitched forward on the floor, knowing what would come next. Pain flared as my back and side made contact with the hard wall.

Jaw gritted, I reached out and called to my starlights. Okay, so I hurt everywhere and felt like I'd fallen into a meat grinder, but I could still spindle some magic. I wouldn't go down like a coward. I was a Merlin, damn it. I would not be pummeled by a half-naked, angry, and delusional giantess.

Instincts hit, and I leaped to my feet just as a

towering female with a mouth that could swallow my head whole, came rushing at me, her fists ready to punch me to death, just like she'd threatened.

Good thing I hadn't let go of my starlights.

My body flooded with the tingling starlight energy that gushed from my core and raced along my hands.

The floors shook with the weight of Catelyn as her massive body came at me, floorboards splitting and lifting—a renovation nightmare right there.

She raised her fists and lunged.

A blast of white light fired forth from my outstretched fingers, hitting the giantess in the chest and covering her body in a sheet of white light.

A shriek of pain came from the giantess, her enormous limbs flailing like she was attempting a backstroke as she sailed across the apartment with a boom, hit the far wall, and disappeared through a sheet of drywall.

"Is she dead?" Shay appeared next to me, her eyes on the great big hole in the wall across from us.

"Shay." I stared at her incredulously. "I told you to get out." What the hell was she still doing here?

Shay glanced up at me. "I didn't want to leave. She wanted to kill you. I can help."

"I know you want to. But fighting a giantess is like fighting a dinosaur. I'm not even sure *I* can defeat her. She's really, really strong."

Of course, Catelyn chose that precise moment to make her appearance again.

"Witch! I will kill you!"

The giantess stepped out of the hole in the wall with plaster, dust, and drywall fragments covering her hair, face, and body. Then she cried out and charged.

I sighed. "I'm getting too old for this crap."

The giantess was almost on me, those big legs propelling her faster than I thought possible.

"Get back!" I pushed Shay down, planted my feet, and pulled on my Starlight magic.

Again, the power of the stars answered.

I joined my wrists together and pushed out. A beam of brilliant white light fired. It hit the giantess on the left side of her chest. It didn't send her sailing back but just managed to knock her off-balance for a few seconds.

Precious seconds.

"Let's go!" Grabbing Shay by the arm, I hauled her with me and out of the apartment a little too hard. For a second, I feared I'd dislocated her shoulder. "The ceiling height is low. She can't come through here."

The massive explosion behind us said otherwise.

God, I hate it when I'm wrong.

The giantess crouched low on all fours, reminding me of a large, angry gorilla. In that stance, she'd lack some mobility in her limbs, but it didn't stop her from coming at us. Her eyes weren't the eyes of my friend. They were crazed, filled with grief and fury for me.

The giantess rushed into the hallway. She stopped, seemingly having just noticed my kid sister.

Her lips curled into a grotesque smile, her eyes cold and calculating, widened with a sick delight at the prospect of smashing Shay's brains that had bile rising in the back of my throat.

"Get to the stairs and get out! Now!"

Frantically, I pushed Shay toward the staircase.

But the giantess was too quick.

Just as Shay hurried to the stairs, she looked over her shoulder and tripped.

My whole world slowed at that moment. The events happened in slow motion: Shay falling down, the giantess reaching for her, and me just standing there like an idiot and watching.

So I did the only foolish thing I could do.

Before my mind had caught up to my legs, I sprinted forward and threw myself at the giantess, my arms out like I was going for a bear hug. Could I squeeze her to death? Doubtful.

I hit the giantess and hung on like a baby chimpanzee. She flinched, not having expected that, and her growl told me was not happy.

I looked up at her and smiled. "Thought you could use a hug."

"*Argh!*" she bellowed, pulling me off and shaking me like I was a blood-sucking leech.

I caught a glimpse of Shay hunkering in the stairwell, her eyes round with fright, just as the giantess flung me across the hallway like a rag doll. I hit the ground and rolled to a stop. Ouch. I was going to need lots of Valen's healing touch after this. Not that I was complaining.

Still, I wasn't beaten yet. And I had Shay to think about. I pushed myself up while the giantess crouched at the same spot.

A hollowness hit my gut at what I saw on her face. Catelyn's eyes were on Shay, her face distraught and her eyes wild. Our gazes met, and for a moment, I thought I saw a small recognition, but then she narrowed her eyes at me and showed me her teeth like a hissing cat.

Then she went after my little sister again, chunks of drywall falling where her back grazed the ceiling.

Crap. "Here! Here you big ugly giant! She had nothing to do with your parents. It was all me. Me! I did it! I killed them!"

At that, the massive woman halted, her eyes blazing with cold, corrupt rage.

"Yeah, that's right. It's me you want." I glanced over at Shay, trying to tell her with my eyes to get the hell out of here, but the kid was stubborn. It seemed we'd both inherited that gene.

The giantess screamed in frustrated rage. "*I will kill you!*" She took huge, crab-like crawls toward me, pulling herself forward faster than before.

And then I was moving. I lurched and gave the giantess a solid kick in the gut. Grunting in pain, she stumbled back, but it didn't last long.

"Look out!" cried Shay.

"What?"

I hurled myself backward and hit the floor in a roll. The air moved above my head. The next moment, something hard struck me in the back, just as I was assaulted by the giantess's hot breath. We hit the ground together, me headfirst on the ground as dirt and God knew what else slid over my face.

Hissing through my teeth, I rolled, not waiting for the giantess to crush me to death. I slipped from under her weight and pushed to my feet. She swatted a massive fist at me, like I was an annoying horsefly, but I sidestepped and kicked her in the knee as hard as I could.

She barely flinched, but that managed to make her angrier. Her eyes shone with wrath and a savage hunger to crush my brain into mush.

"Great." This had to stop.

Resolute, I drew in my will and pulled up every bit of power I could muster in that instant as I threw my right hand out—and let go.

The beam of dazzling white light hit the giantess smack in the middle of her forehead. I was aiming for her chest, but whatever.

She staggered back, stunned for a moment. And then I watched as her eyes rolled into the back of her head, and she fell face-first on the floor.

An echoing boom blasted around us as the impact lifted me off the ground. The next thing I saw, the giantess's body flashed with a light, and then her features, her limbs, started to morph and shrink until she was in her human size again.

Shay was next to me in the next second. "Is she dead?"

"I don't know." I'd struck her hard, really hard, with a crapload of my Starlight magic. "Let me see.

You stay back," I warned as I moved forward and knelt next to the hopefully unconscious giantess. I reached out and pressed my fingers to her neck.

"There's a pulse." I was both relieved and a bit anxious. I wasn't looking forward to when she woke up again.

I stood up and rushed back into her apartment.

"What are you looking for?" Shay ran next to me.

"I need something to cover her up." I rushed into one of the bedrooms, found a white bathrobe, and grabbed it. "And we need to tie her up. See if you can find some rope or tie wraps." I didn't like it, but it wasn't like I had a choice.

I walked back out to the hallway and laid the bathrobe over Catelyn. I didn't want to have to think about whether she'd been the one who'd killed those witches and her parents. All the evidence pointed to her, and I'd seen the madness in her eyes. But was it the same madness as the others lab-made paranormals or just a flash of temporary insanity at seeing her dead parents?

That I was going to find out.

But first, I grabbed my phone and called Valen.

CHAPTER 12

I sat on the couch of my old thirteenth-floor apartment, my hands wrapped around a cup of hot coffee as I pondered the events involving Catelyn. Valen had showed up ten minutes later. After we'd done our best to clean up some of the rubble and mess, we closed the door to the apartment and left. Valen had carried the still-unconscious Catelyn, now with tied wrists and feet, to his Range Rover Sport and set her in the trunk space.

"We're not calling the Gray Council?" Shay had asked. She knew more than I did at her age about our world politics, and I wasn't about to lie to her about my suspicions, that not all the members were trustworthy.

"No. I don't trust them. We can't risk getting the Gray Council involved. Not until we know more." Knowing that bastard Clive, he might use this to take Catelyn away and maybe even Shay.

That's why I'd called the human authorities, an

anonymous 9-1-1 call from the restaurant nearby. Her parents were human, after all, so this should be a case for the human police to handle. However, it wasn't only a human case, not really. It was more paranormal than anything. But better they handled it for now.

Once we'd decided that Catelyn would be safer at the hotel—also the best place for us to keep an eye on her while we tried to figure out what had happened and why she did what she did—Valen had carried her to my old apartment on the thirteenth floor. Some tenants threw glances our way, but no one stopped us or paid more attention. Guess carrying unconscious paranormal women around was a regular thing on the thirteenth floor.

Still, word spread like an airborne virus on this floor, so naturally, the whole gang showed up a few moments later.

"I can't believe it," said Elsa as she rushed in. "And you think she killed her parents? No. I don't believe it. Catelyn could never kill her parents. She loved them. She moved out to be with them."

I shook my head and glanced at Shay, who was very quiet next to me. Catelyn was her friend, and I knew the whole experience was traumatizing. She was only eleven, and even though she was a witch and had experienced hardship at her age, she shouldn't have been a part of seeing Catelyn wanting to kill her.

I thought about reaching out and squeezing her

shoulder, but then I thought better of it. I didn't think she'd want that.

"Believe it," I said instead, glancing over at the older witch with a frown on her face. "I was there."

"You think that madness is taking control of her like the others?" Julian sat in one of the armchairs, his eyes on the bedroom door where Catelyn was still asleep.

"Maybe." Images of Catelyn's dead parents flashed in my eyes. "You'd have to be mad to do that to your parents. Well, parents you loved, and I know she loved them. No one in their right mind could do something this horrible."

"But she was fine," said Elsa, the disbelief and denial still on her face. "She was one of us. She could control the shifting. She didn't show any signs of violence. Not once. Never."

"I don't know what to say, Elsa. All the evidence points to her," I said. "She moved out. Maybe she started to act differently, but we weren't there to see it happen." Maybe we should never have let Catelyn go. If we hadn't, maybe none of this would have happened.

"We should have kept her here." Jade's voice was high with emotions. "We would have seen if something was wrong. We could have helped her. We could have stopped her."

"I don't know if any of us could have," I told her. "There's no cure for this. She was made like this, like the others. I thought she was different from the other lab-made paranormals since they'd used Valen to create her. I don't know. Because of his healing abilities? I thought she was clear of that madness."

"Apparently not," said Julian. He looked around, a frown on his handsome face. "Where's Valen?"

"He went back to the apartment to make sure the police showed up and not the Gray Council. If they saw what happened... we'd never see Catelyn again."

"But it's not her fault." Jade pulled the front of her Def Leppard T-shirt, her Cher outfit nowhere to be seen. "You said it. She wasn't herself. She could plead temporary insanity."

"You watch too much TV," snapped Elsa. "There's no such thing in our world. They'll just lock her up or worse."

Jade sucked in a breath. "You think they'll kill her?"

Elsa's face paled. "No. I think they'll study her and do terrible, terrible things."

I knew exactly what kind of terrible *things* she was referring to. The Gray Council had taken all the lab equipment and files from Adele's transference workshops. They could have just destroyed them, but they didn't. I'd always wondered if they would try and use it to create their own paranormal armies like Adele had planned. I was pretty sure that's why they kept everything.

I shook the thought out of my head. I needed to focus on Catelyn for now. I'd think about that later.

"I need to sit down." Elsa moved to the dining area, grabbed a chair, and hauled it into the living room. "I can't believe this is happening. She was doing so well. But... what do we do now? If, like you say, there's no cure, what do we do when she wakes up?"

I had thought of that. "Do any of you have sleeping spells or potions? We need to keep her in her human form until we figure out what to do. Sedated would be best." The longer she could sleep and not think about the horrific events, the better.

"I'm on it." Julian stood up. "I've got a sleeping potion. More like a sleeping candle. You light it up, and the fumes act like a sleeping gas, halothane vapor. Lasts about four hours."

"Good. Can you get it now?"

"Be right back."

I watched as Julian disappeared through the open door. I'd barely had two sips of my coffee before he returned, carrying a blue candle. Without a word, he popped into Catelyn's bedroom and shut the door.

"I don't understand all this," said Jade, her anxiety raising her voice. "You think she killed those two people in Valen's restaurant too?"

"They died the same way. Same broken neck. Maybe she got a bout of mania and killed them without even realizing she was doing it?" I'd admit it was a lousy theory. And I was still skeptical about her using magic to drain her victims. But at this point, Catelyn was our only suspect.

"Without a motive or a real reason, it all seems a little off." Elsa rubbed her locket with both hands. "Did you try and talk to her? I'm sure if you'd talked to her, she would have come willingly with you."

I shivered at the memory of Catelyn's pain at the sight of her parents. Then, like a switch, the Catelyn I knew was gone.

"Believe me. I *tried* to talk to her. It didn't work. She went into a dark place." I knew that place. I'd been there before. "She attacked us. She wanted to kill us. Me and Shay." I looked at my sister again. Her head was hanging low with her tablet in her hand, but the screen was black. She wouldn't look at any of us. "It could have gone badly. It was luck that I'd managed to knock her out." I was pretty certain my brain would have been mush if I hadn't.

Julian stepped out of the bedroom and closed the door behind him. "That'll do it for another few hours or until the candle burns out." The tall witch came to the living room and sank into his chair.

"Thanks," I told him and sighed. "That'll give us time to figure out what to do."

Julian leaned back in his chair and ran his fingers through his hair. "You're not going to alert the Gray Council. Right?"

"No."

"They're going to find out," said the male potions witch. "Maybe not tonight. But probably by tomorrow they'll hear about those deaths."

"And they'll make the connection to Catelyn," said Jade, her voice quiet and rough, her face pale. "They have all her information. They know all about her parents and where they live."

The thought of Catelyn tied to a magical dialysis machine stirred something in me, and I quickly looked away before my face gave me away.

I let out a long breath, trying to ease some of the tension in my limbs and readying my mind to focus. "So that doesn't leave us much time."

Elsa looked in the direction of the bedroom. "She can't stay here," she said. Her voice faltered a little as she looked back at us, plans forming behind her eyes and her pale skin turning a shade darker. I could tell her blood pressure was rising.

"No, she can't," I agreed, feeling Shay's eyes on me. "This is the first place they'll look for her. They knew she was staying here first, and they know we're her friends. No. We gotta find a place to hide her."

But for how long? As soon as Catelyn woke up from that spelled candle, she would remember what happened to her family and blame me again, and then she'd shift back into her giantess self, and we'd be right back where we started.

"If she's killing people," began Julian. "Maybe contacting the Gray Council isn't such a bad idea—"

"Are you crazy?" shouted Jade. "They'll torture her."

Julian raised his hands. "Maybe. But did you think that just maybe they won't? What if they're the only ones who can deal with someone in her predicament? Maybe the Gray Council is the perfect place for her. Just saying."

"I hate you right now," grumbled Jade, and I noticed Shay giving Julian her mad eyes.

"I don't care. But you need to hear this," said the male witch. "I like Catelyn, I do. But if she's crazy like you said she was, how do you plan on controlling her? How are you going to stop her from killing other people? What if she goes nuts again and hurts one of us? Kills us? What then? What are you going to do? She almost killed you and Shay tonight. Right? I overheard you guys. Next time, you might not be so lucky."

I hated to admit it, but Julian was starting to make a lot of sense. I wasn't ready to give up, though. "Do we know of any potions or spells that could help? Like something to calm her down?"

"Like Valium?" Elsa blinked at me. "I can get my hands on Valium. It will calm her down in her human form. But as a giant, I'm not sure it'll work."

"So we give it to her while she's human," said Jade. "Yes. That'll work."

"So your plan is to keep her high as a kite for the rest of her life?" Julian shook his head. "That's your master plan? I hate to tell you, but it sucks."

Jade jumped to her feet. "You've got a better idea, genius?"

Irritation flicked behind Julian's eyes. "Yeah. Give her to the Gray Council."

Elsa pushed herself out of her chair, and then the three of them started a shouting match. My ears rang as the room descended into a chaos of shouts, cries, and arguments, with Julian the loudest of them all.

I looked over at Shay. "Hey. You okay?"

Shay kept her eyes on the black screen of her tablet and gave me a shrug.

Guilt pulled at my insides. She should have never been there. I wished I knew what she was thinking. This was a lot to handle for an eleven-year-old brain. Part of me wanted to hug her. But would she welcome it? Not sure.

A sudden silence hit, and I looked up to find Valen sauntering into the apartment.

"So?" I stood up as he came to join us in the living room.

Valen's eyes went straight to the bedroom where he'd laid Catelyn on the bed. "She's still sleeping?" His confusion was evident on his face.

"Julian gave her a sleeping candle thing," I told him, not sure what else to call it. "She'll be out for another few hours. She can't hurt anyone. At least, not for a little while."

Valen looked at me and said, "Catelyn didn't kill her parents."

It was like a ball of lead dropped in the pit of my stomach. My mouth dropped open, and it took a few beats to regain control of it. "What? Are you sure?" From the corner of my eye, I saw Shay toss her tablet, her attention on Valen.

"I'm positive," said the giant. "Since I couldn't reach her by phone, I had a buddy of mine, Arther, tail her today. He confirmed she was working at her new job all day, so she couldn't have killed them."

It all started to make sense. Catelyn would have had to be in her giant form to have done that to her parents. And I'd seen what that did to an apartment. When Shay and I arrived, we saw no signs of damaged floorboards or walls.

Catelyn was innocent.

"Thank the cauldron." Elsa clasped her locket in her hands, staring at the ceiling like she was about to offer it to the goddess.

Jade started to cry, and Julian grabbed her into a hug.

Damn, if they didn't stop this, I was going to start my own waterworks.

I blinked fast. "So, Catelyn's innocent," I said, my throat dry and contracting. "She'd just reacted when she saw us, me. She thought I killed her family, and she just went nuts." Totally normal under the circumstances.

Valen gave a weak smile. "Yes. Don't forget, seeing her family murdered, well, she couldn't have been able to control her giant. It takes years for a giant to control their emotions. We do have tempers."

I smiled. "I've noticed." I looked down at Shay. She was staring at a spot on the carpet, her eyes red, and I could tell she was trying hard not to cry. God, she was so much like me. It was scary.

"And Catelyn is a newborn," continued Valen. "There's no way she could have controlled her emotions. Not after finding her parents dead like that. But with time, she will." I could tell by the tone of his voice that he was happy about this revelation, but something still nagged him, and I thought I knew what that was.

My head whipped back to the bedroom door, and I crossed my arms over my chest. "We still need to find a place to hide Catelyn until we figure this all out."

"She can stay with Arther," informed Valen. "I've already made arrangements. He's waiting outside the hotel to take her."

"Okay." I wasn't sure that was the best thing. "Who is he again?"

Valen rubbed my arm, seemingly having sensed my hesitation. "She'll be safe with him. I've known Arther most of my life. He's the main reason I moved to New York. He became pack leader here a few years ago. He's a good man, better werewolf, and he'll protect her like she was one of his pack."

A werewolf pack leader? That made me feel a little better. "So, if Catelyn didn't kill her parents or those witches in your restaurant... who did?"

Valen's expression was troubled. "I don't know. The only connection I can think of is that Catelyn and I are giants."

I shook my head. "But that still doesn't make any sense. Very few know she's a giantess. Us and the Gray Council. So why kill her parents?"

Valen shook his head. "I don't know."

My stomach was a flurry of emotions: anger, doubt, fear, and regret. I was angry at myself, thinking of how quickly I'd blamed and convicted Catelyn, but it was hard to make knowledgeable decisions when a giantess wanted to smash in your skull.

"They're attacking you both," I said, realizing this. "They're attacking your reputation. Blaming you for something you didn't do."

"I agree," said Elsa, her face flushed. "But who?"

"I don't know yet."

My emotions were all mixed until I felt like I was going to throw up. A quiver went through me. Who was this person trying to ruin my friends' reputation? Blaming them for murders they didn't commit?

It felt... it felt *personal*. As though there was a connection to me in all this.

So who? Who would do this? It didn't make any sense. Why were these people targeting my friends?

And then it hit me. Just one person in this world knew me and knew my connection to Catelyn and Valen.

"I know what we're going to do," I told them, my heart hammering with excitement.

"What?" chorused Jade and Julian.

Elsa blinked at me. "Leana? What are you thinking?"

I glanced at my friends, my sister, and finally settled my gaze on Valen and said, "We're going to kidnap Clive."

CHAPTER 13

After Valen had taken a still-sleeping Catelyn into his arms, careful not to inhale those sleeping candle vapors, and transported her to Arther—a handsome, stupidly muscled, blond, forty-something Viking-looking werewolf with piercing blue eyes that could hypnotize most warm-blooded females, waiting next to a black SUV—I made plans.

Said plans included me and my friendly giant breaking into the Gray Council building and kidnapping Clive. Good plan. More like insane.

I called it *Operation Smoking Man*. Cheesy, I know. I happened to love cheese.

Yes, my plan had holes and some dire issues. Mainly, I knew if I went along with this, I'd probably lose my Merlin license or worse—end up in the same witch prison Clive so badly wanted me to move into. But I didn't have any other choice.

Clive was the common denominator in this case, if you want to call it that. Not only had he threatened me, my sister, and Valen, but he was as slimy as they came. I believed him clever enough to pull off something like that. He worked for the Gray Council, so he knew all about Catelyn. Even if he wasn't directly responsible for this, he was connected. And he was going to tell me who, if not him. Like Adele, I was certain he was working for someone whose ass sat on the council.

And I *would* make him tell me.

But the other issue was Shay. She wanted to come with us, and no way in hell would I allow that.

"Please, I want to go with you," Shay pleaded for the fifth time before Valen and I left.

"No."

"Why not?"

"Uh, 'cause you're a kid. And you should be doing homework. You know. Kid's stuff."

Shay gave me an annoyed look. "You don't get homework on your first day."

How the hell was I supposed to know that? "Okay. No homework. Look, it's already late, like, nine or something, and you have school tomorrow. We might be out all night."

"So? I can be up all night too." Shay's face was set in a determined frown. "Let me help. Catelyn's my friend too. I want to help find the ones who killed her parents."

At her tone, and that fierce light in her eyes, I knew why this was so important to her. Someone had also killed her mother. This hit close to home for Shay. Darius had killed her mother to get to her, or her mother had died trying to protect her child from that bastard.

Either way, it was hitting Shay hard. This was way too personal for her. It hadn't occurred to me until now that Catelyn's dead parents were bringing this all up again for Shay. She hadn't even recovered from that ordeal. How could anyone when they'd witnessed their own mother murdered?

It was my job to protect Shay. And I would. Even if it meant she'd be angry with me, then so be it. It was for her own good.

Too many emotions were welling up inside me to keep pretending I was made of steel. I was tough, but I wasn't a robot.

"I want to go, please," she tried again, her cute, tiny mouth pressed in a hard line.

God, I loved that kid. "Shay, listen to me. I know you want to come, but it's going to be dangerous. I can't try to kidnap Clive and worry about his goons trying to kidnap you. He wants to bring you in, you know. Plus, you need a better hold on your magic. I don't even know if it would work at night. We haven't gotten to that part yet."

Shay's mouth fell open, and I could see by the raising of her eyebrows she wanted to comment on that, but then she just clamped her jaw shut.

"Jade, Elsa, and Julian are staying with you," I told her. It was the best thing I could do. "It's just Valen and me. We'll be back before you know it." I seriously doubted that, but I wanted her to believe it.

The sudden scowl on her face told me she didn't. "Whatever. You suck."

Julian snorted as I watched my angry little sister appear to be much heavier by the sound of her loud foot stomps as she disappeared into her old bedroom and slammed the door.

"Ouch," said the male witch. "That's gotta hurt."

"Not as much as losing her would," I told him with a frown and glared at him until he turned away, looking uncomfortable. It was worth it to have her hate me for a while if it meant I'd be saving her life. I turned to Elsa, who was making what appeared to be some hot cocoa for Shay from the sweet aroma that wafted over. "Keep an eye on our escape artist. She's good."

"Oh, I know," said Elsa as she poured the freshly made hot cocoa from her pot into two mugs. "But not as good as I am. I've got the eyes of a hawk and the ears of a fox."

"Didn't she give you the slip too?" muttered Jade with a smile.

"Keep it up, and I'll slip some gnome poop cubes in your hot chocolate," sneered Elsa.

I laughed as I headed to the doorway with Valen. That released a smidgen of my stress level. I was strung out, and my nerves were stretched as tightly as the strings of a guitar.

I hated leaving Shay, but she'd be safe here with the thirteenth-floor gang. However, she would never truly be safe until I stopped Clive, which I planned on doing tonight.

Once we exited the hotel, I climbed into Valen's Range Rover Sport waiting for us out front. The giant pressed the start button, and the SUV roared to life.

It was a quiet ride as we drove for a few minutes to the Gray Council building. I hadn't been there since the time Darius had tried to kill me. Not like I wanted to go. But Valen told me that his informants, whoever they might be, confirmed that Clive had an office on the second floor. Also, according to said informants, the chain-smoking witch practically lived there. It was a good place to start.

"How do you want to do this?" came Valen's deep, rich tone.

Me and my plans. "The usual way. We wing it." I shifted in my seat, trying to rid my back of the stinging pain, but it didn't work. Valen had offered to help alleviate the pain with his healing magic, but I'd brushed it off. The excitement of doing something proactive had momentarily disguised the pain. Now I was regretting it.

Valen chuckled. His dark eyes fell on me and held me for a moment, and then he stared back at the road ahead. "You did a good thing with Shay."

I snorted. "Doubt that. I forced her to go to a new school, and now I'm basically grounding her for her own good. How is that a good thing?"

"She doesn't see it that way. She's too young. But she needs to understand that she's just a kid. And she shouldn't be involved with these kinds of situations."

"I know that. Try telling her that."

A smile stretched along Valen's hot and oh-so

kissable lips. "She'll get over it. Elsa's really good with kids. And the others are there with her too. She'll see that she's not singled out, and she'll come around."

"I know. Shay's a great girl. And way too smart for her own good."

Valen laughed. "Tell me about it."

"And I'm delighted our bedroom walls are magically soundproof."

Valen laughed harder. "I'm glad too."

I rolled my eyes over the giant. He had such a manly quality; his protectiveness, though not too overbearing, was comfortable, and I gladly accepted it. It was nice to know that such a man was looking out for my little sister and me. He'd opened his life to us, his apartment, and everything else. He was amazing with Shay. He had that fatherly or big brother thing down to a T. I envied that.

It was harder for me. I wasn't ashamed to admit it. My entire life had changed when Shay came into my life. It wasn't always rainbows and sunshine either. But I wouldn't change a thing. Now that she was in my life, I couldn't picture it without her.

I blinked fast, my throat constricting with emotions. "You know, I've never really thanked you properly for letting me and Shay live with you."

The giant cut me a look. "I thought you did that a few hours ago," he quipped, a smug tone in his voice.

Heat pooled around my middle. "Ha. Ha. No, I'm serious. Not just any guy would take in a woman with her eleven-year-old sister." My ex would have thrown me out on my ass with her. He might even have taken the time to laugh. Yeah, such an asshole. Glad Valen had pummeled him a few times, yet I still had the weird feeling I hadn't seen the last of Martin.

Valen turned, and our gazes met. I could see the muscles in his jaw tense. His eyes held traces of a hidden meaning as they focused on me. He was trying to tell me something. But what?

"I'm not just any guy," he said finally.

"You're a giant. I know. I just... I just wanted you to know how much I appreciate it. Shay too. She loves it there. Living with you. She loves you, you know."

Valen's expression went still, and I had no idea what he was feeling, but he sort of stopped talking.

Hmmm. What was that about? "I know she can be a handful," I said, thinking she was just like me at that age. I was worse.

"Shay's a great kid," said Valen after a moment. "And she's stronger than she lets on."

"Oh, don't worry. I know." And a sneaky little bugger. "Her father—*our* father—hasn't been around for a while. I wonder why that is." He was supposed to show up every week, but he'd been absent. And I could tell it was affecting Shay. She must be feeling forgotten or abandoned.

"Busy with angel stuff?"

I raised a brow at the giant. "What angel stuff? Picking out his halos? Plucking his wings?" Did angels even have wings?

Valen's lips curled at the corners. "You have an odd sense of humor."

"That's why you *loooove* me," I teased. Wait—had either of us ever said the L word? I was pretty sure we hadn't.

My heart stopped. And then started up again.

He gave me one of his *I know you want me* smiles, and said, "I think he knows she's in good hands. Don't worry. I'm sure he has a good reason."

"Well, he'd better. 'Cause the next time I see him, I might not be so polite."

I rolled my eyes over the giant's handsome yet rugged features, finding him sexier and more appealing the longer I knew him.

"I'm sorry you had to shut down your restaurant," I said after another beat of silence.

"Not your fault."

"I don't know. It sure feels like it."

"Clive will tell us," said Valen.

"So you agree with me that he must be involved?" Elsa, Jade, and Julian hadn't been convinced of my theory. Though they didn't object to me going to kidnap and most probably "hurt" Clive to get answers, they believed my theory had holes— mainly the connection between the murders and the Gray Council being involved.

After Darius, you'd think they'd be more open to the idea that not all governing members were good.

Still, it had me thinking. If not Clive and the Gray Council, who else had it in for me? Or maybe this was really about Valen? I wasn't convinced. I'd deal with Clive first and see where his mouth took us.

I stared out the window, trying to focus on our critical situation with the Gray Council, but I found my thoughts jumbled and not wanting to listen.

I bounced in my seat when Valen pulled the SUV into a large parking lot. The clock on his dashboard displayed 10:12 p.m. as he found an empty spot and killed the engine.

He turned to look at me. "Ready to wing it?"

I smiled. "Hell, yeah."

We clambered out of the Range Rover and headed for the double glass doors at the entrance of the building. It looked the same as the last time I'd been here, like a typical gray stone and forgettable mid-high-rise building. It emitted a small pulse of magic, the glamour that kept the humans at bay.

Only bad memories came to mind when I associated myself with this building. I hated it.

"We going in all stealthy?" I grinned, maybe too happy to be doing this with Valen.

The giant chuckled. "Yes, ma'am."

"You sure he's here?"

"My informants told me he hasn't left yet."

"How knowledgeable of them." And how many of these informants did Valen have?

The giant pulled open the glass doors easily and went in first.

I followed closely behind. "Don't they lock their doors?" I glanced behind me, finding it strange, perhaps suspicious, that they weren't locked.

"They know that no human will wander in, so why bother?"

True. I followed the giant into a large, two-story-tall entryway with towering windows and went straight to the staircase instead of the elevator. Of course, I had to cut a glance at the black metal door next to the elevators, the door that led to the jail cells below where I'd spent three days.

My anger soared. I couldn't wait to get my hands on Clive. I wanted to discuss soooo much with him. I could barely contain myself.

Valen took the stairs, two at a time. I did the same for the first four stairs and then climbed them one at a time the rest of the way. I wasn't going to exert myself before facing Clive. I needed all of my strength.

Still, I reached the top of the platform only a few seconds behind Valen. The giant pushed open the door, and we stepped into the hallway to the second floor. Gray carpet padded our shoes as we strolled down the corridor.

I flicked my eyes at the doors that lined the corridor. "Do you know which door?" I whispered.

Valen nodded, and I followed him a few more steps until he halted before a plain gray door. A metal plate with the inscription *Clive Vespertine, Gray Council Investigator,* hung next to the door.

A hum of voices caught my attention. Chants. Murmurs, in low voices, came from behind that door, being repeated over and over, like in an incantation.

The air grew tight and heavy with magic, gaining momentum as they chanted in raging, rampant tones.

Well, well, well, Clive. What do we have here?

I smiled. *Operation Smoking Man, here I come.*

The giant turned to look at me and whispered, "Do we knock?" The tiny smile on his lips told me he already knew my answer.

I cocked a brow and matched his smile. "Hell, no."

Valen stepped aside. "Ladies, first."

Still smiling, and with my heart pounding with a mix of adrenaline and excitement, I grabbed the door handle, turned it, and pushed in. I opened the door as quietly as I could and stepped inside.

And let me just say this. I was *not* expecting the scene before me.

The office was of moderate size by New York City standards, lit with nothing more than a few candles on the tile floor, projecting onto the walls dark, vague, and creepy shadows.

The first thing that hit me was the overwhelming scent of candles mixed with the stench of blood. Next was the large stone circle in the middle of the room with six chicken heads spread evenly around it and the head of a black goat in its center above a blood-drawn triangle. Runes that I recognized as Dark magic—more specifically, demon letters and symbols —were written in fresh blood inside the circle. These symbols were used to summon demons. The air hummed with energy, visible as clouds of fluttering sparks, like static, danced along the surface of the circle.

Crowded around the stone circle were seven hooded figures.

And, of course, under their cloaks they were all buck naked.

Swell.

CHAPTER 14

It was difficult to keep a straight face as the cloaked figures—a mix of young and old, male and female—all turned, shock in their expressions, and looked my way. The potent scent of petrichor and vinegar had the cartilage in my nose stinging. Dark witches.

And standing slightly apart from the circle, wearing some amulet and holding what looked like a wooden staff with runes and symbols etched into the wood, was none other than my buddy Clive.

His lips were parted as though in the middle of an incantation, the expression of surprise and disbelief plastered all over his face. It had me all giddy inside.

I did *not* want to see Clive's junk. Too late. My eyes traveled down, and I couldn't help the laugh that bubbled out of me.

"Now *that* explains everything."

Clive's face turned a few shades darker. "You have no idea what you've just done."

"You've got me there, Clivy," I mocked. "I mean, sheesh. This is just as awkward as watching a sex scene on TV with your parents. We've all been there."

"You'll pay for this."

"Funny you should say that," I told him. "What the hell *is* this? I thought witches gave the whole naked thing up a century ago. Unless... unless this is some creepy orgy? Clivy. You nasty, nasty witch."

The male witch's hateful gaze zeroed in on me. "*You* are the vile one here. Not me."

"I seriously doubt that, given your history. But seriously. What is this? Looks to me like you're dabbling in magic you don't understand. And what's with the nakedness?" I laughed again. I couldn't help it.

"You have no idea what *real* witchcraft is," he said, his voice dripping with condescension. "You're not even a witch. You're nothing. You'll never harness power like we can. You're just a human playing at being a witch."

I shrugged. "Not like I haven't heard *that* before. Got something better?"

Valen looked at me. "Are we going to throw insults all night, or are we going to fight?" I could tell by the gleam in his eyes that the giant was anxious to pound Clive's head in. After all, he was responsible for shutting down Valen's restaurant and offing Catelyn's family. Well, that's what I was going for. As such, he deserved a good ol' head pounding.

"In a minute, honey," I told him, my eyes back on Clive. "I'm enjoying seeing his naked ass squirm."

"Clive," warned one of the females, the only one with dark skin. "What do you want us to do?"

I snorted. "Yeah, Clivy. Please tell us." I glanced around at the naked witches, all Dark witches by the intense scent of vinegar in the air that was making my eyes water. I wondered if any of them or if all of them were involved in the killing of Catelyn's family and those two dead witches in Valen's restaurant.

"Your intrusion just made my job so much easier," said Clive, that arrogant smile back on his face.

"Mine too. You need to seriously rethink your wardrobe, though. You might catch a chill." My eyes flicked to his willy. "Looks like little Clivy is cold."

One of the male witches propped his hands on his hips and stuck out his large beer belly like that was supposed to scare me. Maybe it did a little bit.

Someone hissed at me, most probably the same female who'd spoken. I didn't know many guys who hissed.

"You have no right to be here," said Clive, not bothering to hide his junk with his robe. "I'll have your Merlin license for this. Believe me. You're done. You're finished."

"Yeah," I said as I took a few more steps forward. "Thought you'd say that. The thing is, after *I'm* done with you, I'm pretty sure I won't have a license anymore anyway. So who cares, right?"

Clive narrowed his eyes at my threat. He folded

his palm, and when he opened it again, a tall flame danced above it.

"Nice trick," I told him, seeing Valen stand next to me, still in his human form. "But it's not going to save you." I tapped into my starlight and held it. There wasn't a cloud in the sky, only stars, so I was good to go. "You're going to tell me why you're trying to blame Valen for those murders. I know it was you. Killing Catelyn's parents? That was a low blow."

Clive, still naked, grimaced. "You know nothing." His pale eyes looked from me to Valen. "You're seriously outnumbered. If you want a fight, you're going to die."

"I don't think so." I hated this guy, but I wouldn't kill him until he confessed what he'd done and told me who else was in on it with him. Only then could Shay be safe, and we could have our lives back.

I would have preferred fighting a fully clothed witch, but you couldn't always get what you wanted. Looked like it was going to be a half-naked witch fest.

Clive turned his palm toward me. "You're going to regret this."

"Not as much as you'll regret interfering in my life."

The feral, yet rotten smile Clive gave me was frightening. His lips moved, twisting and rolling phrases as he worked his Dark spell. He was either going to toss me that fire magic, or he was going to curse me with something else.

The air had the sudden stink of sulfur and rot. He raised his hands, his lips still moving as a wild, whirling wind rose around him, catching his cloak and billowing it around him to give us a full view of his teeny pecker and skinny chicken legs. That image would be imprinted on my eyelids for the rest of my days.

"Tokziat!" cried Clive as he flung his hand at me.

Okay, he had some magic, but so did I.

With a burst of my will, I yanked on my Starlight magic and clapped my hands once.

A white, glowing disk sprang in front of me like armor. Clive's fire magic hit my brilliant shield and bounced off.

The surprise and anger on Clive's face at my shield made me feel looooads better.

I stood my ground, my starlight pumping through my veins like a shot of adrenaline. "You're going to have to do way better than that," I told the male witch.

"Ichtzir!" cried another male witch. He thrust his hand at me, and a tendril of purple energy came firing out.

It hit my shield, making it tremble and shimmer, and then it fell.

"Okay. That was better."

The same male witch smiled. "That's for ruining our séance."

"You're welcome," I told him, never letting go of my starlight. "We just want Clive, but if you interfere with my plans of taking his naked ass, I'm going to hurt some of you."

The same witch, let's call him Long Dong Silver for obvious reasons, stepped forward, bits swinging. "You're dead. And so is your freak."

I made a face. "Freak? Says the witch that looks like he's about to star in some homemade porno."

Next to me, Valen snarled, and with a quick pull of his muscled arm, he ripped off his clothes. Then, in a sudden flash of white light, his eighteen-foot body stood instead of his typical six-foot-four frame—a six hundred pound, heavily muscled creature that could easily kill a person with a kick from his tree-trunk legs.

A few months ago, Valen would have had to think twice about revealing his giant form. Not anymore. Not when practically the entire community knew of his existence, especially this bunch of lowlife witches.

His frame was massive. Good thing the ceilings were high. He fit but barely.

"Whatever you do," I told him. "Don't jump."

Valen, the giant, flashed me a sly smile. *"I'll try."*

He was the only one in the room whose naked-ness I didn't mind looking at.

The air grew tight and heavy with sudden energy, a power that was gaining momentum and growing into a feral, raging current. The Dark witches' power.

Just then, the Dark witches swooped around the room, circling us. Voices chanted in dark, languid tones. Long Dong Silver took two strides toward me and hurled both hands forward, dark curses forming on his lips. A thunderbolt of purple energy rushed at my face.

Crap. I hurled myself backward and hit the floor in a roll. The air moved above my head, and I had a moment of burnt-hair smell shooting up my nose. From the corner of my eye, I saw Valen take on the other two witches. They hit him like semiautomatic weapons with their magic. The giant faltered for a second, but he straightened and hammered the closest male witch. He did not get up again.

"Set phasers to stun," I shouted at the giant. Hopefully, he understood my *Star Trek* lingo. I'd be in enough trouble after assaulting Clive and his groupies. I did not want to add *killer* to the list.

Valen gave a nod and turned to advance on the other witch.

I turned to face Long Dong Silver. Blue eyes burned under his thick brow, and he flicked his wrist.

I spun to my knees and pulled up every bit of power I could muster in that instant as I threw my right hand out. A blast of Starlight magic hit the witch—right in his peepee.

I *swear* I didn't mean to hit him there. My senses just sort of took over.

Long Dong Silver froze in place, his hands going to his crotch. He cried out and then went down with a grunt.

I heard a snap and turned in time to see the giant knock the body of another witch to the ground.

Damn. I didn't want to hurt any of them. I just wanted Clive.

I spotted the chain-smoking witch behind two other witches, the same female who'd hissed at me and the beer-gut witch.

Yanking on my starlight, I rushed over.

The female witch stepped in my way. Her lips twisted into a sneer. "You're finished. You're gonna cry like a baby." The Dark witch spread out her hands like she was going to offer something to the goddess.

"Hmm. Maybe next time when you fight an opponent, how about you put some clothes on?"

She laughed. Her confidence annoyed me. "So, you're a prude?"

"I'm not a prude. I just choose to keep my wiggling bits covered. Face it. You're not twenty anymore. No one should see that."

The witch snarled at me, and I knew I'd hit a chord with her. "Adele was my friend. You killed her. It's payback, bitch."

Here we go again. "No, I didn't. She got her own stupid ass killed. Now step aside. I've got a bone to pick with your boss."

The witch made a face. "You'll have to come through me."

"Fine." I pulled on my starlight and let go. Beams of white light shot from my hands and hit the witch right in the chest. The power poured out of me, leaving me a bit short of breath.

She stumbled back, the starlights exploding all over her. I knew they wouldn't kill her. They'd just burn her a little and hopefully put her out of business tonight.

Pulse hammering, I lurched around, looking for Clive, but found Beer-Gut standing in my way.

A growl escaped him. "You're going to pay for that."

"We'll see."

He stepped closer, his pulse of magic sending the hairs on the back of my neck standing straight up. "Your star magic is weak. I'm stronger than you. Bigger."

"Maybe."

His face twisted into an ugly grimace. "I've got the power of demons behind me," he added smugly, stepping closer still. "What you got?"

"This—"

I kicked out and hit him as hard as I could in the meat clackers with my foot. That's two in a row. What did that say about my fighting skills?

He cried and fell to his knees, his hands covering his precious manhood. Then I kneed him in the face. The witch fell back, black cloak furling as he dropped to the floor.

"See? In this case, bigger doesn't mean better—"

Green flashed before my eyes. Something smacked my side, and searing pain flared. I went sailing down hard on the floor. Instincts kicked in, and I whirled, coming up on my knees, my hands glowing with starlight.

Agony stabbed me in the head as ice picks

plunged into both temples, and I gritted my teeth so I wouldn't cry out.

When my eyes met Clive, his lips twisted in a sneer as he finger-gunned me. Bastard. Okay, so this witch had some skill. But I was nowhere near finished.

Big hands wrapped around my middle, and I was lifted off my feet and set down.

"*You okay?*" asked the giant, his voice booming.

"Never better." I was fine, just irritated that it was taking so long.

I glanced over at Clive again. He was smiling now. Why was he smiling? Valen shifted next to me, and I knew he was also worried at the smile on the witch's face. He should be pooping his pants, not looking victorious.

And then I saw why.

Clive and the two last of his naked pals joined hands as they chanted. The air grew thick with power as green and purple tendrils of energy flew between them like a glowing rope. Their eyes emanated the same power. I knew what this was. I'd seen it before. They were joining forces, combining their power.

Clive's grin widened, the smile of a man who truly believed he'd won, and I was about to die. "This is for Adele."

I rolled my eyes. "Not this again. Give it a rest."

"After I'm done with you," continued Clive, "I'm going to tear apart your sister. Such a pretty little flower. Not for long." The sadistic smile he gave me chilled my heart.

Not Shay.

A mix of anger and fear rushed through my core. The image of my dead little sister leaped into the forefront of my thoughts.

Shay. She's all I could think of. My chest fractured at the thought of losing her.

And then something inside of me snapped.

As one, a combined, intertwined tendril of magic fired out of the witches' chests like a massive beam of purple and green light. Clive and the two remaining witches cried out, and that energy beam came directly at me.

I felt the air next to me move as the giant came to my aid. But I didn't need help. I knew exactly what I was doing.

I'd never felt this kind of rage before. I couldn't even describe it, not really.

The witches' beam came at me, but instead of cowering back or taking cover, I pushed out with my starlight. I used them like exhaust shooting out of a jet engine, and shot sideways in a blur.

The room rocked as an explosion hit the walls behind me, what should have been me.

I glided up and away, kind of like a Marvel comic character. I'd never done this before. Never thought I *could* do this. Fly. I *was* flying. There was no other way to describe it. It was pretty amazing, though I didn't have time to *marvel* at my skill. I had to end this now.

Still hovering, I spun around in time to see the giant grab Clive's sidekicks and smash their heads together. With a dull thud, he tossed them like discarded old clothes. No idea if they were alive or not. I didn't care.

Saving the best for last, I raised a finger gun, smiled at the last standing male witch, and shot a starlight beam right at his head.

Clive's head jerked back. His legs lifted off the ground, and he fell on his back.

I let go of my starlight and hit the ground, not quite the awesome landing I was going for. I popped up and walked over to the witch, seeing his chest rise and fall.

"Not so tough, you bastard." I refrained from kicking him.

"He's alive," said the giant, his loud footsteps nearing.

"Yeah," I agreed, a smile pulling my mouth. "Too bad for him."

CHAPTER 15

After Dark *was* dark, in a matter of speaking. Only a few lights glimmered in the sleek, modern restaurant. Namely the one next to the bastard tied to the chair.

The restaurant was still closed, so no one was inside except for the three of us.

"Wake up," I yelled, snapping my fingers next to his ears, but I wasn't getting much of a reaction from the unconscious witch. Then I did what any smart, badass, now-flying witch would do in this situation.

I backhanded him across the face as hard as I could.

"What? What's going on? Where am I?" Clive flicked his gaze around the office. It landed on me momentarily and then snapped to Valen, who was back in his human form. With his arms pulled back and clasped behind him, the chain-smoking witch didn't look so threatening. He was still naked, though. I wasn't about to look for a pair of pants for him, so we'd basically wrapped him up in his black cloak like a toga. His junk was covered, which was all that mattered. I couldn't have a serious interrogation if his wiener kept peeking at me.

I snapped my fingers in his face. "Here. There you go. Have a nice nap?"

"What have you done!" The male witch pulled at his restraints, the chair sliding and bucking with his effort. "Oh." He laughed as he stopped straining. "You just signed your death wish, you stupid bitch." His laugh vanished, replaced by a frown. "What did you do to me? I feel… different? What is this? What did you do?"

"Oh, those." I clapped my hands together in mock happiness. "Those are so awesome. Let me tell you about them. See, they're cuffs that stop you from doing your little magic tricks. You know, kinda like the ones you put on me. Remember? Well, I happened to find a witch who made some for me. Not the same, but pretty close. You like?"

"You'll go down for this." The male witch coughed and then said, "Assaulting and kidnapping a Gray Council investigator? Your whole family will go down too. You're screwed. This is the day you'll wish you'd never met me." He started to laugh again. It annoyed me, but I let him.

I looked at Valen. He stood next to me, eyeing the witch like he was hoping he could take a swing at him. All in good time.

"Shall we begin?" I asked my uber-sexy giant.

The giant looked at me, his brow raised in question. "This is your show. I'll follow your lead."

"Excellent." I stepped forward until I was face-to-face with Clive.

Clive narrowed his eyes at Valen. "I'll have you thrown in jail for assisting a kidnapping. You're all going down for this."

"The only authority you'll have after I'm done with you is to wipe your own ass. Because you'll be in jail. Not us." I wasn't sure Clive would see the inside of a jail cell, but I didn't like the fact that he was threatening my giant.

"We're going to start with some questions. You do like questions. Right? I mean, you ask questions for a living. Oh, and you perform naked rituals. Cute."

"I'm not talking to you," sneered the male witch. "You'll never get me to say anything. You think I'd never been interrogated before? I'm trained for this. Clearly, you have no idea what you're doing."

"We'll see about that." True, this was my first kidnapping and torture, but I had it all planned. I wouldn't let him out of that chair if he didn't give me the answers I was looking for.

I reached out to my starlight. The air buzzed and pulsed with energy as I pulled on the stars' magical elements. Power sizzled against my skin, and then a ball of radiant white light floated over my palm.

"Is that supposed to scare me?" said Clive with a snort.

I smiled. "It is."

"It doesn't."

"Oh, but it will." I took a breath and blew on my palm. The sphere burst into thousands of tiny, glowing orbs of light that attached themselves to Clive like a swarm of bees.

He jerked, his expression shifting as he struggled with his composure. He was trying to act as though having my starlights over him like a second skin didn't affect him, but it did.

I waited until his entire body and face were covered with my tiny starlights. "Okay, then. First question. Did you kill those witches in Valen's restaurant? And Catelyn's parents?"

Clive clenched his jaw. "I'm not telling you nothin'."

"Have it your way." I stretched out with my senses to my starlights and willed them to *burn*.

The witch grimaced for half a second, and then his mouth opened in a silent howl followed by a wail of pain as my beautiful starlights cooked his skin.

I'd have to add torturing to my list of skills. Looked like I was moving up in the Merlin ladder.

Still, I wasn't thrilled about burning this bastard, and he was right. I'd most probably lose my Merlin license after this. But he'd threatened Shay, and I wouldn't stop until he gave me some answers. I wasn't going to kill him. I wasn't that psychotic. But *he* didn't know that.

I let go of my starlights. "Hurts. Doesn't it?"

Clive's eyes burned with fury. "Fuck you."

"Bet you're dying for a cigarette, huh?"

The male witch hung his head but wouldn't answer.

I looked over to Valen to see if my torturing tactics repulsed him. He kept his face blank. His posture, though, showed that he was anxious to use his own methods, like his giant fists.

"Did you kill those witches?" I tried again.

Clive sighed to hide the fear that tightened his posture. He looked up at me, and defiance burned in his eyes. "Torture me all you want. I'm not talking. I'm not a rat."

"Oh, but you are a rat." I yanked on my starlights and pushed my will into them.

Clive wailed in pain, tears streaking down his face.

"Tell me why you killed those witches," I demanded again. "Was it to blame Valen for it? What did Valen have to do with the Gray Council?"

Clive screeched and thrashed in the chair, and the scent of burnt hair made bile rise to the back of my throat. Yeah, that was gross.

He jerked, his head shaking as he kept muttering the same word over and over again—*no*. Then he froze with a frightening suddenness, and his body eased into relaxation. And then his shoulders shook as he began to laugh.

"Told you so," said the male witch, a smile in his voice. "Not giving you nothin'."

Valen edged closer to me. "You want me to give it a go?" He cracked his knuckles, showing me the delight he would get from knocking Clive around a bit. He would enjoy that *way* too much.

I released my starlight. "Not yet." I gave him a short smile. Part of me wished we were back upstairs, enjoying the new "magically soundproof" walls. But I needed to do this. "I'm just getting warmed up."

I pulled my focus back on Clive. The parts of the skin on his face, hands, and other places I could see were red and blistering. It must have hurt like hell. "Like I said. I'm just getting started, but all of this could stop if you just began to cooperate."

The witch pulled his lips into a grin. "You're wasting your time."

"We'll see about that." I shrugged. "Okay, then." I willed my starlights again and said, "Who are you working for? Who on the Gray Council wants Shay?"

Clive laughed. "Fuck you."

"Thought you'd say that." I channeled my starlight. The energy poured out of me in a rush.

The witch threw back his head and wailed in utter rage and pain. A sound like a series of tick-tick-tick reached me, and I realized it was his teeth clattering. Clearly, he was hurting, a lot, but still he wouldn't talk.

After another twenty minutes of starlight torture, Clive was still not talking.

Breathing hard, I sagged with a bit of fatigue. Channeling so much energy through me like running a marathon, and a sudden weakness in my limbs made me sway.

But I wasn't giving up. Not today. Not ever. And not when Shay's life was at stake.

I pushed harder on my starlight. "Tell me who killed those people? Was it you? Tell me, damn it!"

Clive's entire body shook and convulsed as he took the pain. Drool trickled from the corners of his mouth. He looked at me, still shuddering, and managed to smile.

That's when I knew he wouldn't talk. Like he said, he was probably trained to endure that kind of pain. What type of organization did that? If the Gray Council was responsible for this, I wasn't sure how I felt about them.

The witch's expression shifted, slack replacing his smile and his features growing distant. Then his head fell forward.

"Damn it." I let go of my starlight. "I think he just passed out."

"He won't talk," said Valen, echoing my thoughts exactly. "He's trained for this. He can take more, but I'm not sure you can."

I raised a brow. "I can do this. I'm not tired."

The giant looked at me, his expression going a little bit softer. "That's not what I mean. This... You've never done this before. And if you keep going, it's going to have an effect on you."

"It won't," I lied. I could already sense some inner turmoil.

Valen reached out and pulled me into his hard chest. "I don't care if this miscreant dies. I care about you and how this is going to affect you. You can't

177

keep doing this. It changes a person." He went quiet, and I was left wondering if torture was something on his list of skills as well. Seemed to be.

It meant a lot to me that he cared so much, not so much for Clive here but for what might happen to me after the fact. I let myself breathe him in for a moment, pretending everything was right in our world. That would be just too easy.

Reluctantly, I pulled back. "Let's take a break."

"Maybe we should just stop. He's not going to talk."

"Oh, he will." If my starlight didn't work, I had other means to make him blab.

"Leana," said Valen, his smile fading and his eyes turning grave.

"I have something else that might work," I told him. "Something we haven't tried. We might have to wait a few more minutes until it's ready."

Valen raised his brows. "Until *what's* ready?"

As if on cue, the sound of the front restaurant door closing got my attention. A moment later, Julian appeared in the doorway of Valen's office.

"Here," he said as he handed me a vial with a light-green liquid. "This is the truth serum I told you about."

I grinned as I took it. "Guess it pays to have a potions witch as a friend. Thanks."

"It does." Julian looked at Clive. "Dumbass. I hope he knows he did this to himself."

As we'd arrived at the restaurant, and while Valen hauled an unconscious Clive into his office, I'd called Julian and asked him if he had anything resembling a truth serum.

"I do. I'll need about twenty-five minutes to cook it up," Julian had told me over the phone.

"Okay. We're at After Dark. Valen's office." I'd hung up, feeling marginally better about my torture attempt, knowing if my tactics didn't work, Julian's just might. Even if Clive had been trained to endure all sorts of physical torture, I didn't think he'd have much to bargain for with a magical truth potion. He was already magically incompetent with my fabulous anti-magic cuffs. The truth serum would work. It had to.

"I've made some adjustments for it to work with those cuffs." Julian looked at me. "Call me if you need anything else."

"I will. Thanks."

"No problem." With a last smile in Clive's direction, Julian strolled out of the office.

"You had Julian cook up a truth potion?" Valen eyed the vial in my hand.

I flashed the giant a smile. "Are you impressed with my torture skills?"

"Maybe." Valen chuckled. "I might be wrong. Maybe you were meant to do this."

Damn. I did not want to think about that. "Okay. Guess we should wake him up."

"I got it." Valen grabbed the glass of water on his desk and flung it in Clive's face.

The witch flinched and batted his eyes, and I saw

them finally focus on the giant. He took in his surroundings, remembering where he was.

Clive spat some water out of his mouth. "I can do this all night. I won't talk. Your magic can't make me."

"You're soooo proud of that. Aren't you?" I rubbed the vial in my hand with my fingers. "But this will." I held the vial in front of his eyes. "You know what this is?"

Clive's eyes rounded, telling me that he did. "It's illegal. You can't use it on me."

"Is it?" I stared at the vial, wondering if that was true. Was Julian cooking illegal potions in his apartment? Of course he was. "I don't care. You're going to talk now. Valen, open his mouth, please."

Clive clamped down on his jaw, but as soon as Valen wrapped his big, manly hands over the witch's head and tilted it back, his jaw snapped open as if nothing was holding it back.

"He's ready for you."

"Thanks, babe." I leaned over the witch's head and had to bite back a squirm. Staring down into someone else's mouth was pretty disgusting. Resisting the urge to gag, I thumbed off the cork from the vial and dumped its contents down Clive's throat.

He gagged and coughed, but Valen forced his jaw shut and kept it clamped until he swallowed every last drop. Once satisfied, the giant let go of Clive and moved to the side.

"How was that? Good?" I mocked, having no

love for this witch. Part of me wished he'd choked on it.

"It's not going to work." Clive's face was red, blotchy, and blistered from my Starlight magic. Nothing a healing ointment couldn't cure. "I have innate counter-magic in me. You're wasting your time. No truth potions can work."

"We'll see." I checked the clock on my phone, having forgotten to ask Julian how soon I'd see the effects of a truth serum and how long I might expect it to work. In ten minutes? A half hour? Immediately? I was hoping for immediately.

Clive was still smiling that smug smile of his, but I didn't care. It was now or never to test Julian's handiwork.

"Who on the Gray Council are you working for?"

The witch blinked, his eyes seemingly going out of focus. "Freida Pavlov."

Oh, shit. It was working. Beaming and trying to control my sudden excitement, I looked at Valen. "You know her?"

Valen's expression closed off. "She's a vampire. An old one."

"Vampire?" What the hell was going on? I turned back to Clive, seeing his head loll to the side with a string of drool hanging from the left corner of his mouth down to his chin. Swell.

"She's not someone you want to cross," warned the giant, and I sensed the worry in his tone that only increased my own.

"What does she want with Shay?" I asked Clive,

though I had an inclination I already knew the answer.

"She wants her power. All of it," answered the witch, his voice a little low and slow, like he was talking in his sleep.

My heart was thumping not with excitement anymore but with dread. "Why does she want Shay's power?"

"So she can rule over the rest of the council members," droned the male witch.

Of course, she did. "She wants them to fear her?"

"Yes."

I took a breath. "But Shay's unique. You can't kill her and assume to harness her power. It doesn't work like that. She can't die."

"Freida can control her. She'll obey. She'll do as she commands."

What the hell did that mean? "Like a slave?"

"Yes."

That bitch. I needed to take care of this ancient vampire. "Who else on the Gray Council wants to use my sister?"

Clive blinked a few times. "Only Freida."

I raised my brows in surprise. "She's the only one?"

"Yes."

I glanced at Valen before looking back at Clive. "Who else on the Gray Council wants me in prison?"

"Just Freida," answered Clive.

"So, just Freida and Darius?"

The witch's mouth flapped open. "Yes."

Okay, then. One down, one to go. "I'm glad we're having this chat. It's almost like we're friends."

"We are not friends," muttered the witch.

"Thank the gods." This was good information. Hell, it was amazing. I had a name and now a confession that she wanted to use my little sister's power for herself. It would have taken me days, maybe even months, to gather the names of those on the council who were frauds. But I wasn't finished. "Why did Frieda have you kill those witches in Valen's restaurant?"

Clive blinked. "She didn't."

"What?" I leaned closer. "Who killed them, then?"

The male witch hesitated a moment and then said, "I don't know."

Yeah, that was strange. "Who killed Catelyn's parents? Who murdered her family?"

Again, the witch hesitated like he was trying to think. "I don't know."

I reeled back, looking at Valen for support. "What the hell?"

He gazed at me, his eyes intense. Not for the first time, I wished I could read his mind, but he seemed just as confused as I was.

Dread hit. Maybe Clive was playing me. Perhaps this was his clever self trying to pretend he was magically induced by the truth serum but wasn't? No. Julian was a hard-core potions-and-poisons witch. He knew how important this was. He wouldn't give me a dud potion.

Still, I had to test this theory. "Clive. Do you have

a small penis?" No man in his right mind would say yes to that. Unless spelled, of course.

"Yes," came Clive's voice in that same sleepy tone.

Valen shook his head at me. "You're crazy."

"Better crazy than boring. Clive," I tried again, not liking how nervous and high my voice was. "Did the Gray Council have anything to do with those murders?"

"No," answered the witch.

Holy hell.

I leaned back, my pulse hammering. If the Gray Council wasn't responsible, who was? Who had killed those witches and Catelyn's parents?

I had no idea how I was going to figure this out. I just knew I couldn't give up.

Looked like I had a hell of a lot more work to do.

CHAPTER 16

I stepped through the front gates, my legs stiff and tired, but my body was more exhausted from the lack of sleep.

After our little torture episode with Clive, I barely slept. How could I? First, because some ancient vampire wanted to get ahold of my sister, and second, because I had no idea who had killed those witches and Catelyn's parents.

I was back at square one. It wasn't even a square. It was an oval. The only thing I could come up with was Valen's list of enemies, but even that didn't make a whole lot of sense. For one, what did they have to do with Catelyn? Unless they thought she was his sister or giantess friend? Or maybe they just hated giants?

Basically, I had nothing to go on.

After getting all I could out of Clive, Valen and I decided to take him back to the Gray Council, where we'd abducted him. Once we'd finished with our questions, the male witch had dozed off, snoring loudly.

"He gave us classified Gray Council information about this Freida," Valen had told me on our way back to the Gray Council building. "I think he'll be too ashamed to reveal his betrayal of her to the vampire. He'll keep his mouth shut. You can bet on it."

That I believed. He was too arrogant to let his peers know he'd blabbed. He'd bragged about how the "physical" torture wouldn't have an effect on him. But he hadn't accounted for Julian's truth serum. In the end, it had worked. Thank you, Julian.

And so we'd dumped a snoring Clive in the middle of his ritual circle. The other witches were gone, so it was just him.

It didn't give me all the answers I wanted, like who'd killed Catelyn's parents and who was trying to blame Valen for those two dead witches. But at least it was good enough for now. And on the plus side, I didn't think I'd be seeing Clive around for a while, which meant I had a clear path to my own investigation.

But Shay was still not safe from the clutches of that vampire. I was going to investigate this Freida. I'd already forgotten her last name. I'd start right after I dropped Shay off at school.

"You're acting weird," said Shay, walking up the steps to Fantasia Academy, next to me.

I thought it strange that I didn't see any other

kids with their parents on their way to school. Maybe they'd already come and gone.

"Hmm? Oh, sorry. Lots of stuff on my mind." Like this vampire Freida. I'd seriously thought of keeping Shay home with me today, but she'd told me she wanted to go, which surprised me. She *liked* this school.

Plus, from what I'd read in the rules and regulations catalog Shay had brought back with her yesterday, no one was allowed on the school's premises, not even the Gray Council, except for faculty and the students. So I knew she'd be safe there for a while until I figured out what to do. We always had the option of running.

Shay shrugged. "Whatever."

I sighed. "Please don't be mad at me. I know you wanted to come last night, but trust me, you didn't want to see what we saw." Like lots of naked witches. Plus, I was glad she wasn't there to witness the torturing. No kid should see that. But I realized it was more that I didn't want her to see me in that light. I cared about what she thought of me.

Shay stopped when we got to the front doors. "Did you find him?"

"Yeah."

"Did you get what you were looking for?"

I pursed my lips. "Yes and no. More of the yes, little bit of the no."

Shay frowned at me. "You're so weird."

I grinned. "I know."

The front door swung open. I'd plastered on a

fake smile, expecting to see the same oily bald member of the school's staff. Instead, a woman stood there. Magic pinged my senses, but I couldn't figure out if she was a White or Dark witch. I was hit with a strong feeling of familiarity. She looked... familiar to me. Had I seen her somewhere? Could be. I had a terrible memory. I was even worse with names. I might have met her before and wouldn't even remember. Hanging from her neck was a pendant with the most beautiful blue stone I'd ever seen. An oval-shaped jewel in sapphire blue was held in place by four dragon claws.

I pulled my eyes away from her pendant and found her looking at me.

Her gaze settled on me briefly but then widened as she focused on Shay. "Ah, hello, Shay. Nice to see you again."

"Hello, Ms. Barclay," said Shay, her cheeks touched with pink. With the polite tone in her voice, I could tell she liked this teacher. Good. That was good.

Ms. Barclay had long, blonde hair, which she kept neatly back in a half updo. Wrinkle free, she looked to be in her forties and nicely fit, though a bit on the thin side. Large gray eyes settled on me. "Thank you for being on time today."

"Uh... right. You're welcome." *You're welcome?*

Shay snorted. "God, you're weird. See you later."

"Later." I waved at her back as she walked past Ms. Barclay and disappeared behind the doors.

"See you soon, Leana," said Ms. Barclay as she shut the door in my face.

I lowered my hand, staring at the door for a beat. After a minute or so, I sighed and whirled around. And my face smacked into Jade's head.

"Ow. What are you guys doing here?" I jerked back, seeing Elsa, Jade, and Julian standing behind me.

"We followed you," said a cheery Elsa, her green garden clogs peeking from under her long orange skirt.

I rubbed my forehead, where I could already feel a throbbing lump. "You followed me?"

Jade laughed, rubbing the opposite side of her head, which was wrapped in a pink headband at the moment, her pink plastic loop earrings swaying. "You have a really hard head." She wore a pastel-blue jumpsuit tied with a broad white belt around her waist. And with her blonde hair pulled on the top of her head in a high ponytail, she looked like she'd just stepped off a time machine from the eighties.

"We did." Elsa pressed her hands to her hips, beaming as she admired the school. "I've always wanted to see the inside of Fantasia Academy." She looked past me to the front of the building. "My son Dylan wasn't accepted. I think that had something to do with Adele. After Cedric refused to let her bully him, well, he lost his job, and we lost our good name."

I lowered my hand, remembering Elsa telling me

that story. "I'd love to take you on a tour, but we're not allowed in. Not even me."

"I know. Isn't it cool?" Jade was staring up at the school with dreamy eyes, like she'd do just about anything to be able to attend.

I grabbed hold of my friends and pulled them away from the school before Ms. Barclay saw us through one of the many windows. When we'd stepped beyond the gates, I asked, "But why did you follow us?"

"Well, after what you told us last night, we did some of our own digging on your vampire friend, Freida," said Elsa.

I'd told them every conversation worth mentioning, I had with Clive.

"Thanks, guys," I exhaled, appreciating that I would have extra help on this case. It looked like I was going to need it. "And? Is she as evil and conniving as I imagined?"

"Worse." Elsa looked over her shoulder and then lowered her voice. "Apparently, she was responsible for the mass human deaths in Chicago in 1809 and then in Boston in 1812. Thousands died. Humans claim it was some sort of yellow fever, but records show that it was her. She and a group of vampires massacred all the humans they could get their hands on. A real bloodbath."

"Literally," added Julian.

I felt sick. "And they let her sit her ass on the Gray Council?"

"She's had a change of heart," mocked Jade, a hand to her chest. "Well, that's what the records say."

Two thirtysomething human females walked by, eyeing Julian like he was sex on a stick. But the handsome witch didn't even notice them. Yeah, he had it bad for Cassandra, the twins' mother.

"Bull," I said, reeling in my focus. "We all know people don't change. Not really. And not that much." If she was a murderess psycho with a thirst for human blood back then, I was positive she still was. "I can't believe they would put someone like her on the Gray Council." I looked at my witch friend, her red hair swaying in the morning breeze. "Where did you get all this information?"

Elsa grinned and tapped the side of her nose. "I've got my sources."

"She means her friend, Luciana, who used to be the Gray Council's secretary back in the nineties," said Jade. "She retired, like, fifteen years ago."

Elsa frowned at Jade. "The point is, you don't want someone like her to get ahold of your sister. Fact is, she's the worst there is. No empathy, no love for humans or any other paranormal race except her own. She only cares about vampires. We're all lesser beings to her. She's a real piece of work."

I raised a brow. "Wonderful."

"Have you heard from Catelyn?" Julian was watching me.

"Not yet," I told him, both Elsa and Jade leaning in closer. "Valen's gone over to Arther's place to check up on her."

"You think she'll be safer there than with her friends?" Elsa had that look on her face that told me she disapproved. "She was fine with us. I think it was a mistake to take her away from her friends. How can being with a group of strangers be better?"

"You didn't see her when she found her parents," I said. "She wasn't herself. You don't want a crazed giantess in the hotel. She'd destroy the entire thirteenth floor. Easy. And she'd kill people."

"Not if we were there to help her," insisted Elsa, and I could tell this was really bothering her.

"It wouldn't help," I said, feeling some guilt at having dropped Catelyn off with strangers. "From what Valen's told me, Arther's taking her north tomorrow. Somewhere remote. Somewhere far from the human population. So if she changes, and I know she will, she won't harm anyone."

"But she might harm herself," said Jade.

True. "Valen's promised me that his friend knows what he's doing. I have to trust him. He cares about Catelyn. He wouldn't just hand her over if he didn't trust them to take good care of her."

Elsa pressed her lips tightly, shaking her head. "I don't like it. Will we ever see her again?"

Good question. "I'm sure we will." I didn't think so. My chest tightened at the thought, but with Catelyn gone and secure from harming anyone, I could concentrate on the other issues without having her as a distraction.

"I wonder…" I began, getting my thoughts together while inhaling all the exhaust fumes from the passing cars and cabs. "If Darius and Freida were working together to get ahold of Shay, they would have to share that power. Right? But I don't see Darius as the sharing kind. This Freida either."

"They would have offed each other," said Julian, like it was the apparent plan. He looked at us. "As soon as opportunity struck, they would have tried to kill one another. And the victor would have had full control of Shay."

I shivered at the thought of anyone having control over that little girl. No one should have control over anyone. Period.

Julian gestured with his right hand. "You can't share power. Not these types."

"And you think she's the only vile vampire on the council? No others?" asked Jade. "There could be others. What if they're all bad?"

I had thought of that. "Not according to Clive. Darius and this Freida are the only two who were after Shay. I don't know if the other members had other dark agendas, but where Shay is concerned, it was just the two of them."

"You believe him?" asked Elsa as she jammed her hands in the pockets of her skirt.

"He was under the influence of Julian's truth serum."

"Right. Well, aren't you a clever one," said Elsa, looking over at a smug Julian.

"So that leaves one powerful vampire," I said, wondering if that was worse than a powerful witch. I didn't know what she looked like, where she lived, or where her hangouts were. I had lots of work ahead of me if I wanted to build a case against her. If what Clive said was true, there were just two bad apples on the council. Well, one, now that Darius was out of the picture.

And I had to get rid of her before she tried anything with Shay.

"Let's go." Elsa ushered us all down the street with her. "We'll talk more back on the thirteenth floor. I can make us a nice brunch. With After Dark being closed and all, that doesn't leave us much choice. So, the hotel it is."

I glanced back at the school before turning away and following the others back to the Twilight Hotel.

I still had the unresolved murders hanging over my head. As far as I knew, there hadn't been any new deaths, but that didn't mean it was over. And Valen's restaurant was still closed because of it. It wouldn't reopen until they were solved.

And somehow, I had to stop a powerful, ancient vampire who happened to sit on the Gray Council.

Easy peasy.

CHAPTER 17

After we strolled through the hotel's lobby, still with the seventies' disco theme in full effect, I dodged behind a very large were male, when Basil threw his glance our way. At first, I thought he saw me and would force me to work to greet the guests again, but we made it to the elevator without interruption.

I'd wanted to say hi to Jimmy, who looked marvelous in a bell-bottom ensemble and a fringed leather vest, but I was too afraid Basil would see me.

Once we hit the thirteenth floor, we all clambered inside my old apartment. I went straight for my office area, which was a simple desk, laptop, and whatever books I was reading, all pushed against the far wall next to the dining room.

"I think I'll make some egg-and-grilled-ham sandwiches," said Elsa as she opened the refrigerator door, which to my surprise, was always stocked with food that I never bought.

"Yum. I'll help." Jade followed Elsa into the kitchen while Julian stretched on the couch and flicked the TV on.

I stared at the back of Julian's head for a moment, my thoughts on Clive and how wonderful that serum had worked. How easily the words came flying out of that chain-smoking bastard.

"Julian," I called and waited until he turned around. "That truth serum. You got any more?"

The male witch smirked. "You planning on using it on a certain vampire female?"

"Absolutely." If I could get my hands on her and get her the tonic, I could get her to confess. On video. If I could do that, we were golden.

"Sorry, Leana, but it won't work on her."

"Why not? Because she's an *ancient* vampire?" That was news to me. But then again, I didn't know much about ancient vampires, especially those who wanted to use little girls to their benefit.

"No, not because she's ancient," answered the male witch, his expression pensive. "Because she's a *vampire*. Truth serums, or any kind of mind-inducing, mind-manipulation potions I know of, don't work on vampires."

I raised my brows. "Really? Wow. I really need to keep up with my vampire 101 reading." I was basically clueless. But I was more ignorant about how truth serums and other potions worked.

"Yeah." Julian turned around and stared at the TV. "Something to do with their blood. Like their blood acts as a countermeasure against that. Imagine their blood is a virus and kills all other intrusive viruses."

"Bummer." Huge bummer. I had already envisioned Freida tied to a chair and spilling the beans on camera. Guess I'd have to think up of another way to make her talk.

I doubted she was a loner-type vampire. She probably had an entourage with her at all times, which meant it would be even harder to try and—what? Trap her? Kidnap her like we did Clive? Clive had been easy, even though we had to fight a few of his naked pals. I had the feeling Freida would be a hell of a lot harder to reach.

First, if I wanted to face her, I needed to know where she lived or hung out. Maybe she had a vampire lair? And maybe I watched too much TV.

"How's Cassandra?" I asked Julian and saw his shoulders jerk.

When he turned around, I saw a flush on his cheeks. "She's good."

I raised a brow. "She is. Isn't she?" I caught Elsa smirking in the background and Jade with her hand on her mouth, her eyes filled with laughter.

Julian chuckled. "She is. And the twins too. There. Are you done with your interrogation?"

I scoffed. "Not even close." I pointed a finger at him. "Let me remind you of all your questions when we first met. I'll have more for you later." I laughed harder as he turned around, the tips of his ears turning red.

"Here." Elsa appeared at my desk and deposited

a steaming cup of coffee. "You look like you need this."

"Elsa, you're the best," I said as I grabbed the mug and took a sip, savoring the delicious bitter taste.

The older witch grinned. "Tell me something I don't know."

I spurted a bit of coffee as Jade snorted from the kitchen and turned on my laptop. I thought I might as well log on to the Merlin database and see what goodies I could find on Freida.

"So, what about those dead witches?" called Jade from the kitchen, a knife in her hand as she chopped what looked like a tomato. "Any leads?"

I took another sip of coffee. "Not really. The only thing I can think of is that someone wants Valen to be blamed for those."

"But what's the connection with Catelyn's family?" Elsa propped a large bag of bagels on the kitchen island next to Jade.

I shook my head. "That's the thing. I don't know if there even is a connection. I mean, it doesn't make sense. None of this does."

"But there haven't been any more murders." Jade took a hard swing of her knife down on the tomato like she imagined it was the murderer's neck.

"Not that we know."

"Does Valen have a lot of enemies?" asked Elsa as she sawed a golden bagel in half and started on another.

"Apparently, yes."

Elsa narrowed her eyes. "That doesn't sound like Valen. He's such a sweetheart. Who would have a grudge against him?"

Julian cleared his throat. "Uh, even *we* did before Leana jumped his bones."

I spat some more of my coffee. "Hey. That's not fair."

"Just saying that the giant wasn't so forthcoming before he met you," said the male witch. "We ate at his restaurant because the food's amazing. But the guy was a total asshole."

He had a point, but Valen had been going through a lot of personal stuff. "He's not perfect. But I think those who would warrant him harm are the more dangerous and shady types that he probably fought and kicked out of his sector."

"Sticking his giant nose where it didn't belong," added Julian, and I shot him a glare.

"Anyway, the list is *long*, so it might take a while." Like a few months.

"Well, I just think Valen's a wonderful man," said Elsa, her chin high and looking like she was waiting to see if anyone would contradict her. "And I'm glad he found you, Leana."

I grinned. "I'm glad too."

"I mean," continued Elsa, sawing away like a seasoned logger. "He's so much more amiable now than before. And he smiles a lot. I don't think I remember seeing his teeth before you showed up. He has such nice teeth."

I laughed. "This is a strange conversation." I

dragged my finger on my laptop's mouse pad and opened a browser. I typed in the Merlin database web address and waited for the home page to appear. Once it did, I typed in my ID and password and pressed enter, and then—

INVALID CREDENTIALS.

I stared at the red-lettered message in big, bold letters.

My heart stopped. "What the hell is this?" I stared at the screen.

"What's the problem?" I heard Elsa say.

"Uh. Not sure." I reentered my information, pressed enter, and got the same error message. No way had I forgotten my password. It had been the same one for more than ten years. If I couldn't log on, it meant...

"Oh, no."

"Oh, no?" Footsteps came closer. "What do you mean, *Oh, no*?" Elsa's shoulder brushed up against mine as she leaned in and gawked at my computer. "*Invalid credentials?*" she read. "Leana? What does that mean?"

I let out a long breath as my heart jump-started again. "I think... No, I know my Merlin license has been revoked."

"What?" cried Elsa and Jade simultaneously, making me jerk in my chair.

"What are you talking about?" Julian's voice rang louder as he also appeared on my other side, just as Jade bumped into Elsa.

I leaned back in my chair and pointed at the nasty

red letters. "It's either I've lost my license, or I've been put on suspension. Either way, it doesn't look good." Damn it. I didn't need this crap right now.

Elsa clasped her locket. "But that doesn't make sense. Don't they send out warnings before they do that? *Can* they do that?"

"They can," I answered, still staring at the screen. "But usually, I'd get an email or a letter."

"Did you check your email?" asked Jade, her voice dripping with anxiety.

"Not yet." I opened another window and checked my mail. "Nothing here. Just junk email. It's possible this was just issued. I might get something within the next twenty-four hours."

"Well, that's just awful," grumbled Elsa. "It has to be a mistake. Can you appeal it?"

I shrugged. "Not sure. I've never had to appeal it before." I'd never lost my license.

"Why did it happen to *you*, specifically?" Julian crossed his arms over his chest. "Who has the authority to do this?"

Only one person I knew who would. "Clive."

Elsa and Jade both sucked in a breath through their teeth.

"Didn't you tell us last night that Clive wouldn't say anything?" Julian loomed over me.

"I did." I'd told the gang everything that had happened with Clive and that we'd disposed of him because we felt he would be too ashamed to say anything.

"You were wrong about him," said Julian. "He

blabbed. Maybe he told Freida. If he did this," he said, pointing, "you can bet your ass he told her."

I looked back at the screen. Anger tightened my gut. "I'm not sure. No. I don't think he did. If he had told Freida, there'd be some Gray Council officers here arresting me right about now. I think this is the only thing he could do without bringing any attention to himself." It was the only way the bastard could stop me from discovering more about his vampire mistress.

"That slimy son of a bitch," accused Jade.

"Yeah, and worse." I drummed my fingers on the desk. "Now I can't log on and investigate Freida. This is why he did it. To make it harder, maybe impossible, for me to look into her. I won't be able to link her to any devious organizations, nothing." Damn that cigarette-smoking witch.

"But you can get it back, though. Right?" Elsa watched me. "If he can't back up his claims without dragging his vampire boss down, he has no leverage."

"True," I exhaled. "But it will still take a while before I can get my access to the database back. Maybe weeks. I'll just have to figure out another way to learn about Freida."

Jade tapped my shoulder. "Don't worry. We'll help you. I'll reach out to my friend Margorie Maben. She's married to Oscar Maben, who sits on the Gray Council. Remember? She was the one who told her husband about Adele wanting to destroy the hotel."

"Right. I remember," I said, vaguely remembering that conversation.

"We've been writing more regularly since that night. You'll see. There are other ways we can get the scoop on that vampire."

"Thanks." Warmth calmed my senses at her comment and her willingness to assist me. I knew my friends would help, even if I didn't ask for it. It was hard to imagine working a case without them.

"But first, let's eat. Brunch is ready." Elsa returned to the kitchen, Jade right behind her.

I stood up, staring at my screen as I heard Julian following the witches to the kitchen. You couldn't hack remotely into the Merlin database. That I knew for sure. It was magically protected with wards, things human computers didn't have. I'd have no choice but to appeal this decision. That would take weeks.

After a nice meal of Elsa's egg-and-grilled-ham sandwiches, we all leaned back in our chairs, stuffed and a few pounds heavier than when we'd first arrived.

A ping sounded, and Jade pulled out her phone. "Margorie just wrote me back."

I sat straighter in my chair. "Oh. And?"

"This ought to be good." Elsa pushed her chair back. "I'm going for some wine."

I pulled my eyes away from Elsa's red hair and looked back at Jade. "What did you ask her exactly?"

"Everything she had on Freida," answered Jade,

her eyes gliding over the screen of her phone. "Okay. She lives in some mansion in Upstate New York."

"Her lair," I mumbled.

"She doesn't have the address, but she says she's going to look into it," said Jade, speaking fast. "Says her husband doesn't like her. Apparently, she's not well-liked."

"Must be that vampire breath," said Julian. He shrugged when we all looked at him. "What? All vampires have bad breath. It's a known fact."

"I didn't know." I looked at Jade. "What else?"

"She's been trying to enforce Darius's replacement with one of her vampire buddies, and the rest of the council members are not happy about it. They're supposed to vote in a new member. You can't just choose anyone."

"Freida doesn't seem to care." And I had a feeling she usually got what she wanted. "Anything else?" So far, it wasn't much. I wanted the address to her house. With that, I could make plans. I could organize a stakeout.

Jade's face brightened. "Oh. There's a meeting tomorrow morning. Ten a.m. At the Gray Council building." She looked at me and said, "And Freida will be there."

"Okay, that's good." I nodded to myself. "Anything else?"

Jade shook her head. "No. That's it."

"Are you planning to kidnap her in front of the entire council?" asked Julian, looking at me like I was mad.

"No." But the thought had crossed my mind. "But it'll allow me to see what she looks like. But more importantly, how many bodyguards will be with her."

"Smart." Elsa was looking at me proudly. "And that's why you're the Merlin. You think up that detective stuff."

Was a Merlin. That was more accurate. No, I was still a Merlin. I didn't need a plasticized ID to prove it.

"And then I'll follow her," I continued. "If I'm lucky, she'll lead me straight back to her lair." And then... and then I hadn't thought that far ahead just yet. I'm sure Valen would like to be informed of my future plans that involved a so-called ancient vampiress.

"A lair filled with vampires?" Julian shook his fork at me. "Are you insane?"

"I thought we'd covered that before."

Julian stabbed a piece of tomato with his fork. "Leana, use your head. She's powerful. The vampires with her will be too. What are you going to do? Barge in, starlight blazing?"

I shrugged. "Something like that."

"Are you mad?" Julian's voice rose. "You won't last a minute in there. These vampires will be strong, more resilient, and more dangerous than you can imagine. Some might be just as old as she is. We don't know. You need to think this through because if you go in there all hotheaded and emotional, you'll die."

I narrowed my eyes, not appreciating his _emotional_ comment. "I'm kidding," I said, though I wasn't sure I was. With the threat on Shay, I wasn't sure I wouldn't go in there blasting me some vampires with my starlight—all emotional. I had to do something. I had to protect my sister from this vile vampire female.

I would follow her tomorrow, and then I'd decide how to approach this. I smiled. This was very good.

A loud tread came from down the hallway, and when I turned around, I saw Valen rushing over to us.

I grinned, feeling better now that I had a plan and would soon know where Freida kept her coffin. "Hey. What's up? You look worried."

"It's Shay," said the giant, and my heart about stopped.

"Oh my God. She took her?" I jumped out of my chair.

Valen waved a hand at me. "No. She's fine. Well, no, she's not. The school called me. She's sick so we have to pick her up. They said they couldn't reach you."

I let out a shaky breath. Damn. I yanked my phone out of my pocket with a trembling hand. "Crap. Phone's dead." I fumbled away from the table and rushed over to my desk, looking for my charger. Once I found it, I plugged in my phone. "My phone is charging. Is she okay? Is it serious?" I asked as I walked back.

"They wouldn't tell me much over the phone,"

said the giant. "They just said she had a fever, and regulations were that she be kept away from the other kids so that whatever she had wouldn't spread. I'm parked in front of the hotel."

Poor Shay. That's all she needed now, to be singled out as the virus carrier.

"Go." Elsa pushed me lightly. "Go get Shay and bring her back. We can have Polly take a look at her if it makes you feel better, but I'm sure it's nothing."

"Yeah," I told myself, though I didn't believe it. Shay had been fine this morning. "Okay. Be back in a bit."

I followed Valen out, all thoughts and plans of kicking Freida's ass vanished as I only had room for one thought.

Shay.

CHAPTER 18

Valen's Range Rover Sport pulled over to the curb at the school's front gate. Before he killed the engine, I'd popped open my door and dashed out.

I didn't have to go far. Shay sat at the top of the steps alone.

Anger flashed in my gut. They left a sick eleven-year-old girl alone outside?

"Shay." When I reached her, I sat next to her and immediately pressed my hand to her forehead.

She slapped my hand away. "I feel fine. Don't make a scene." She glanced over her shoulder like she suspected the teachers were watching.

"That's not what the school says. And you do feel hot." Hotter than I would have liked. Her face was pale, but her cheeks were red, and her temples were a little sweaty. So, yeah, she was definitely coming down with something.

"I think Ms. Barclay is overreacting," said Shay. "She didn't have to call you guys."

"She did. Come on. Let's get you home. Well, back to the thirteenth floor. Polly'll take a look at you."

"Hey, squirt," said Valen as he reached us. "How you feeling?"

Shay shrugged. "Okay."

I looked at Valen and shook my head. The concern in his eyes told me that he knew it was worse than she was letting on. But Shay was stubborn, like me. She didn't want people to fuss over her.

"Let's go." I tried to take her hand, but she yanked it out of my grip. Instead, she followed Valen back to the Range Rover. Guess she was still mad at me for not letting her go with us to find Clive.

Sighing, I followed Shay and Valen down the walkway and climbed into the Range Rover.

The SUV's engine roared to life, and Valen stepped on the accelerator. We sped off.

My seat belt pulled as I whirled around in my seat. "How are you feeling? Seriously?" Was it my imagination, or were her cheeks redder?

Shay was staring out the window. She shrugged. "Same."

"You look a little hot. Are you hot?"

She gave me a one-shoulder shrug.

The engine's hum grew steady as I kept my eyes on her. I was glad the school had called. Shay was sick. More than she was letting on.

I pulled myself around, finding Valen's gaze on me.

"It's just a cold or something," soothed Valen, his eyes back on the road. "She'll be fine."

"Hmmm." Poor Shay. Being sick on her second day of school must have been hard for her. Hopefully, with some rest and whatever Polly had for colds, she'd be right back at that school in no time. Especially since she genuinely seemed to like it there.

"So, did you make any friends yet?" I asked, though I kept my eyes to the front on the road.

"I don't know," came Shay's reply.

"What are the classes like?"

"Like classes," she answered.

I looked at Valen, who was smiling. Was he enjoying this? Yeah, he was.

"What kind of magic are they teaching you?" I asked, still staring at Valen. "You're not a White or Dark witch, so I'm just curious." I was more curious to know if my teaching methods were correct.

"You mean, are they teaching me the same way you did?"

Yup, the kid was perceptive. "Yeah. Are they?"

"No."

"No?" I spun around in my seat. "So, how are they teaching you?" Shay wasn't an elemental witch, so they couldn't be teaching her how to draw up powers from the earth. I wanted to know how they were doing it.

"We meditate," said Shay.

"Meditation? That's it?"

Shay blinked at me. "It's my second day."

"Right. Sorry." I turned around, not knowing where my brain was. Of course, they would have to start slow, and meditation was a great way to calm oneself and learn how to control your emotions. It made sense they would start with that.

When I glanced over at Valen, he was still grinning. "What?"

"Nothing," answered the giant, though that smirk never left his lips. Okay, so he thought I was going a little overboard with my questions. Maybe I was.

I pulled my gaze away from his smiling face and stared out my window. I needed to start making plans about Freida. I knew where she was going to be tomorrow. It was perfect. And what was also perfect? Having a giant as an ally.

The SUV's engine was barely an audible purr over the ringing of thoughts and emotions in my mind.

"I have some new information about Freida," I told him. "I know where she's going to be tomorrow. There's going to be a Gray Council meeting, and she's going to be there."

"How do you know this?"

"Jade's Facebook friend told her. The one with her husband on the council." I decided not to mention the minor mishap with my Merlin license. I didn't want to talk about that in front of Shay because I didn't want her to worry.

"What do you want to do about it?" asked the giant.

"Follow her. See where her lair is or whatever," I said. "Thought you could come with me."

"Right. Because you need a ride?"

"Yes. Is it that obvious?"

"Little bit." The giant chuckled.

I shifted in my seat. "So, we have a lot to talk about later. And Shay? You'll be resting on Polly's orders, in bed, so you can't be angry with me this time." The last thing I wanted was for my little sister to be upset again at being left behind. But this was grown-up stuff, my job, and I couldn't have my little sister hanging around a dangerous vampire lair.

"Shay? Did you hear me?" I rotated in my seat. "Shay?" Her head lay against the glass, her eyes closed. "Shay," I said again. Was she sleeping? I rolled my eyes over her. The skin around her cheeks wasn't red anymore but more like a sickly green. That wasn't normal.

"Is something wrong?" I heard Valen ask.

"Shay!" Now I was shouting. "Shay, wake up! Wake up, Shay." A nauseating mix of dread and fear shook my knees. I took a deep breath and held it to avoid getting sick. "Why isn't she waking up? Valen. She's not waking up!"

"We're almost there," said Valen, as he took the next right, the thinnest ribbon of fear in his low, controlled voice.

"She's awfully pale," I said. Terror was heavy on me, like a boulder in the pit of my stomach. Why wasn't she waking up? What was happening to her?

"She was fine. She was talking. What's wrong with her?"

"I don't know," said Valen. "Looks like she might have passed out from the fever."

Do people pass out from fevers? I had no idea. I wasn't a healer, and I knew close to nothing about healing remedies and that sort of thing.

Panic cascaded over me. This was definitely *not* normal. She was fine this morning. She was her grumpy self. And now this?

My lips parted as it dawned on me. "She's cursed." As soon as I'd spoken the words out loud, I knew they were true. It was the only explanation. No way was this a typical cold or flu to have acted this fast. Shay was a healthy kid with no health problems, not even allergies. I wasn't an expert, but I didn't know of any virus that had you okay one minute and then passed out in about two hours.

"What?" Valen's voice was high with tension. "Are you sure?"

"Yes. Someone cursed her," I said, my throat tight as I tried to control the tsunami of emotions threatening to drown me. "Someone did this to her."

I couldn't believe it. I felt a dizzy spell hit me like I had way too many glasses of wine at the same time. This was so insane. Who would want to hurt Shay? She was just an innocent kid. Did this have something to do with her ability to control the sun's power? Was this Freida? Or was Clive getting back at me? He was a witch, so this type of curse should be easy enough for him to conjure up. But why would he if his mistress had wanted to use Shay's power? No. It wasn't him or the vampiress.

I snapped off my seat belt and leaned back to grab her hand. I flinched. It was ice-cold, literally like touching an ice cube.

"She's so cold, so cold." I blinked the tears in my eyes. "Hang on, Shay. Please hang on."

"Who would do this? She's just a kid," growled Valen, breathing hard like he was doing his best to control his anger.

I gritted my teeth, unable to answer. Not because I feared I would break down in a slop of tears but because of the anger simmering in my gut. This was one of those times when I wished I was a different kind of witch. A White witch so that I could conjure up a healing spell, a magical spell to counter the curse. Hell, I'd even conjure up a demon and make a deal with it if it could heal my sister. I'd give it *anything*.

But as a Starlight witch, I could do nothing but watch as my sister's health seemed to be draining away. My starlight didn't heal. It was useless.

Cursing a little kid was a cowardly act. A young person without the knowledge and means to defend herself from something alien to her. And when I found these bastards, heads would fly.

"We're here."

My lips trembled, and I nodded, my voice having left me. I jerked in my seat as Valen pulled his Range Rover Sport to the curb in front of the Twilight Hotel, the space reserved for guests, but who cared.

I pushed my door open, jumped out of my seat, slammed the door behind me, and ran over to the other side of the SUV. Valen was already there, and he pulled an unconscious Shay into his arms.

Without a word, I galloped over to the hotel's front doors and held them open while Valen carried Shay inside.

"Shay?" Elsa crossed the lobby and came rushing over. "What's happened to her?"

"I think she's been cursed," I told her, my heart hammering so hard I feared I might give myself a heart attack. "Can you get Polly? We'll take Shay upstairs."

"I'll get her," said Jade, who'd appeared moments later behind Elsa. I stared as she rushed off toward the dining hall.

"Leana? What is going on here?" Basil came strutting toward us. "Why are you making a scene?"

"Get her in the elevator," I told Valen just as Basil joined us.

"The guests are looking," he hissed, glancing over his shoulder and plastering a fake smile at a group of curious onlookers who were ogling the little girl in Valen's arms.

I liked Basil; he was a great boss, but if he stopped me or Valen, I would lose it. I was high on emotions. I couldn't be blamed for what I could do.

"Basil," said Elsa as she hooked her arm around the hotel manager's arm. "I wanted to show you a defect in the carpet. I'm afraid it's an eyesore."

"A defect? Well, I can't have that," said the male witch as Elsa pulled him away.

When I turned around, Valen was at the elevators, and I rushed over to join him.

"How is she?"

"Still not waking up," he said.

I could feel more guests' eyes on us, but I didn't care. At this moment, there was only me, Shay, and Valen. Nothing else mattered.

"What happened to Shay?"

I turned around and found Jimmy walking our way.

"She's been cursed," I told him, seeing his eyes rounding at my words. Jimmy knew all about curses, having lived with one for decades. "That's what I think." I swallowed and added, "Jade went to get Polly. I just hope she can help."

"Polly's amazing. She'll help," said Jimmy, though I wasn't that comforted since she had been unable to remove his curse. I shook the thought from my head. This was not the time to second-guess her skills.

With a ting, the elevator doors swished open. "Tell Jade and Polly we've gone up. Jimmy?"

Jimmy was staring out at something with his jaw clenched, and I could see a mixture of hate and fear in his eyes.

"Jimmy?" I followed the direction of his gaze. He was staring at a thin, blonde woman I recognized.

"You know Ms. Barclay?" She stood there, her eyes on us, and she was smiling.

"That's not Ms. Barclay," said Jimmy as he looked at me. "That's Auria. The sorceress who cursed me."

I felt like someone had just thrown a bucket of ice in my face. My blood went cold.

I turned and looked at Valen. "Take Shay upstairs. I'll be right back."

I heard Valen call out my name, but I could barely hear it over the white noise ringing in my ears. I focused on Auria, seeing her still smiling as she turned around and walked toward the front doors, disappearing through a crowd of guests who had spilled in at the moment.

I put on a burst of speed, fed by adrenaline and the fear of losing my sister. I reached the doors, pushed them open, and hit the sidewalk.

"Auria!" I shouted, spinning around and searching for that sorceress.

But the sidewalk was empty.

She was gone.

CHAPTER 19

"When did you first notice a change in Shay?" asked a generous woman with red cheeks. Her blonde hair was neatly tucked under a toque. She usually sported a smiling face. However, at the moment, her expression was carefully guarded.

"Uh…" I stared down at Shay lying motionlessly on the couch, her skin pasty and pale and her breathing shallow. "Only when I saw her on the steps of her school. She looked like she had a fever."

"Not before?" Polly, the hotel's healer and chef jammed her hands in her white, stained chef jacket pockets, stretching the buttons to their limits, and pulled out what looked like a small ointment jar. She twisted the top and smeared a white, cream-like substance over Shay's forehead. Her lips moved in a spell, and magic twanged my senses.

"No. She was fine this morning. I wouldn't have let her go if I thought she was sick. She didn't look sick. We walked to her school together, and she was normal. Fine."

My eyes found Valen standing across from me. His big, muscled arms crossed over his broad chest, and his face was skewed in a mask of fear and anger. He loved Shay, as did I, and I could see the turmoil of emotions behind his dark eyes. We didn't have to exchange words to know we were feeling the same thing.

"Well, that gives us a time window," said Polly. "You said you arrived at her school at nine, and then Valen got the call around eleven thirty. Which means she was hexed or cursed during that time."

"Is that supposed to mean something?" My voice came out a little rough.

Polly looked at me, her features blank. "It means you caught it in the early stages."

"And that's good?"

"Yes. It'll give us more time to figure things out before... before the magic deepens and Shay takes a turn for the worse. The weaker her body is, the harder it will be to cure her of this. So, we need to act fast."

I nodded, blinking rapidly. My throat burned as I tried to swallow. "Anything you need. Just tell me. Just... just please help my sister." The last word came out in a small shriek. The idea of losing my sister was too hard to imagine. The image of Auria's winning smile just now in the lobby flashed in my mind's eye. She'd come to see her work in action, come to rejoice in my reaction. She wanted me to know this was her.

As soon as Shay was okay and stable, I was going to hunt that sorceress. When I was finished with her, she was going to curse the day she ever laid a finger on Shay.

A hand squeezed my shoulder. "It's not your fault, Leana," said Jade.

"It is. Auria cursed her because of me." If Shay died, it would be *my* fault.

"No. Me," said Jimmy, standing on my other side. "If you hadn't gone after her for that book, none of this would be happening. If you want to blame someone, blame me."

I glanced at Jimmy, seeing real pain etched in his features. "This is not your fault."

"And it's not yours," he said.

"It's the damn sorceress's fault," said Elsa, coming around the couch to get a better look at Shay.

The only one missing from our gang was Julian. He was probably with Cassandra. He'd be here if he knew something had happened to Shay.

Polly dabbed the last of that ointment and stuffed the jar in her pocket.

"What does that do?"

Polly kept her eyes on Shay. "It'll tell us what sort of curse or hex we're dealing with. She'll have a better chance if we know what the sorceress did to her."

"But how could she curse her at the school?" I wrapped my arms around my middle, trying to calm my heart. It didn't work. "I thought the school was protected from that kind of stuff. Someone would have seen her curse Shay, no? No one said anything about Ms. Barclay cursing my little sister."

"Well," said Polly, her large middle expanding as she took in a breath. "If I were to guess, she probably put the hex or curse in something that Shay touched or ingested. Could be something as mundane as a glass of juice or even a pen. The magic would have transferred without alerting the staff and without anyone knowing until Shay started to show signs."

I rubbed my eyes. "If I had kept her from going to that school, she'd be okay. Why did I have to push her? I should have never let her out of my sight. Why did I force her to go to that damn school?"

"You can't blame yourself for this." Valen watched me. "She would have found another way to get to Shay."

"He's right," said Jimmy. "Auria's resourceful, if not insane. She would have found another way to curse Shay. Trust me. The school was just a means to an end."

I stared at my sister's gray lips, fighting a sob that threatened to escape. I kneeled next to the couch and grabbed her tiny, ice-cold hand in mine. When I glanced back at her face, the ointment on her fore-head had shifted and turned black. I could see tiny specs of yellow. I looked up at Polly. "It's black and yellow. What does that mean?"

The healer glanced at me. A hint of worry crossed her expression. "Yellow means it's a curse."

I knew as much. "And the black?"

"Most witches, and in this case sorceresses, work

their curses to cause misfortune and harm on whoever it's placed on," answered the healer. "This looks to me like the Mark of Death curse—one of the most difficult curses to perform and the deadliest."

"Looks to you? What the hell does that mean?" I stared hard at the healer. "What does that mean?" I repeated. "Is it or isn't it? You better not tell me that there's no cure or counter-curse."

Polly looked at me, and I could tell by the shifting of her mouth that she was struggling with what she was about to tell me. "A counter-curse for the Mark of Death curse is rare. I don't know anyone who survived such an attack."

"Rare, but not impossible. Right?" I was going to strangle her with her own hat if she said there wasn't anything we could do to save my sister.

The healer dropped her gaze to me. "Auria is known for conjuring up her own intricate curses. She uses elements most witches never heard of. I said it *looks* like the Mark of Death curse because that's what it appears to be, but it's different. It's been altered. It would help if I knew what elements she used. Auria is an accomplished and mighty sorceress. I'm not sure—"

"Don't say it," I snapped at her. "Don't even try." I was about to go mental on her.

"I'm saying that Auria's powerful," continued the healer, though she was looking warily at me. "Curses are her forte, what she excels at. Look what she did to Jimmy. We couldn't even break the curse until you figured out what she'd used."

I thought of something. I pushed to my knees, dashed into my old bedroom to the dresser, pulled out the first drawer, grabbed a book, and ran back out. "Here," I said, giving it to Polly. "This is Auria's grimoire I stole from her. It's where we found the counter-curse for Jimmy. There's got to be something in here about the Mark of Death curse."

"Her book!" Elsa clapped her hands together. "I forgot you still had it."

Both Elsa and Jade were looking at Polly, with hopeful expressions on their faces, as she took the book and moved away from us so she could look through it. This was it. If anything could tell us what that horrid sorceress used, it was her own damn book.

After what felt like an eternity, Polly came back. The book of curses lay flat in her arms and open. "The Mark of Death isn't here."

"What? That's impossible." I went to grab the book from her, but the healer snatched it away from me.

"It's not," she said, practically growling. She glared at me until I lowered my hands. "She must have worked this recently. If this is her old book, she probably has a new one."

My heart broke. I felt the little hope I'd clung to slip away. "So…" I couldn't bring myself to say the words. That Shay was lost to me…

"Let me try."

We all looked at Valen.

"It's not a cure, but I might be able to relieve the fever and remove some of her pain," said the giant.

My chest contracted. "Anything, please. Please help her."

Silence hit the room as we all watched the giant kneel next to the couch. He took a deep breath and then placed his right hand over Shay's pasty-and-pale forehead.

I held my breath, not sure why, as Valen closed his eyes, his brow furrowed in concentration. A soft, golden glow stemmed from his hand, his giant healing magic, the same magic he'd used on my ankle. My senses quivered with the magic emanating from Valen.

Not sure what to expect or how long this was going to take, I moved closer until my knee bumped into the couch, staring down at my sister's face.

But after a minute or so, I didn't see a change. She still looked deathly ill.

Valen let out a breath through his nose and leaned back. I could see a trickle of sweat going down the sides of his temples like he'd eaten something really spicy or this had taken a chunk of his energy and effort.

Yet Shay didn't look any different.

"Did it work?" asked Jade, pulling my thoughts out of my head.

My throat contracted. Valen had tried and failed. "I don't think so. She looks the same—" My heart stopped. "Wait a second... her skin is getting some color back."

Sure enough, Shay's pallid, almost gray-colored cheeks shifted, slowly turning pink. The next thing I noticed was her lips as they blossomed back to their rosy color as well.

And then her lids fluttered and snapped open.

CHAPTER 20

"Shay?" I leaned forward, nearly climbing over Valen in my attempt to get closer. "How are you feeling?"

Shay frowned. "Okay, I guess. Why are you staring at me like that?" Her eyes flicked around the room. "What am I doing here?"

I threw my arms around her neck before I could stop myself and pulled her into a hug. We hadn't established yet if we were going to be the hugging type. I didn't care. All I could think of at this very moment—she was alive. And Valen had healed her.

"I can't breathe," came Shay's voice against my head.

"Sorry." I pulled back and released her, quickly wiping away the one tear that leaked out of my right eye. Then I turned and assaulted Valen with my mouth. I kissed him deeply, passionately, and quickly. I tried to tell him everything I felt in the kiss—the gratitude, the desperation, the love. He kissed me back eagerly. All those pent-up emotions were making me dizzy and a little crazy. I wanted to rip off his clothes and jump on him right now to show him how much I appreciated what he'd done. His grip tightened on my waist, and I knew he understood exactly where my thoughts were. Naughty, naughty thoughts.

"Ew. Get a room," said Shay.

I pulled away and laughed. "You're okay. You're okay." I glanced at Valen. "How? I... Thank you."

Valen smiled, and that's when I noticed the dark circles under his eyes. He looked a little pale. "I'd do anything for this little squirt."

A big sob spun me around on my knees, and I saw Elsa and Jade bawling their eyes out as they hugged.

"What happened?" Shay pulled herself up to a sitting position on the couch. She stared at me, and I could see a bit of alarm in her big green eyes.

"Someone cursed you," I told her, guilt hitting me like a sledgehammer. "It was Ms. Barclay." At her scowl, and when she opened her mouth to protest, I added, "She's not who you think she is. She's a sorceress."

"An evil sorceress," said Elsa, and then she blew her nose in a tissue.

"Her real name is Auria," I told Shay. "She once cursed Jimmy years ago, into a wooden toy dog. He could never leave the hotel. Ever. Not until we found the counter-curse and saved him."

Shay blinked and stared at Jimmy. "Wait. You used to be a toy?"

Jimmy flashed her a smile. "I was. A wooden toy beagle."

Shay shrugged. "Cool."

I pushed off my knees and sat next to her on the couch. "The point is, she's vile, dangerous, and vindictive."

"But why would she want to curse me?" asked Shay. Her voice cracked, and I knew this information was upsetting her.

I sighed. "Because it's payback for breaking the curse she'd used on Jimmy. And also because I kicked her ass. She wants to hurt me," I added, knowing it to be true. "I took something from her, so now she tried to take something from me."

Shay stared at her fingers as she spoke next. "But I'm okay. Right? I'm not sick anymore. I don't feel sick."

I smiled. "No. Thanks to Valen." My eyes fell on the giant again, and my heart swelled at the emotion that crossed his features. "You're fine."

"That's not exactly true," came Polly's voice.

I whipped my head around, and my smile faded at the troubled expression on Polly's face. "What? What are you talking about? Look at her. She's fine. She's awake, and she looks healthy." I could feel some irritation flaring. My sister had gone through enough. I didn't want this healer scaring her.

Polly came forward and touched Shay's forehead. "Her fever broke." Then she took out some instrument from her coat pocket that looked like a blood pressure monitor kit, grabbed Shay's arm, wrapped a flat part around her arm, and began pumping. After a moment, Polly removed the contraption from Shay's arm and turned her gaze to the giant. "You've been holding out on me," she accused with a smile.

Valen let out a low chuckle as he stood. "I wasn't sure my magic would help."

"It did."

"And? She's okay, right?" I looked over at Shay, my chest tightening again, and squeezed even further as Polly didn't answer right away.

"I know she looks fine to you," answered Polly after a moment. "And she probably feels fine, but she's not."

I gritted my teeth. "What are you saying?"

"I'm saying…" Polly exhaled. "That the giant's magic peeled away at the fever and most of the sickness and gave her a bout of energy—for now. It's only temporary. The curse is still there. Still very much alive in her body."

I felt like Polly had just punched me in the gut. "So, you're saying she'll feel sick again? That she'll…" I couldn't bring myself to say the words.

I took Shay's hand, and this time, she didn't try to pull it away. Her hand felt warm, not at all like before. It felt normal and healthy. Maybe Polly was wrong, but the tiny voice inside my head told me she was right.

If this curse was anything like Jimmy's, it needed a counter-curse, not just giant magic.

"Let's just say she's a sick little girl," answered Polly. "Curses are complex magic. Auria's curses, well, they're in a league of their own."

Moisture gleamed in Shay's eyes as she kept her focus on her lap. I knew she was fighting back the tears. Damn it.

I squeezed her hand gently. "We're going to figure this out. Don't worry. I promise."

Blinking fast, Shay just shrugged, but she still didn't pull away. And that was doing all kinds of things to my emotions, which were already hanging by a thread.

I looked up at the healer. "How long until the curse is back in full effect." What I really wanted to know was how long Shay had left to live, but I couldn't use those words, not in front of my little sister.

"Well," said Polly as she jammed her hands in her front pockets. "I would have to say, considering what's at stake and the level of complexity in Auria's curses, and also judging by Shay's skin color, the loss of the fever, her steady blood pressure... no more than twenty-four hours."

My heart leaped. Good. That was better than I had hoped. "Tell me what you need. Tell me what I need to do to eliminate this damn curse."

Polly looked at me. "Without knowing the true elements of the curse, the only way to save your sister is if you get Auria to tell you *what* she used. Then we can make the counter-curse."

"She'll never tell me." This was like the situation with Jimmy all over again.

Polly shook her head. "No. She won't. At least not willingly. You'll have to make her."

"I don't have a problem with that. I kicked her ass once, and I'll kick it again." Obviously, I was powerless to face a vengeful sorceress during daylight, but as Polly said, I had twenty-four hours, give or take a few. I could wait for sundown, and then the old bitch's ass was mine.

"Leana." Jimmy had a strange look on his face. "Didn't you notice something different with Auria?"

I thought about it for a moment. "Yeah. She was a lot younger." And that's why Ms. Barclay had looked so familiar to me. Because I'd been staring at the old sorceress, just a younger version of her. "I can't believe it. I thought she was a teacher. She didn't even look like the sorceress I'd seen. No amount of plastic surgery could achieve *that*."

"Exactly," said Jimmy. "When you fought her, she was old. Right? That's what you told me."

"More like ancient and ready for her ashes to be blown away in a breeze. Why?"

"I don't know how, but she's found a way to rejuvenate herself," said Jimmy, a worried edge to his tone. "She's not the old, fragile sorceress anymore."

I raised a brow. "I never thought of her as fragile, though she did smell." I wrinkled my nose, remembering the nasty odor of an unwashed body. It had been pretty disgusting. Like she hadn't bathed since the sixties.

"You're not listening." Jimmy gave me a hard stare. "She's going to be much more powerful than before. She's back in her prime now. She looked just like that when..." He hesitated, his face hard as he most probably recounted a dark memory. "When she'd cursed me."

"And we *un*-cursed you. She's not invincible. No one is." And I was going to prove it. I wasn't going to be put off from seeking out Auria. I would find her, and when I did, I would *make* her tell me what she used on Shay.

"You need to be on your guard," said the assistant manager, a slight edge to his voice. "Don't be fooled by her. Whatever she says, she's a liar. She loves to play games."

"I will."

"We'll help." Jade pointed to herself and then to Elsa. "We're coming with you. And before you say anything, you can't say anything to stop us."

"Yes," agreed Elsa, and I gave her a warm smile, well, as much as I could. "We can create a diversion while you concentrate on that bitch."

I raised my eyebrows. "You bet your ass I will. Fine," I added with a smirk, and I was glad they were coming with me. I could use the backup if what Jimmy said was true. I glanced at my little sister. "Are you going to be okay without me for a while? I won't leave just yet, only in a few hours."

Shay gave me another one of her signature shrugs. "Yeah."

I hated leaving her when she was infected by

some curse from Auria. But I didn't have a choice. If I wanted to save her, I had to find the sorceress and the elements used in the curse.

"Will you drive us?" I asked Valen.

The giant opened his mouth, but Polly cut him off.

"Valen stays here," ordered the healer, and we all looked at her. But when I looked at Valen, he didn't seem surprised. "I need his healing magic. It'll keep Shay from… It'll keep the curse at bay." She looked at Valen. "You up for that?"

Valen looked at Shay when he said, "Anything for this little squirt."

At that, a smile stretched over Shay's face, the first I'd seen in a good while. At least Valen would be with her. And I knew he'd protect her like she was his own kid.

That gave me the comfort and strength I needed to kick some ol' sorceress's stinky ass.

Get ready, Auria. I'm coming.

CHAPTER 21

The Manhattan Bridge looked just as I remembered when I was here a few months back—big, imposing, and quiet. We stood on Cherry Street under a dark sky. The sun had disappeared just as we'd arrived by cab. It was dark. It was perfect.

"This is where she lives?" Jade threw her gaze around the pier and neighboring streets, her hands on the pair of roller skates that hung down from her neck like a scarf.

"Why? Not what you expected?" I looked over my shoulder, making sure there were no wandering humans.

"I don't know. I imagined her living in a hut with a fire in the middle while she chanted and scribbled her curses."

Elsa laughed. "She's a troll. She deserves to live under a bridge. Ah. Look. There's a door."

I followed Elsa's gaze, and sure enough, I saw an outline of a door carved into the stone. Just as before.

Although this time, she hadn't bothered to hide it with a glamour. Not sure I liked that.

I looked at my friends. "Be on your guard. She's no mere sorceress." No. She's a real stinker.

Elsa sliced a gaze at Jade before answering. "We can manage. We both have the power of the elements. Don't worry about us."

"Okay." I glanced back toward the door just as I pulled on my Starlight magic and held it. "Watch out for booby traps," I said, stepping forward, toward the stone pier.

"You think she knows you're coming?" asked Elsa, and I noticed her rubbing her locket like she was hoping a genie might spring out and help her.

"Yeah," I answered. "She knows." She'd *wanted* me to see her back in the hotel's lobby so she could gloat. She knew I'd show up back here eventually.

"So what you're saying is we're walking into a trap?" Jade's blue highlights reflected in the moonlight.

"Most probably. You can wait out here if you like."

"Not a chance," said Jade, looking determined. "I want this sorceress as badly as you do. I love Shay. We all do. And what she did, well, she deserves what she gets. Besides, I have a personal score to settle with her." She raised her brows, and I knew precisely what personal score she was implying. She meant Jimmy.

"Glad you feel that way. Let's go." Putting my

shoulder against the door and using my weight, I pushed it open and stepped through.

We found ourselves in the same short hallway with a low ceiling that I remembered. The air thrummed with a familiar magic—Auria's magic. It wasn't strong, more like an echo of her power, but it was still there. Was this the first booby trap? It didn't feel like a curse. Not wanting to take any chances, I yanked on my starlight. Energy crackled against my skin—the energies from the stars tingling over me. I gave a burst of my starlight, lighting up the hallway with white light as it ate away at the darkness.

I sent out my senses, searching for a curse, a hex, anything. My starlights couldn't detect any curse. Weird, but that didn't mean there weren't any. Maybe my starlights couldn't sense them. Yet.

"Ugh. What's that smell?" Jade pressed her hand to her mouth, looking like she was about to hurl.

Elsa had the same reaction, given the grimace on her face, and by the slight darkening of her skin, it looked as though she was holding her breath.

"That, my friends, is the stink of Auria," I said, trying to breathe through my mouth. I thought it was worse that way, though, because I could practically taste it on my tongue.

Just as I remembered, the place reeked of mildew, cat pee, and other fouler things I'd rather not think about. Wrinkling my nose, I stepped over the dirt-packed ground chamber that was dimly lit by glowing flames from a few wall torches.

"Which way?" asked Elsa, looking like she

wished she had stayed at the hotel where the air was breathable.

I laughed. "Follow the stench."

"This is *soooo* gross." Jade brushed her hand against the stone wall and pulled it away, rubbing something between her fingers. "Looks like she didn't believe in housekeeping."

Elsa coughed. "Smells like she didn't believe in bathing."

I clenched my jaw to keep from laughing. This was serious. I needed to focus. Besides, sooner or later, we would get used to the smell. So what did that say about us?

We kept going in silence. I had a feeling the girls didn't want to talk and open their mouths to the foul odor. I ducked under a stretch of cobweb and continued, all the while holding on to my starlights. I sent out another burst of starlight, feeling for anything cold and untoward. And again, my starlights felt nothing apart from the cold stone walls and the thrum of the earth's vibration beneath our feet.

The floor inclined where a rise in the cave led to a larger chamber. I let a rush of my starlights fly into the room, illuminating a small kitchen area with a table covered in melted-down candles, cauldrons, and a stained cot pushed against the far wall next to bookcases crammed with books.

It looked exactly the same, all except for one important detail.

Auria, the sorceress, wasn't here.

"Is this it?" asked Jade. "This is her home?"

I let go of my starlights. "Yup." Layers of dust ran over shelves packed with various jars of suspicious objects. "I just love what she did to the place."

"Where's the bathroom?" Jade looked around the chamber.

"You're stepping on it."

"Ah!" Jade screamed and started to shake out her hands and legs like she'd stepped on an ant hill and they were crawling over her.

Elsa grabbed her and hauled her around. "Are you done? We're supposed to be on a mission here."

I wouldn't exactly have called it a mission, but who cares.

"Okay. Okay." Jade brushed the hair from her eyes. "I'll need to bathe in bleach when we get back."

Though Elsa hadn't commented, she was staring at her garden clogs, probably wishing she'd worn her rubber boots instead.

"She's not here," I told them, looking around. "I really thought she'd be here."

"So did we," said Elsa. "What do you think that means?"

"No idea." Jimmy had said she liked to play games. Perhaps this was the beginning of one of them. I stared at the long table covered with books and melted-down candles. "Quick. Look for a book of curses."

I rushed over to the table while Jade and Elsa hurried over to the tall bookcases crammed with books.

"What does it look like?" Jade pulled out an old book, and the pages fell out when she flipped it open.

"I don't know. Look for something that has written-out curses." I grabbed a small book with a gleaming red leather cover. It looked new. New enough to be her new grimoire? Heart throbbing, I flipped it open. The corpses of flat, dead butterflies and moths spilled out. "Gross."

After what felt like hours, the three of us had gone through every inch of that den, and we never found even a simple book of spells, let alone a curse book.

I wiped my brow with the back of my hand. "She removed all her magical tomes. She must have took them with her."

Panic hit. Auria was not here, and neither was her book. Now what? How was I supposed to find the ingredients to a curse without either of them? My heart rate shot through the roof. I couldn't panic right now.

Jade exhaled. "Well, that was a bust." She kicked a path through a mountain of old rags and books.

Elsa seemed to have noticed my dismay. "Don't worry. We'll find her. We'll search the whole city if we have to."

"Yeah." I sighed, tension pulling me tightly. "I think we might have to."

"Let's get some fresh air before I pass out," said Elsa, beads of sweat forming on her forehead and upper lip.

"Good idea."

The three of us headed back out, the thumps of our steps echoing around us, but I could hardly hear them. I was too busy trying to think of where Auria could be. Why else did she show up at the hotel if not to taunt me? My gut told me she wanted me to find her, which meant she had to be somewhere I would *think* of looking.

And then it hit me.

"The school. She's at the school." Of course, she was. Why hadn't I thought of it before?

Both witches stopped right before the door to our freedom of fresh air.

Elsa looked at me with a determined brow. "Then let's go get her."

I smiled, glad they were with me. It made things less boring, if you will. A year ago, I would have never imagined working a case with two other witches. Now, I couldn't see myself working a case without them.

Feeling a pulse of excitement, I pulled open the door—and cursed.

There, in the middle of Cherry Street, stood three hooded figures. Green tendrils of magic dripped from their hands. Dark witches.

The one in the middle took a drag of his cigarette. Clive Vespertine.

Now, *this* was interesting.

CHAPTER 22

I stepped out from Auria's lair, Jade and Elsa right behind me. It was dark, and the three hooded figures stood in the shadows, their bodies blanketed under long, dark cloaks. Their auras and the thrum of magic they emitted were a dead giveaway that they weren't human, not to mention the green magic that coiled around their fingers.

Jade wrinkled her face like she was sucking on a lemon. "Is that..."

I grinned. "Clivy. My favorite chain-smoking bastard."

The council investigator frowned but said nothing.

"Oh great, just what we needed. More trouble," muttered Jade.

"What on earth is he doing here?" hissed Elsa. "I thought he wouldn't be a problem anymore. I thought you and Valen took care of him."

"Looks like we didn't do a very good job of it."

Though I was *really* curious as to why he was here. I thought Valen and I had made it clear to him to stay away from me *and* my sister. I cleared my throat. "You've been following me again," I told him. "How very pervy of you."

The male witch stepped from the darkness and flicked his cigarette butt on the ground.

"You were always such a littering bastard." That part of him really bugged me, like the entire world was his ashtray. From the corner of my eye, I saw Jade kneel down and slip on one of her roller skates.

The chain-smoking witch pulled his lips in a sneer. "You thought you could attack and kidnap a Gray Council investigator without any repercussions?"

"Pretty much. My thoughts exactly. Yeah."

The other two witches snickered, and when one of them shifted, I noticed a particularly large abdomen protruding from his cloak, or rather, beer gut. I'd recognize that sizable belly anywhere. It was Beer-Gut witch from that ritual last night. And if I had to guess, his pal was also one of those witches from that night.

"Well, you were wrong," said Clive, gazing around the street. "And now you're going to pay for what you did to me." His tone dripped with malice and fury and a bit of... yes, humiliation. From the folds of his cloak, he pulled out a flat metal box and plucked out a cigarette. He put it to his lips and added, "I took your Merlin license away."

"I noticed."

"That's power. Control. Something you lack." Clive lit his cigarette. The end blazed red as he puffed on it and then dropped the lighter and metal box inside his cloak.

"Control?" I chuckled. "You call control how you blabbed top-secret information to me last night? You blabbed. No control over that tongue of yours. And man, oh man, did you blab. Once you started, you couldn't shut up. You went on and on and on…"

"You used an *illegal* substance on an officer of the council," he snapped. The streetlight reflected over the vein that throbbed in his forehead.

"I thought you were an investigator?" I said, making Jade snort.

Clive's attention snapped to her and then over to Elsa. "What is this? Your reinforcements?" he mocked, and his two minions laughed with him. "A senior citizen and a middle-aged loser on roller skates?" He laughed harder, and so did his cronies.

Anger cemented my gut. "Age doesn't really matter unless you're a cheese or a wine." Yum. I could go for some wine and cheese right about now.

Clive took a drag of his cigarette with a mischievous smile and a dark playfulness in his eyes. "I don't give a shit who you're with. If they interfere, they're going to die. Just like you."

I clenched my jaw. "Wow. So you're here to kill me? Is that what it comes down to? I thought as a member of that Gray Council you worship, you weren't allowed to take a life."

"Oh, I can. It's in the small print." The smile Clive

gave me was truly serpentine. "I can kill, but it must be in self-defense." He looked behind him at his pals. "And if there are witnesses, I am in my rights."

"Leana," said Jade, and I heard the anxiety in her voice. "What do you want us to do?"

"I wasn't planning on having you fight these bastards," I said. One sorceress wasn't so bad, but three Dark witches might be a problem for them.

Elsa gave me a reassuring pat on the back. "Oh ye of little faith, Leana. I wasn't born yesterday. I might have a few more wrinkles than I would like, and my neck looks like it belongs on a turkey, but that only means I'm wise and strong. Youth is not an accomplishment."

"Amen, sista," said Jade. "Too bad I don't have my curling iron," she added, her eyes on Clive. "I'd love to shove it up his arrogant ass."

I laughed. I really shouldn't have been laughing. We were about to duel. Weren't we?

"Once you're out of the picture," continued Clive, that fury never leaving his eyes, "your precious little sister is all mine."

My heart dropped. "You leave her out of this," I hissed and stepped forward as a hot rage entered my bloodstream.

Clive's laughter sent another wave of fury through my limbs. I gritted my teeth. I hated the bastard.

The cigarette-smoking witch tsked. "Oh. Did I offend you? Did I touch on a *sensitive* subject? Always so emotional. You females are *so* sensitive."

I cocked my hip. "Yeah. I'm sensitive to the fact that you're the asshole whose ass I'm about to kick." If he thought I was shaking in my witchy pants, he was wrong.

His face was lit only by the streetlamps, but it was enough to see his glower. "Well then..." He flicked his cigarette. "Ready to put your witch skills to work?" He looked eager as the shadows danced over his features, his eyes narrow and dark.

"Bring it," I snapped, pulling on my starlights.

"It was a mistake for you to assault me," said Clive, lifting his hands in a display of magic and power. "A very *big* mistake."

"Oooh. I'm shaking like a leaf," I said, wiggling my upper body, but it came out more like shaking my hips as though I was gyrating. Needed to work on that.

"I'm going to enjoy killing you, you little bitch," hissed Clive.

I pointed a finger gun at him and winked. "Yes, I'm a bitch. Just not yours."

"Good one," laughed Jade, and the air around her thrummed with her magic. As she muttered a few words under her breath, a faint yellow light emanated from her fingers.

Elsa stepped forward, speaking in low, deliberate syllables. Her entire body blazed in energy as she summoned her White magic, words spilling from her.

I took a breath, spindling my own Starlight magic as I focused on the chain-smoking witch. "You shouldn't have threatened my sister."

Clive shook his head. "I can do whatever I want. I'm a Gray Council *investigator*."

I snorted. Couldn't help it. He made it sound like he was the king of New York or something, which was laughable.

He winced. Guess he didn't think it was funny.

And then they closed in on us.

Three fireballs of green magic sailed toward us.

But I was ready.

I sidestepped and flung out my hands.

A sheet of starlight intercepted the witches' magic. A boom shook the earth around us as the magics collided. The fireballs faded, but when I looked back at Clive, his lips moved as he prepared another spell.

Clive stretched his palm outward, and a tidal wave of power roared toward us. I sent out another volley of my starlights. Again, the magics collided, and some of my starlight absorbed the witch's power, but not all of it.

I growled, bracing myself as the assault of the witch's magic hit. I tottered, almost losing my footing, but I straightened, my arm muscles shaking with the effort. Pushing through the battering power, I willed my starlights and kicked out, blasting the last of the witch's magic and him with it.

It hit Clive, and he went sailing forty feet back. But the bastard landed in a roll and got up. His brow furrowed, and he snarled at me, clearly thinking his magical mojo bested mine. Nope.

So I smiled. "Sorry, I got all *emotional*," I said with finger quotes.

The sound of wheels crunching on asphalt neared, and Jade rolled to a stop as she spread her arms. "Let's see what you've got, bitches," she intoned, widening my smile. Having Jade and Elsa with me was a definite necessity.

Carefully pronounced Latin came from Beer-Gut, and green energy dripped from his hands. The air was thick with sulfur—the scent of Dark magic. I barely had time to blink as he hurled another ball of green death at us.

"Move!" I shouted, as we all lurched sideways, missing that green ball of death by inches.

And then Jade rocketed forward on her roller skates, muttering a spell as she spun around Beer-Gut faster and faster.

He flung out his hands again, and a tendril of green magic flew at Jade. But she was quicker, and his shot went wide.

She ducked and then zoomed in the opposite direction, finished in a spin, and then hurled a blast of her own elemental fire magic at him.

Beer-Gut cried out as it hit, and he fell backward to the ground, disappearing under a wall of magical flames.

Jade grinned. "Middle-age my ass."

The flames dispersed. Beer-Gut clambered to his feet and staggered a moment. Coils of smoke rose from his cloak and the top of his head. He snarled and raised his hands, tendrils of electricity twisting between them.

A cry came from behind me, and I saw Elsa battling Clive and the other witch on her own.

"Go," said Jade, her eyes on Beer-Gut. "I've got this."

Without another word, I rushed over to Elsa's aid. Clive saw me, scowled, and then threw his magic at me.

I flung myself to the ground, causing my breath to escape me as I hit the asphalt. The green energy ball exploded behind me on the stone pier.

I looked up and saw Clive. A sick, deranged kind of laugh that sounded remarkably like a hyena ushered out of him as he turned his attention on Elsa. Her back was to him as she countered the other witch with blasts of red and yellow fire magic.

Clive snickered at me and then hurled his magic at Elsa.

"Elsa, behind you!" I shouted as I pushed to my feet, channeling my starlights.

Elsa spun, her arms raised as she summoned her defenses, but not fast enough.

Lashes of green hit her. Teeth bared, Elsa's face twisted in pain as she stumbled back and fell, the smell of sulfur replaced by the scent of burning flesh. A scream of pain ripped from the witch's throat.

"You bastards!"

Snarling like a beast, my anger fueled my magic until I could see only death and destruction. I was going to fry these cloaked bastards.

I lunged toward Clive and lashed out with my starlight. A beam of light shot toward the chain-smoking witch. A green, semitransparent wall rose over him just as my starlights hit... a shield. I cursed as I saw that my starlights couldn't penetrate his shield.

I didn't wait a single second because I knew Clive was busy summoning strong magic just to keep that shield up. He'd be busy for a little while, so I turned to the other bastard.

I felt the air move, raising the hairs on the back of my neck. The other witch, let's call him Dickhead, was summoning his magic.

"Oh, no you don't."

Fuming, I charged, flinging my hands as I ran.

His lips moved as he channeled his magic.

The good thing about Starlight magic was I didn't need to waste time mumbling spells and incantations. It was insta-magic. And it was fast.

Before Dickhead could finish his spell, a ball of starlights hit him in the chest. He let out a cry of surprise as he stumbled back, white flames rising high over his head. He shouted a word I couldn't decipher, and then he fell to the ground, the scent of burnt hair filling my nose.

"You fucking bitch," came a familiar and vicious voice.

I lifted my gaze to see Clive facing me, his shoulders stiff with tension. He was pissed. Excellent. That made two of us. Now we could dance.

I caught a glimpse of Jade rolling to a stop next to

Elsa and helping her up. Beer-Gut, the witch she'd been fighting, lay in the street, and it didn't look like he was going to get up anytime soon. Pain was fresh on Elsa's face. She was alive, but she was hurt. She needed a healer. She needed Polly.

"You'll fry for this," growled Clive, anger lacing his words. "Adele should have killed you, but it doesn't matter. I'll finish the job, and I'm going to enjoy it."

"Lovely." I fixed my gaze on the witch, my hatred oozing out of my pores. "But remember, you attacked first," I panted, planting my feet as I focused all my energy on Clive.

The witch let out a laugh. "Your star magic is worthless. Magic from the stars? You're a joke." He chuckled. "There's a reason there aren't many of you. It's because your magic is weak. Obsolete."

"Tell that to your friend I fried with it." I flicked my finger in the direction of Dickhead, in case he didn't get that part.

"You're not a real witch. Witches manipulate energies from the elementals and power from demons. *That's* magic." He shook his head, the movement slow and patronizing. "You're pathetic. You're nothin'. And I will end you."

I smiled wider, knowing I was getting under his skin. "And here you said I was the *emotional* one."

The witch came at me in a burst of speed, his dark cloak billowing behind him like giant bat wings.

Unintelligible Latin spilled from his mouth, or maybe it was incomprehensible to me because my

Latin was a little bit rusty. A wind rose, slapping my hair against my face and into my eyes. He was putting all his energy into his attack.

This was his killing strike. The big one. He wanted to end me.

I watched as if in slow motion as the witch spun his magic. I heard my name. Jade, maybe?

As Clive pointed out before, I was emotional. And magic thrived on emotions. Like feeding it steroids.

So I let my emotions consume me, fueling my magic.

Shoots of green tendrils soared from his outstretched hands, vehemence blazing in his eyes, but I was ready.

With all the pent-up energy from my *emotions*, I swung my starlight directly at his green tendrils.

At first, I wasn't sure if my magic would do anything. But then, as the two different magics collided, mine kept going, pushing like a freight train. Instead of knocking away Clive's beam, my starlights rammed into his magic, crushing and flattening it until nothing was left.

Clive's mouth hung open in utter shock. "Impossible. How?"

I wanted to rub it in, but instead I used that moment to strike again. Hard.

Clive was knocked back with force as I slammed him again with my starlight. He hit the ground rolling, wailing, and thrashing, coils of my starlights wafting off his cloak and clothes like smoke from a fire.

Though I couldn't see it, I had a feeling his skin was sizzling too. Good. Let him roast a little. And then he was still.

"My bad," I said with a shrug. "Here I was all *emotional* again."

I walked over to him, seeing his chest rise and fall. He was alive. Part of me wanted to kick the sonofabitch. But I had other, more important, things to do.

I yanked out my phone.

"Who are you calling?"

I turned to see Jade and Elsa shambling my way.

"I'm getting an Uber to take you back to the hotel," I said, my fingers sliding over my phone's screen. "You need Polly to look at you." Elsa was bleeding from the side of her head, and she was pale like that fight had taken a toll on her energy. Jade was holding one of her roller skates with its wheels ripped off and was favoring her left leg. Blood seeped from both knee areas of her jeans.

"Aren't you coming?" asked Jade, hopping over to me and trying to spy what I was writing.

"No." I pocketed my phone. "I'm going to the school. I'll hail a cab when I reach Fifth Avenue."

"Alone? No, you're not," said Elsa, her face twisted in distress.

"Yeah, we're coming with you," voiced Jade.

I looked at my friends, my heart warming at the sight of these two witches. They'd fought fiercely. These witches were badass, but they were injured. "Thanks, but you can't come with me in your state." I raised my hand at the protest bubbling on Elsa's lips. "You're hurt, and in your condition, you'll only slow me down." Or worse, get killed. "You can't face Auria like this."

"Can't you wait for Polly to heal us?" By the tone in Jade's voice, I knew she was asking for a long shot. She knew I'd already made up my mind, and there was nothing she or Elsa could do to persuade me.

I sighed. "Polly's good. But she can't heal you in ten minutes. And Valen needs to keep his healing magic for my sister. Shay is running out of time. Polly said we had about twenty-four hours, but what if she was wrong? She'd also said that Auria was the queen of curses and that her curses were extremely hard to decode. What if Shay gets sick again much sooner? I can't take that chance. I need to go now."

"We understand," said Elsa, lowering herself on the curb with a strenuous effort. "I don't think I've got much more fight left in me."

I winced at the pain that flashed over her face. Maybe having them come with me hadn't been such a good idea after all.

"What about them?" Jade pointed to the three unconscious witches.

"Leave them," I said. "Let the human police deal with them." At this point, I couldn't care less about keeping our paranormal ways secret from humans.

"Leana," said Elsa, looking grim. "Be careful."

I gave them a tight smile. "I will. See you later."

And with that, I rushed ahead, leaped over

Clive's stupid, unconscious and still smoking body, and jogged down Cherry Street.

CHAPTER 23

Fantasia Academy looked creepier at night than it did in the morning sun. It had more of a Gothic feel, the turrets like knives pointing up into the night sky. Its stone glimmered in the moonlight like black frosting on a cake. Pretty. *I think I like it better at night.*

The iron gates glowered down at me as I made my way up the walkway and to the front oak doors framed by gray stone. I stole a look over my shoulder, expecting someone to jump me. I had no idea if Auria was a solitary creature or if she had a handful of her sorcerers and sorceresses with her. I didn't know much about her, except for the fact that she cursed Jimmy and now my sister, and she was a vengeful being.

I sent out a bout of starlight just in case, watching my little spheres shoot out like hundreds of fireflies, but all I gathered back was the quiet hum of humanity. No magical beings.

I turned and faced the school. "Maybe you're inside."

I hadn't decided how I was going to make Auria tell me what ingredients she'd used to make that curse on Shay. She had refused to tell me what she'd used on Jimmy, so I knew this would be a challenge. How did one force an evil sorceress to reveal her curse? I couldn't kill her. I had to force her somehow. But how? Guess I would have to think of something fast.

I cursed myself for not asking Julian for his truth serum before I left. It might not work on ancient vampires, but I had a feeling it could have worked on Auria.

Too late. I was already here, and I didn't have time to go back and wait for Julian to make me a new batch.

I stared at the door and wondered for about two seconds, as my hand reached out for the handle, if it might be booby-trapped. My witchy instincts said no. She wanted to face me, to fight me. She was waiting for me inside.

"Let's do this, Auria."

I yanked open the door—more like heaved it *very* slowly and with great effort. It was a lot heavier than it looked. Either that or I had zero upper-body strength.

I pulled it enough to slip through and sneaked inside, my heart racing as I prepared myself mentally for what I was about to face—a full-on sorceress-witch duel. Well, most probably. I got that Auria was mad. It had been a suspicion in the back of my mind that perhaps someday she might retaliate for the ass-whooping I'd given her. I'd always assumed she'd come for me, or perhaps she'd forgotten about me, given her ancient age. It never occurred to me that she'd go after Shay.

I shut the door behind me and glanced around. The first thing that woke my warning flags was the lack of security. More like the lack of wards that would surely attack intruders.

If this school was anything like I thought it was and had read about, it was a highly secured magical facility with only one objective—to protect the students.

And right now, it wasn't doing that. It had let me walk in without so much as a slap on the wrist. This was all kinds of wrong.

But magic did chime my senses as I walked into a large foyer with high, decorative ceilings like something you would find at a grand hotel. It was more of the prickling of charm magic closing around the building, shutting it off from any supernatural access —the school's glamour. I also got some tingling magic from the walls that seemed to reach out from everywhere at once, circling me and resonating in rhythm like the beating of a giant beast's heart. The heart of the school.

Soft yellow light spilled from a few wall sconces, enough to let me see properly. And it was quite the view.

I'd wanted to see the inside of this place. And

here was my chance. Too bad it wasn't under more pleasant circumstances.

A grand, winding staircase, richly carpeted in red and gold and leading to the second and third floors, served as the room's centerpiece. The school was massive. Everywhere I looked, I was met with lustrous polished wooden doors and railings, exquisite drapery, chairs, and side tables.

It was glorious and majestic, like a grand hotel somewhere in Europe. But even its noble presence couldn't make me shake the cold and relentless feeling of dread crawling up my spine.

My shoes sounded loudly on the dark, polished wood floors, and I could barely hear the throbbing of my own heart. Was I nervous? Hell yeah. Especially because the outcome would determine what happened to Shay. I wasn't ashamed to admit it.

So far, so good. I feared the staff might have added more protective wards inside the school, but since I didn't combust into dust, I took that as a good sign and kept walking.

The hallway was lined with various doors, and from what I peeked, the classrooms had pupil desks and a much larger desk across from them where I imagined the teacher sat. I would have loved to study here, and I understood why Shay loved it. It was unique, and I was pretty sure most of the kids who attended were exceptional too. And in their uniqueness, they formed a bond.

I checked another three rooms on the first floor.

Again, I saw no sign of Auria. If she wasn't here... I was screwed. I didn't know where else to look.

I approached a set of double doors leading to the last room I hadn't checked on this level. Light seeped from the space below the door and the floor.

Isn't this interesting...

Keeping my starlights close, I pushed the doors and stepped through.

The room was large, perhaps the size of the hotel lobby, and by far the most spacious classroom I'd encountered so far.

I treaded into a large workroom teeming with shelves crammed with books, glass jars, and twenty individual desks topped with cauldrons. Some still steamed and smoked, unidentifiable *things* floating inside them.

It was a potions lab of sorts, but more like a potions room where students could learn the art of potion making. Julian would have loved this room.

Of course, it was the room where Auria would make her stand.

A woman lounged in a chair across from me, her feet up on the wooden desk, looking mildly bored. She wasn't the elderly woman, bent with age and old as dirt, when she looked up at me as I entered. Nope. This was the young teacher I'd met, Ms. Barclay. She had a powerful quality to her that I felt as soon as I walked in. She'd done an excellent job of hiding it when I met her the first time. If she hadn't, I would have suspected something irregular. Or maybe I would have thought she was just a powerful teacher.

She'd ditched the school's attire and wore a gown of flowing black silk in a medieval style with long sleeves and a tight bodice that showed off her cleavage. Tucked between her breasts was the same pendant and glowing blue stone.

Auria rolled her eyes. "Took you long enough." She swung her feet off the top and made her way around the desk.

"I'm here about the curse you put on my sister." No point in beating around the bush.

Auria snorted. "Yes. I thought that would get your attention."

"Picking on little girls... That has to be a new low for you." I stayed where I was. I wasn't a fool. The distance between us was good. It would give me some time to figure out how to get her to blab about the curse she used on Shay.

Auria's gray eyes sparkled with a feverish glee. "Ah, I get it. You went to my old home. Well. I don't live there anymore. Haven't for a while."

"Really? Could've fooled me. I thought you liked to live in your own filth."

Auria smiled. It was cold, false, and dangerous. Her power danced over her skin, a silver light cresting over her like tiny waves, with sparks of energy flashing in the room's light.

I gestured a hand up and down her body. "So, how did you do it?" I figured she would know I'd ask this, and judging by the stretch in her smile, she was happy to share.

Auria pressed a manicured hand to her chest, her

nails a little too long to look tasteful. "What? You mean, how did I make myself young and beautiful again? To be the object of desire of every man?"

"Sure. Whatever." I wanted to keep her talking so I could figure out my next move.

"Well," began Auria as she dragged her finger along one of the student desks. "Only a true proficient in the arts of curses can manipulate the life force of others—and take it." She made a fist for show, like I didn't already get that.

I raised a brow. "You don't say?"

Auria ambled around the desk, inching closer to me the entire time. "You see, to make oneself young again, one must find a valuable host."

"Are you saying you're a tick?" She was kind of an insect in my mind, and not the pretty kind.

Auria flashed me another of her false smiles. "It took a few hosts to get to the level I needed. Each time I drained them, each time I took from them and made it mine."

I was hit with a sinking realization at her words. "You killed those witches in Valen's restaurant? It was you." Of course, it was.

A sickly little feeling of dread rolled through me. It all made sense now. She just told me. She'd drained those poor people of their life's energy and somehow manipulated it into her, like charging up a battery. She'd powered herself up.

And then another thing I realized with a start was that the woman I'd seen running out of the restaurant's bathroom had looked familiar. It was

Auria. Only older than she was right now in front of me.

I shook my head. "You broke their necks to make it look like a giant killed them. But why there? Why Valen?"

Auria's mouth twisted in disdain. "Because I wanted you to suffer. That night when you came to my home uninvited, you attacked an old, defenseless woman," she accused, her features twisting to make her look more feral.

"You were old but never defenseless."

"I'd heard of your relationship with the giant. Oh yes. It's no secret what he is. I wanted him to be blamed and be sentenced to death. I wanted you to pay for what you did to me that night. Taking something away that you loved, well, that was a great plan."

"So you went after Valen."

Auria's mouth stretched in a savage grin. "People are afraid of giants, always have been, always will be. They're... unnatural. Shouldn't exist."

"Right, because you're so *natural*." What was this, a species thing? "So..." I blinked, trying to make sense of this. "You killed Catelyn's family? You wanted Valen to be blamed for that too?"

Auria grinned like I'd just paid her a compliment. "Yes, that was me. You like that?"

"No, you psychotic bitch," I seethed, remembering Catelyn's pain all too well. "You're insane."

"I'm a woman with a plan is all," she added, her lips spread like she was trying to dry out her teeth.

Her eyes focused on me. "You have no idea what it feels like to take another person's life energy, see the fear in their eyes when they know they're about to die." She shivered in delight. "What a high."

I hated this bitch. "You can't get away with this. I won't let you."

Auria threw back her head and howled. "Oh, Leana. I must thank you. I haven't had this much fun... well... since I cursed that wretched Jimmy."

I gritted my teeth, feeling a slip of my control. "You're evil."

Auria giggled like a schoolgirl. I recognized a surety in her manner and expression as something more than just a rampant ego. It was pure madness. Plain and simple. The bitch was insane.

The sorceress spun around and leaned her back on one of the desks so she was facing me. "And you know what else?"

"Why do I get the feeling even if I say *no*, you're going to tell me anyway."

She pointed a long, manicured finger at me. "I knew you were smart. See. The thing with taking that life energy—"

"You mean stealing."

"Is that it makes you stronger," she said. "And more powerful. The witches gave me their power. The humans? Well, it wasn't much, just more of a rejuvenation scream." She laughed. "But it was necessary, to follow my plan." Her eyes widened on me, and the air sizzled with energy. Hers.

The air shifted, and I felt a wave of energy

cascade over me, cold and unfamiliar. My heart thrashed madly in my chest, and raw fear flooded into me. The stone set in that pendant around her neck glowed a bright blue. Somehow I knew that wasn't good.

"And I'm going to do the same thing to you," she said in an airy tone like she was sharing good news with me. "Your power will be mine." Her smile was victorious. "And then you're going to die."

Well, shit.

CHAPTER 24

Auria's fingers twitched as she prepared whatever curse she was going to throw at me.

I wasn't about to just let her kill me. But I had to be careful about how I proceeded. I had to be innovative. I still needed her to rid Shay of the curse she'd cast on her.

Somehow I had to subdue her and jam a truth serum down her throat. How I would force the liquid down her esophagus was another matter. Good plan. I just didn't know how to execute it.

"You won't be able to use my starlights," I said, contemplating how I was going to overpower her but coming up short. "It's not how it works."

The sorceress laughed and then tsked. "Maybe not. But they will feed me with more strength and power." Her whole body shuddered as her power washed over her. "Have you ever seen the life go out of a person's eyes, seen the fear when they know they're about to die and can't do anything about it?"

"Can't say that I have."

"It's invigorating and so, so delicious."

I wanted to throw up. "Sex is invigorating. You're just crazy."

She stood staring at me for a few seconds. "Witches are so judgmental. You call it crazy. I call it being empowered."

"No. I can't go any higher than insane."

A flash of anger contorted her features. Auria hadn't moved, but great power thumped me from above as if she was getting ready to pound me with it like an invisible hammer.

"Wait!" I threw out my hand and put on my best, fake I'm-afraid-of-you face. "What about that curse you put on my sister?" A ribbon of tension squeezed around my chest.

Auria pushed off the desk, her power thrumming so I could almost see it, like a veil coiled around her. "What about it?"

Might as well just say it. "Pretty powerful curse. What did you use?"

The sorceress cocked her hip. "Nice try. A true sorceress never reveals the elements of her curses, silly."

I planted my feet and held on to my starlights. Feigning weakness wasn't going to cut it. "I'll give you anything you want. Name it." It wasn't wise to bargain with a mad sorceress, but I'd do just about anything for my little sister.

Auria took another step forward, the sapphire stone around her neck glowed and pulsed, throbbing with power, and I could see her hair lifting off her shoulders. "You have nothing that I want. Except your life," she added with a laugh.

"Come on. There must be something else you want. Money? Men? Women?" What? I was desperate. I needed her to tell me.

The sorceress frowned, and I thought I got a glimpse of her much older self for just a second in a mask of lines and creases and age. But then it was gone. "You stole something of value from me."

"Jimmy? You can't steal a person."

"My book, you idiot," she seethed, her eyes on me, and I could see the raging storm of fury behind them.

"Do you want it back?" Maybe I should have brought it with me to bargain with. "I'll give it to you... if you tell me what you used to make that curse. It's yours."

"Really? Just like that? You would give it back?" Auria watched me. Her eyes were unsettling.

I let out a puff of air. "Obviously, I'll have to try the counter-curse first to make sure you're not lying. Then if Shay's better, I'll give you back your book."

"How do I know you're not lying?"

"You don't. You'll just have to trust me. I'm a witch of her word."

"Hard pass," said Auria, her expression disinterested. "I have no more use for that book. And I'll never tell you what I used. Never. Your sister is going to die. You're going to die. And that giant of yours is going to die. Die. Die. Die."

"You're wrong," I growled through my teeth, my anger tightening my gut until I thought I would scream. I was going to force her to tell me.

"I'm not," she mocked, her tone final. I didn't like it.

I stretched my arms and flexed my fingers, preparing for the battle that was about to begin.

Auria's eyes narrowed, and her lips curled in a wicked smile. "Are you ready to meet your doom, Starlight witch?"

I rolled my eyes. "You really need to work on your insults. 'Meet your doom'? That's so cliché. But then again, you're a cliché."

She scowled. "I'll show you who's a cliché." And with a wave of her hand, she sent a bolt of blue energy hurtling toward me.

I dodged to the side and countered with a blast of my white starlight, but Auria was too quick, deflecting it with a flick of her hand. We circled each other, both of us waiting for an opening.

"I have to admit, Auria," I said, grinning wickedly, "your outfit is on point today. Did you raid Maleficent's wardrobe?"

Auria glared at me. "I'll have you know, this is the latest in sorceress fashion. Clothes don't win battles."

"Well, you should really try it sometime. A killer outfit can do wonders for your confidence."

Auria snarled and sent another blast of energy toward me, but I'd anticipated it.

Pulling on my starlight, I countered with a beam of white star magic.

The two magical energies hit, tangling in the air above the classroom. They twisted and clashed as they fought like intelligent creatures, but Auria's magic was greater. It broke through my starlight beam.

And came straight for my head.

I raised my arms, and a barrier of starlights materialized and stretched across the floor and over my head, deflecting the attack back at her.

She stumbled back but quickly regained her balance. "You'll pay for that, witch!"

I grinned. "Oh, I don't doubt it."

"You call yourself a witch, but you're just a mistake. A glitch in our world. An anomaly," Auria sneered and gave a laugh. "More like a glorified fairy."

I pursed my lips in thought. "Haven't heard that one before. But fairies are awesome. They can fly, do magic, and make wishes come true."

Auria scoffed. "That's nothing compared to the power of a sorceress, the real dark arts."

"Oh, please," I said, rolling my eyes. "Dark arts are so overrated. I mean, who wants to go around summoning demons and sacrificing goats? That's so 1600s."

Auria sneered. "You think this is a joke?"

"No. But it's way more fulfilling than this power trip you've got going."

Auria's face slowly flushed scarlet, rushing up from the light skin of her throat and over her cheeks.

A growl escaped her as she sent a blast of blue energy toward me. I barely had time to dive to the side to avoid the attack. After hitting the floor and rolling to my feet, I leaped up and braced myself to defend against the sorceress's magic that kept coming.

We stood there, facing each other, both of us breathing heavily.

Okay, so she was faster and more powerful than I'd anticipated. I could work with that.

Auria scowled and sent another wave of blue energy my way. I dodged it easily and shot a beam of starlight back at her. She deflected it with an armor spell, and we continued to trade blows, each of us trying to gain the upper hand.

As we fought, I couldn't help but think about how ridiculous we must look to anyone watching. Two grown women flinging magic at each other like kids throwing snowballs.

"Is that the best you've got?" Auria taunted, a smirk on her face.

I grinned back. "Oh, I'm just getting started."

My heart raced as I approached the sorceress. She was a formidable opponent, so I knew I would have to use every trick in my arsenal if I wanted to defeat her. And I had to do it quickly. I didn't know how long Shay had until the curse consumed her again, and she would be beyond Valen's help.

"You'll never win this," Auria said with a leer as

she twirled a lock of her long, blonde hair around her finger. "You're too weak. The smart thing to do is give up."

Like hell, I would. I took a deep breath and prepared to unleash my magic. "Let's get this over with. Shall we?"

Auria laughed. "Oh, you're in such a rush to die. Are you?"

I scowled at her. "I'm not going to die. I'm going to beat you."

Auria raised an eyebrow. "Is that so? Well, let's see what you've got."

With a flick of my wrist, I summoned a burst of starlight, hoping to blind Auria and give myself the advantage to knock her out. But she was too quick, dodging out of the way and firing a bolt of blue energy back at me.

It hit. The force of the blast sent me flying backward. I landed on my feet, a bit shaken but otherwise unharmed.

"You have some skill. I'll admit that. For a make-believe witch," Auria taunted. "But you're going to have to do better than that if you want to beat me." She fired a barrage of blue bolts at me.

Focusing on my magic, I hurled another starlight shield over me like a vast glittering shell. A hiss sounded as Auria's attack bounced harmlessly off my protective armor.

Auria chuckled. "That won't save you."

"So far, so good."

With a wave of her hand, a massive gust of wind

shot out. It hit my shield and broke through, sending me tumbling backward, my protective wall shattering into a million tiny stars.

I blinked in confusion for a second. She shouldn't have been able to break my protective shield that quickly and easily.

I scrambled to my feet, panting with exertion and with a bit of uncertainty. "Okay, you got me there, but I'm not giving up yet."

Auria smirked. "Oh, I wouldn't expect you to. You witches are so stubborn."

I summoned another burst of starlight, this time aiming it straight at Auria's feet. She stumbled, her concentration momentarily broken.

Ha! I took advantage of the moment and lunged at her, sending a powerful punch straight to her jaw. She staggered backward but recovered quickly and retaliated with a blast of her blue magic that sent me hurtling through the air.

I crashed to the ground, my head spinning, but I refused to give up. I rose to my feet, my eyes blazing with determination.

"You're not going to beat me," I growled.

Auria chuckled. "We'll see about that. Won't we?"

Standing my ground, I planted my feet and summoned another shield of starlights. They rose over my head like a sheet of gleaming crystals.

I heard Auria laugh, and I thought it strange how confident she was. Way too confident. And then she threw another curse at my starlight barrier.

Her magic sailed through my armor like it was

made of butter. The curse hit me, flinging me across the room like a rag doll. I hit a wall, my breath escaping me as I slid sideways to the floor. *Ow. That. Hurt. I think my ribs are broken.* I couldn't breathe. Worse was the searing pain I felt as my skin burned. The scent of burnt flesh rose in my nose. I howled as the arc of her curse jumped inside and then out of my body, burning the whole way.

I heard the scraping of her high-heeled shoes coming closer before I saw her. With my head and ribs throbbing in pain, I pushed myself up on my knees. Every breath sent a wave of nausea through me. God, it hurt.

I opened my eyes to find Auria standing resolutely, her fingers wreathed in blue energy and her smile promising more pain, an echo of her power.

If I had any doubts about whether Auria was a powerful sorceress before, I didn't anymore.

My starlights hadn't protected me. It was the first time in my witch life they hadn't. And that scared the crap out of me.

"I've made some adjustments," she said, looming over me and seeing my confusion. "See, I can adjust my curses to match my enemies' strengths. You. Well, it was Starlight magic, magic from the stars. So, well, I made sure I could counter it."

Well, that explained why my starlight was acting up.

Auria gripped her pendant, staring at it in amazement and adoration as power spun through her.

I blinked up at her. Instincts kicked in, and I

reached out. I didn't know what possessed me to do it, but I grabbed her pendant and yanked it off her neck with as much force as I could muster. The chain snapped, and I held her pendant in my hand. It pulsed and was warm.

Auria's demeanor changed. Panic filled her eyes. "Give it back."

Should I? Hell no. I had a feeling this was countering my magic.

In a deranged rage, she flung herself at me, nails out like claws.

I rolled, barely having time to escape her clingy fingers. I kicked out, my shoe hit the side of her jaw, and she fell back. I pushed to my feet just as she staggered up.

"It's mine. Mine. Give it back!" Her eyes narrowed, lips and fingers moving. I knew she was just about to curse me.

Not this time.

I pulled on the starlights, feeding them with all of my emotions—fear, fury, guilt, everything I could— and directed them at the sorceress.

A large burst of white light blasted out of my hand and hit Auria in the chest.

She flew back and hit the wall. Okay, so that was a bit hard, but not hard enough to kill her. Just restrain her—hopefully, knock the mad bitch unconscious.

I rushed over, seeing her lying on her side and unmoving. "Auria? Get up." I hadn't hit her *that* hard. Had I? No. I'd made sure not to kill her. So why was she all banged up?

Her eyes rolled until they focused on me. "No…"

And then something weird happened.

Her face shifted like it was made of clay, going from one expression to the next until her skin started to stretch and pull and age. Her hair went from a healthy blonde to a gray and then white until only wisps remained on a nearly bare scalp. Her strong, younger body thinned, the muscle mass on her arms and legs that I could see withered and shrank, clinging to her bones. The skin was paper-thin, like tissue. Dark veins showed through.

She'd aged right before my eyes. "Oh my God."

She looked… She looked older than the first time I'd seen her. She'd looked old then, but now she looked like a corpse.

I stared down at the pendant still clasped in my hand. "This. This was making you young? Making you strong?" More like it had trapped the energies of those dead people, and it was releasing them to her, keeping her vital and young. Without it, she was vulnerable and old. It was creepy and gross.

Auria's cracked, thin lips moved. I leaned in, trying to hear what she said, but then all I heard was the whoosh of her last breath. I pulled back. Her dead eyes stared back.

Damn it.

She was dead. I'd killed the sorceress Auria.

And by doing so, I'd also killed the only person who could save my sister.

CHAPTER 25

"I tried putting the pendant back on her chest, but it didn't work," I told the gang back on the thirteenth floor. I had done exactly that, not knowing what else to do after I checked her pulse five times and even slapped her.

Auria was dead.

"I killed her. I killed my only chance at making Shay better." What a colossal mess. I'd gone there in the hope of making her talk. Not kill her.

"And this was feeding her power?" mused Elsa, holding up Auria's pendant close so she could see it clearly. She had a dressing plastered on the side of her head where she'd been bleeding, but otherwise she seemed fine.

Jade was sipping a cup of coffee with her leg up on a chair and her knee bandaged. I was happy they were okay. But it didn't help that I felt like a giant ass.

When I'd returned to the hotel, Elsa and Jade

were there, and so were Jimmy, Polly, and Valen. No one had left. Not seeing Shay, I had a moment of panic.

"She's fine," Valen had said, seeing the terror on my face. "She's sleeping. She's okay. Tell me what happened."

Then I'd just blurted the events with the sorceress, feeling more and more like a massive failure. I'd lost my cool. I'd gone too far. And now, Shay would pay for my folly.

"It could have happened to any of us," said Valen, trying to make me feel better. He took my hand to lead me to the living room just as I saw Polly enter Shay's room.

I let myself fall on the couch. "I have experience. I knew what I was doing. I didn't hit her with a killing hit. But she just…"

"Shriveled up and died," said Elsa. "It's because you removed the pendant. If you hadn't, she might have killed you. You said she'd adjusted her magic to defeat your starlight. But when you separated it from her, you made her weaker. You took it away, exposing her to your magic with nothing protecting her. She'd put all her power into that thing. It's no surprise that she died. Maybe she would have died regardless if you had struck her or not. Once you took that off of her, that was it. Like taking away her oxygen."

"You pulled the plug on her," said Jade, looking a little happy and sad at the same time. "Too bad I missed it." I knew she'd wanted to settle a score with the sorceress because of Jimmy. Guess she missed her chance.

Jimmy stood behind her, his hands on the chair's headrest. "I'm glad she's gone," he said and kissed the top of Jade's head.

"I'm not." I rubbed my eyes. I shouldn't have killed her.

Valen pulled out his phone and walked away into the hallway, his voice a muffle and too far away for me to hear. I wasn't sure who he had called, but I had an idea.

"You said Shay's okay?" I looked up and glanced at Polly as she came out of Shay's room and closed the door. "Has she had a relapse?" Not sure what else to call it. Curses weren't my thing. In fact, the only real curse I'd ever been involved with was the one Auria had put on Jimmy.

The healer shook her head. "No. Valen's healing magic worked better than I'd hoped. I think it's time Valen and I had a long chat." Her eyes moved to the giant. His back was to us, and he was still talking on the phone. Polly glanced back at me. "She's doing fine."

"But she's not cured," I said, the desperate hope almost painful as it clenched around my heart.

"I'm afraid not," said Polly, and I could hear the sadness in her voice. "I just checked her. She's still sleeping soundly, which is good. No signs of a fever. But the curse is still in her body."

I sighed. "I was hoping the curse had broken somehow with Auria's death, and Shay would be rid of it forever." By the grim look on Polly's face, I knew that would've been a long shot.

Polly was nodding as she came around the couch to face me. "Maybe at the hands of an inexperienced sorceress, which Auria was not. She made sure her curses would last even if she was dead."

"She's an evil bitch, even in her death, to do something like that," commented Jade, and I had to agree with her. Who thinks up stuff like that? Apparently, Auria did.

I swallowed hard, feeling pressure along my temples and stiffness along my shoulders. "What now? How can I help Shay? Will she... she..." My voice cracked. How could I help my little sister now when I'd destroyed the only person who could? Yes, Auria wouldn't have given me the elements of the curse freely, but I'm positive I would have found a way to make her talk. Now she was dead. And the dead don't talk back.

Polly was quiet for a moment, and I could sense that everyone was waiting for her to answer. "Well, her reaction to Valen's magic is very positive. I think if we monitor her closely, and with a daily dose of Valen's magic, she'll be all right."

"Wait a minute." I sat straighter, my gaze flicking to Valen and then resting back to the healer. "Are you saying that the curse is manageable?"

"Yes." Polly stuffed her hands in her front pockets. "Think of it like having type 1 diabetes. You need your daily insulin shot. Well, that's where Valen comes in. It's a good thing you know a giant," said Polly with a wink. "Make sure he stays close."

You can bet your ass he will.

My eyes burned, and it took tremendous effort not to start bawling. "Okay. So she can live a normal life."

"She can. But…" Polly's eyes were intense. "But it's not forever. Shay could one day start showing signs of the curse. I just don't know, and I don't want you to think she's cured because she's not."

"But it'll give me time to find one." Yes. This was it. I would look for a cure and not have to worry about Shay's condition worsening. I met the healer's gaze. "Even if Auria's dead, there's a chance I can find her secret recipe. Right? She's not the only sorceress in this state. Someone's gotta know something."

"A coven of sorceresses live here in New York," announced Elsa, and we all turned to look at her. "I can make some calls. Get you to see them."

"Thanks, Elsa," I said, smiling. "If they can see me tomorrow, that would be great."

The older witch smiled back brightly, the idea gathering momentum in her thoughts. "We'll figure this out. Don't you worry."

For some strange reason, I believed her. Things hadn't turned out the way I'd hoped, but there *was* still hope that I'd find the formula of the damn curse and heal Shay of it.

But first I needed a good night's sleep.

I opened my mouth to thank her and yawned at

the same time. "Sorry," I said, still yawning. "Tired. Thanks, Polly. Thank you for everything." Even though I'd accidentally killed Auria, she'd given me quite the beating, and so did Clive and his goons. My body needed rest.

"Glad to help." The healer took a deep breath. "Well, I've got a brunch to plan for tomorrow, so I better get some sleep too. Good night, everyone."

"Yes. We should all go to bed," declared Elsa as she started forward. She stopped mid-step and held out Auria's pendant. "Leana? Do you mind if I hang on to this? I'd like to inspect it more closely. Maybe try a few spells."

I shrugged. "Sure. I've got no use for it." If it couldn't make Shay better, she could toss it.

"See you tomorrow," said Elsa. "Good night, Valen," she said to the giant as he was heading back, and she followed Polly down the hall and disappeared out the door.

I stood up as Jimmy helped Jade to her feet. "You guys okay?"

"I've got her." Jimmy draped Jade's arm over his shoulder, supporting her easily. "I could carry you, you know," he added with a cheeky smile.

Jade's cheeks turned beet red. "Stop. I can do this. Night, Leana. Valen."

"Night." I watched as Jimmy hauled his girlfriend out. And the last thing I saw was Jade lifting her eyebrows at me and then at Valen as she shut the door. Yeah. Not obvious at all.

I flinched when Valen came up behind me and

wrapped his arms around my waist. His body was warm against mine, and I couldn't help but feel a sense of comfort in his embrace. I leaned into him, enjoying his musky scent and warmth.

"You know, for a giant, you have a way of sneaking up on people," I teased.

"It's what I do. Make sure I blend in," he said, his voice low and husky.

I wasn't sure he blended in anywhere. He was just too damn hot, too damn big, and too damn dominating. But whatever.

"What did the Gray Council say about Auria? I'm guessing that's who you called."

"I explained everything," said the giant, his warm breath tickling the back of my neck. "They'll take Auria's body back to the morgue and do a thorough check of the school to make sure she didn't leave any curses behind for the kids."

"You think she's that evil?"

"She's a twisted sort. Just have to be careful."

"Yeah, you're right." I sighed. "So, I'm guessing these trumped-up charges they had on you are gone. Auria killed all those people."

"There'll be an investigation. They have to. But I'm confident they'll find enough evidence to tie those deaths to Auria and not me."

"Good. I don't want to have to see Clive's chain-smoking face ever again."

"You won't."

Why did I not believe him? I had a strange feeling Clive was not finished with me.

"Have you heard from Catelyn?" Guilt was something I wasn't used to feeling. Now, with the remorse of what Auria did to Shay and to Catelyn because of me, I felt like I couldn't get rid of it once it got there.

"Not from her," said the giant. "But Arther called. They had to sedate her."

Fear rushed into me. "What?"

"It's okay," soothed Valen, rubbing my arms. "They didn't have a choice. She started to change. But eventually, she did calm down. She's fine now. She's surrounded by really great people. Don't worry about her."

"I can't help it. Her parents died because of me." And I would have to live with it for the rest of my life. I cringed at the thought of me telling her because I would have to. I couldn't *not* tell her. She might not forgive me, and that's just something I would have to live with as well.

Valen sighed. "Maybe we could drive up on the weekend with Shay? Would you like that? Some fresh air. Wilderness."

I thought about it. "Yes. I think Shay would love that." I really did. "I would have the chance to talk to Catelyn, and it would be nice to get away from everything, even if it's only for a few days."

"Done. I'll call Arther and tell him we'll be up there this weekend. There're some great trails for hiking. And lots of beautiful lakes. We could go fishing."

I laughed. "I never pictured you as someone who liked to fish."

"I'm full of surprises," he purred.

"Yeah, bet you are." I grinned. "We could go skinny-dipping."

"We could," he said, sending kisses down my neck.

I turned to face him, my heart racing with anticipation. "So what now? You want to stay here tonight? I don't want to have to wake up Shay," I asked, a smirk playing on my lips.

He leaned in and kissed me, his lips soft and gentle against mine. I melted into his embrace, my hands snaking up to tangle in his hair. The smell of his cologne filled my senses, and I felt myself getting lost in the moment.

He tasted of promises, security, and devotion. My lady regions pounded in agreement.

After a beat, Valen pulled away, his gaze smoldering with desire. "I can't lose you or Shay. I can't," he said, his voice rough with a need that had my heart pumping and my knees weak.

"You won't. I promise. And Shay is okay because of you."

His face went still, and he fell silent for a moment. It was one of those times when I wished I knew what he was thinking. Was he thinking of his wife? I knew she'd died of cancer, which had devastated him. With Shay sick, like she had an incurable disease, it must be bringing back all those memories and feelings of loss.

"She's a tough kid," Valen said suddenly, breaking me out of my thoughts.

"I know."

"Like her big sister."

I raised an eyebrow. "I do what I can."

He grinned, his eyes shining with affection. "You're strong, fearless. Even in the face of danger, you always keep your cool."

I felt my cheeks flush with pleasure. "I wouldn't say that, but I'll take the compliment." I searched his face. "You know, I couldn't do this without you. I've never had someone like you in my life before. Someone I can count on. A real partner."

He leaned in, his lips hovering just inches from mine. "You deserve to be with someone who'll put you first."

Did he just say that?

He kissed me hard and intently until I could barely catch my breath. A stab of desire flew to my middle as a moan escaped him. I lost myself to the feeling of him, my hands traveling under his shirt and tracing over his hard back muscles. Pleasure unfurled from every cell in my body, making me hot and maybe a little crazy. I breathed heavily as his coarse man-hands slipped under my shirt, his fingers rolling up and down my back. Waves of demand pulsed from his touch, my core throbbing.

"I never thought I could feel this way again," he said, pulling away from my mouth, and my insides twisted. "And I never thought I could love that little girl the way I do."

"I know. She kinda grows on you."

Valen fell silent again for a beat. "You found me

on that street that day. It was almost like you knew I *needed* you."

Okay, cue in the tears. "When you were so incredibly rude and beastly?" A tear slipped out of my eye, and he ran his thumb across my cheek.

"And it's been worth it. All of it. You make me want to be better—a better man, a better giant."

I didn't know what to say, so I just nodded like a fool. I knew if I opened my mouth, I'd start bawling. Better keep it closed.

Valen laughed. "You're also a stubborn beast. I like my females strong and with attitude. A sexy beast with a great ass."

I cocked a brow. "Why, thank you, sir." Ah, found my voice.

The giant exhaled through his nose. His eyes darkened with desire. "I want it. Now." He growled low, cupped my ass, and pulled me against him so I could feel the hardness in his pants, telling me how much he wanted my great ass.

"Oh? Hello."

Chuckling, the giant crushed his lips on mine, and I shuddered under the kiss. I kissed him back with as much desire and longing as I could. He was so warm, solid, and loyal, and I held on to him.

It felt right. All of it. Me. Valen. Me with Valen. Me having sex with Valen.

It was exactly what I needed. To be consumed by Valen, his love, his protection, his sexy beast-hands rubbing over my body.

And as I fell into his embrace, soaking him in, I made a promise to myself.

I *would* find a cure for Shay.

I would rid this Mark of Death curse from my little sister. I would.

Just as soon as I was done with Valen.

CHAPTER 26

My shoes clacked loudly on the sidewalk as I strode south on Fifth Avenue. The morning sun was warm and high in the sky. A breeze rose around me, sporadically sending my hair to tickle my neck. The loud whooshes and honks of vehicles made a comforting background to my rambling thoughts.

The air was fresh—not really. It was filled with its usual aroma of exhaust and garbage. It would be nice to get some fresh air, and I didn't mean taking a stroll through Central Park, though lovely. I meant real fresh, like forest fresh, if that was such a thing. Valen's suggestion of going up to see Catelyn this weekend popped into my mind. I hadn't had a chance to discuss it with Shay yet.

After my intense love-making session with the giant, I'd stayed up until half past two in the morning trying to find everything I could on this sorceress coven, *Ladies of the Light*, that Elsa had mentioned during a phone call hours later. I found them on the Merlin database. Yup, a few hours after Valen had made his phone call, I'd found my account *magically* enabled again and my license reinstated. Well, obviously not magically. Someone had physically reinstated it. So either Clive had done it, or someone *made* him do it. Yeah, the latter made me smile.

And after a few hours of research, it turned out the coven wasn't that far from the hotel. About a twenty-minute cab ride would take me there. Would they receive me? That I didn't know, but I was going to try my damnedest.

Right after I dropped my sister off at school.

I cut a glance at Shay walking alongside me, her Converse sneakers flapping on the sidewalk and her nose in her tablet. I frowned. "How can you see where you're going if you're staring at your tablet?" The new generation astounded me with their tech-savvy ways and text-and-walk abilities.

Shay shrugged as she walked. "It's easy. Everybody does."

"Well, *I* can't."

"That's because you're old."

Ouch. I opened my mouth to tell her that forty-one was *not* old but decided against it. From an eleven-and-a-half-year-old kid's perspective, I was ancient. "How are you feeling? Tired? You know, we could have stayed in today. Watched some movies together? Made some popcorn?"

"I feel fine," replied Shay, still not looking up from her tablet as she strode on.

I dipped my head, trying to catch a better glance at her face. "Are you sure?"

Shay cut me a look. "Why are you being weird again?"

"I'm not."

"You are."

"Just double checking. It's what big sisters do. We double-check stuff. We're double-checkers."

Shay shook her head, and the expression on her face said it all. She thought I'd lost my damn mind. "Maybe you're the one who's not feeling all right."

"Ha. Ha." I watched her closely as she returned her attention to her tablet as she walked. Someone who didn't know her wouldn't have noticed the dark circles under her eyes that weren't there before or the pallid color of her skin. They would think she looked perfectly normal. But I knew better. I knew she might feel fine, but that was temporary. As Polly had said, the curse was still inside Shay and would be until we removed it.

Still, it was enough for Shay to continue to have a life, and for her right now, that was school. It's what she wanted to do, and I wouldn't stand in her way. It made her happy and gave her a sense of purpose, which she needed right now.

I could wallow in my guilt forever, being responsible for doing this to Shay, or I could move forward and do something about it. I chose to do something.

"Valen was thinking of going up north this

weekend to visit Catelyn. She's at some compound deep in the forest. Would you like to go?"

Shay stopped and looked at me. "For real?"

The hope in her eyes made me smile. "Yeah, for real. So? I hear there are lots of lakes and trails we could explore and hike." Not to mention the fresh air might do her some good.

Shay gave me a one-shoulder shrug. "Okay."

My smile widened. "Okay then. Cool. This is cool, right? Us sisters going on a trip together?"

My little sister rolled her eyes. "You're being weird again."

I sighed, not minding at all being called weird. "I'll tell Valen. I think it's just what we all need. A little vacation would do us some good." We started walking again. "It'll be nice to get away and see how Catelyn's doing."

Staring at her tablet, Shay grunted in agreement.

And I really needed to talk to Catelyn. The idea still had my stomach in knots, but she had to know the truth. Valen said she was well-treated there, and she would be like family to them. I really hoped so.

Speaking of family. "Your dad, does he tend to disappear a lot?"

"*Our* dad," corrected Shay. "Yeah. Sometimes."

"So, it's perfectly normal that he hasn't shown up? I thought he said he was going to check on you— on us," I amended before she did.

Shay shrugged again. "He will. Guess he's not worried about us. That's why he hasn't come to see us yet."

"Right." My legs felt heavier as I treaded up the sidewalk. As an angel, he might have the ability to cure Shay or maybe know how to rid her of the curse. Either way, I needed to find out. "How do you call him? Do you even *call* him? How do you make contact? I guess is what I'm trying to ask."

"I don't know," answered Shay. "He kinda just shows up."

"Figures." That didn't help. But there were ways of making contact with angels. I would make a note to do just that after I was back from visiting the coven of sorceresses.

If anyone knew how to manipulate and decode a sorceress's curse, another sorceress would. I didn't know of many sorceresses. They didn't exactly mingle with us witches. Sorcerers and sorceresses ranked themselves higher than witches. They thought of us as small-timers in terms of magic manipulation. See, they had a higher level of magical education, kind of like a PhD in magic. Witches didn't. That didn't mean we weren't as intelligent and capable of equal amounts of magic or being as powerful. Just that some witches learned their magic from their parents, and some went to school like Shay.

I had to study the fundamentals of magic, demonology, basic investigative and intelligence techniques, learn how to manage and run counterintelligence, magical weapons of mass destruction, and criminal investigations—all to become a Merlin. But I didn't spend decades learning high levels of magic.

Sorcerers and sorceresses did, though. It was what set them apart.

So, you can understand my excitement to meet this coven.

"I'm sorry this happened to you," I said, my throat tight. She didn't deserve what had happened to her. None of it.

Shay gave me her signature shrug. "It's fine."

No, it was *not* fine. Most definitely not fine. But I would make it better. I swore it. And I wouldn't stop until I did.

We walked for another few minutes in silence. The cacophony from the busy street and humanity kept us company.

Finally, Fantasia Academy came into view. Cornices and turrets gleamed in the sunlight like giant jeweled fingers. Pretty in the sunlight, but at night the building had more character. I liked it better.

And as soon as Shay looked up from her tablet those few times and spotted it, her pace increased.

"That much, huh?" I tried hard to hide the smile from my voice as I matched her speed walking.

"What?" Shay marched forward like a little soldier.

God, could she be any cuter? "You really like this school." At first, when Valen had mentioned it, I wasn't sure it would be a good fit for her because of her *special* magic. But the giant had insisted she'd like it and that it would be good for her. How right he'd been.

"Yeah. So?" Shay strode on.

"No, I'm happy. Seriously. I'm glad you like it." I let out a breath. "And they're probably going to be able to help you with your magic, seeing as I couldn't."

Shay halted and turned around. "No, they won't."

I frowned. "What do you mean? Did something happen? What aren't you telling me?"

Shay's green eyes sparkled, and then, with a burst of energy, she shone like a brilliant star—just like that day when she'd fried Darius.

Rays of light emanated from her like heat waves. I had to shield my eyes for a moment until the beams diminished slightly so I could see.

Holy crap. Shay could conjure her magic!

My breath caught. "No way."

Shay beamed, her sun magic rippling around her, glowing. "Way."

I wasn't alarmed that she'd just tapped into her Starlight magic, or rather, sun magic, in public. Humans were blind to it. If you weren't a paranormal, you couldn't see it. And it was extraordinary.

I shook my head, a smile creeping onto my lips. "You lied to me. This whole time, you could conjure up your magic. You let me train you. Why?"

The sun's magic shimmered and then vanished, leaving only a smiling Shay.

She shrugged and said, "Because if you knew, you wouldn't want to spend time with me. You're always too busy with work or the hotel. With Valen."

I blinked a few times. "So you pretended to be a dud so we could hang out?"

Shay flashed me a smile. "See ya." And with that, my eleven-year-old sister took off running through the school gates.

"You little shit," I muttered, watching her dash up the stairs and past the waiting oily, skinny male faculty member I'd seen on the first day. He narrowed his eyes at me, and his face wrinkled like he'd bitten into a raw onion.

"Hi, Cosmo," said Shay as she rushed past him.

"Shay," said the staff member called Cosmo in way of greeting.

I raised my hand and waved just as he slammed the door. "Nice." Okay, so maybe they weren't thrilled to have discovered that Ms. Barclay had been an evil sorceress in disguise and had used the school. I couldn't be blamed for that. Yet by the glare Cosmo had just given me, it looked like I was.

But I didn't care. Shay could tap into her sun magic. This was the best news I'd had in weeks. I didn't even care that she'd lied. And I didn't even want to try and understand her reasoning. Who knew what went on in an eleven-year-old's head?

Feeling like things were finally taking a turn for the better, I twirled around and walked back the way I'd come with an added hop to my step. We were safe for now on this glorious sunny day. I couldn't wait to tell Valen and the others about Shay. They could use this bit of good news too—

I sensed them before I saw them.

Cold, powerful magic stirred my senses, a magnanimous presence that shook me.

I halted, slowly turning on the spot and searching for the source of power. I found it.

Through the crowd of humanity, I spotted a group of people, no paranormals, from the sense of energies I got from them. They stood next to a series of parked black SUVs, their eyes fixated on me. From the intensity of their gaze to the absurdity of their beauty and fine clothing, I knew I was staring at vampires. I felt a spike in my blood pressure as I forced myself to keep looking.

One among them stood out.

Tresses of raven hair spilled down past her waist. Her snow-white skin was pulled and stretched tightly over her sharp features, making her a combination of petrifying and beautiful, which was all kinds of creepy.

She wore a white pantsuit that slipped and shifted with her movements like some exotic silk. Her ebony eyes shone with a premeditated coldness, and they were also fixed on me.

Fear slithered through me at the power and dominance she radiated, just standing there. But I pushed it down at the bluntness of her expression. I would not show this vampiress fear.

Her red lips lifted into a sneer as though she'd guessed or sensed my thoughts. Her dark eyes flashed with hatred. Then just as quickly, she smoothed her features back into that arrogant, aristocratic demeanor.

I'll be seeing you, Starlight witch, a female voice spoke into my mind.

With a final look in my direction, she turned as one of the male vampires opened the passenger door to the nearest SUV, and she climbed in. The same male vampire shut the door, got behind the wheel, and started the engine.

Cold fingers of dread crawled up my spine and grasped my throat. With everything that had been going on with Shay and the curse, I had forgotten entirely about the vampiress. But it seemed as though *she* hadn't forgotten about us.

My heart pounded as I watched the SUVs drive away, knowing exactly who that was and what she wanted.

That was the ancient vampire Freida.

And Shay had just given a full-on demonstration of her power, something Freida wanted.

The world shifted and slapped me in the face.

Damn.

Don't miss the next book in the Witches of New York series!

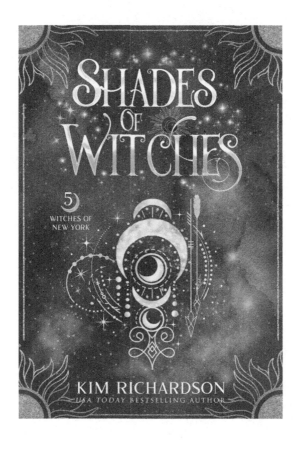

BOOKS BY KIM RICHARDSON

THE WITCHES OF HOLLOW COVE

Shadow Witch

Midnight Spells

Charmed Nights

Magical Mojo

Practical Hexes

Wicked Ways

Witching Whispers

Mystic Madness

Rebel Magic

Cosmic Jinx

Brewing Crazy

WITCHES OF NEW YORK

The Starlight Witch

Game of Witches

Tales of a Witch

THE DARK FILES

Spells & Ashes

Charms & Demons

ABOUT THE AUTHOR

Kim Richardson is a *USA Today* bestselling and award-winning author of urban fantasy, fantasy, and young adult books. She lives in the eastern part of Canada with her husband, two dogs, and a very old cat. Kim's books are available in print editions, and translations are available in over seven languages.

To learn more about the author, please visit:

www.kimrichardsonbooks.com